PENGUIN BOOKS

THE MEMORIAL HALL MURDER

Jane Langton has written twelve Homer Kelly mysteries, most recently *Dead as a Dodo*. She lives in Lincoln, Massachusetts.

THE
MEMORIAL HALL
MURDER

Jane Langton

Illustrations by the author

PENGUIN BOOKS

PENGUIN BOOKS
Published by the Penguin Group
Penguin Books USA Inc., 375 Hudson Street, New York, New York 10014, U.S.A.
Penguin Books Ltd, 27 Wrights Lane, London W8 5TZ, England
Penguin Books Australia Ltd, Ringwood, Victoria, Australia
Penguin Books Canada Ltd, 10 Alcorn Avenue, Toronto, Ontario, Canada M4V 3B.
Penguin Books (N.Z.) Ltd, 182–190 Wairau Road, Auckland 10, New Zealand

Penguin Books Ltd, Registered Offices: Harmondsworth, Middlesex, England

First published in the United States of America by Harper & Row, Publishers, Inc., 197
First published in Canada by Fitzhenry & Whiteside Limited 1978
Published in Penguin Books by arrangement with Harper & Row, Publishers, Inc., 19

LIBRARY OF CONGRESS CATALOGING IN PUBLICATION DATA
Langton, Jane.
The Memorial Hall Murder.
I. Title
[PS3562.A515M4 1981] 813'.54 80-20208
ISBN 0 14 771166 5

Printed in the United States of America
Set in Electra

With the exception of the selections on pages 87 and 220, portions from *Messiah* are
reprinted by permission from George Frederick Handel's *Messiah*,
copyright 1912 by G. Schirmer, Inc.

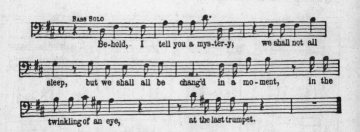

Be-hold, I tell you a mys-ter-y; we shall not all sleep, but we shall all be chang'd in a mo-ment, in the twinkling of an eye, at the last trumpet.

G. F. Handel, *Messiah*

Chapter One

BASS SOLO

Thus saith the Lord, the Lord of Hosts:

Yet once a lit-tle while, and I will shake _____

_____ the heavhs and the earth, the sea and the dry land...

The biggest noise wasn't the muffled sound of the explosion. It was the fall of shattered glass from the rose windows. Blue and red fragments rained down. Little shields of black-and-gold-painted glass bearing Harvard's motto—*Veritas*—burst on the stone steps. The wooden doors at either end of the memorial transept hung swaying on broken hinges.

Across Cambridge Street in the firehouse there were startled cries. Men ran outside and stood looking up at the vast sunlit bulk of Memorial Hall. A bell began sounding a long *claaaaaaaaang*, and then a loudspeaker said, *Box 48, Memorial Hall.*

John Campbell had been typing a letter in his office on the second floor of the firehouse. He jumped up and put on his helmet and coat with the men who were on duty and ran across Cambridge Street, while the sirens of the rescue truck and Engine No. 1 set up a high whine and pulled out of the garage to park across the street. Three of Campbell's men ran to the congested crossings around the firehouse and began rerouting traffic.

Cautiously John Campbell walked up the steps on the south side of Memorial Hall, his rubber boots crunching on the broken glass. A reddish cloud of smoke was rolling out of the broken door.

Only one side of the tall double door had been splintered and smashed. The other was intact, and the poster on its central panel was still fresh and clean.

MESSIAH
an oratorio

G.   F.   *HANDEL*

The Harvard-Radcliffe
Collegium Musicum
Hamilton Dow, Conductor

The Harvard-Radcliffe Orchestra
Jonathan Pearlman, Conductor

*****

Sanders Theatre, Memorial Hall
December 2, 8 p.m.
Free tickets, Holyoke Center

The Chief of the Cambridge Fire Department and two of his fire fighters stepped over the fallen half of the door and peered into the gloom. Water was pouring from the high ceiling. It fell on Campbell's helmet and ran backward down the brim. "There's somebody in there," he said. "See there, on the floor. Eddie, go downstairs and turn off the main valve."

There was no sign of fire. Dampened by the falling water from the sprinklers in the wooden vaults, the cloud of brick dust was thinning, settling on the floor and on the body of the fat man who lay half in and half out of a hole in the floor.

"Jeez, what in the name of Gawd was that?" Crawley, the building superintendent, looked out of the shattered door of his office. Somebody else, a very tall man with a lot of hair on his head, was blundering over the broken doors of the great hall, holding up his arms as a shield against the rain from the ceiling.

John Campbell looked at the tall man and held up his hand in warning. "No," he said. "Get back. You too, Crawley. Everybody out of the building."

The building superintendent withdrew an inch or two and the hairy man backed up a few paces and stopped, as Campbell walked forward and bent over the body, then groaned and turned his head aside.

"Mother of God," said the man at his heels.

John Campbell stood up. "Everybody out, I said. Come on. You heard me. Go on outdoors."

But people were still coming out of the walls. Someone had run up behind him and was digging thin fingers into his arm. "All right now, miss," said Campbell. "That goes for you too. Out with you. You never know if there might be another explosion."

"Ham?" said the girl. "It's not Ham? Oh, no." She was falling back, her hair streaming in the rain from the ceiling, her hands over her mouth. She was whimpering, "Oh, no, no, no, no, no."

The blackened body of the man who lay on the floor was hanging down, draining blood into the hole. Most of the clothing had been burned off. The head was missing.

Chapter Two

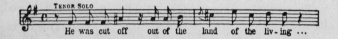

TENOR SOLO

He was cut off out of the land of the liv-ing ...

The floor had thundered like a cannon, and opened up its blazing mouth and thrown him down. He was falling and shouting, and the cannon were firing all around, and he went on shouting and falling until he hit the ground at last and smashed his forehead against a rock. The battle raged over his head, an army trampled his body, and then something immense fell on his back and crushed him. Slowly he struggled forward, squirming through the blinding storm of dust, until he was free of the terrible burden and could rest his bleeding head on his arm.

Then something else slammed down on the back of his head. He lay still while the raging night rolled over him.

Chapter Three

The President of Harvard was drinking coffee at his desk and looking out the window. Massachusetts Hall was the oldest building in the Yard, and the window glass should have been old as well, giving a pleasantly distorted view of the oak trees in front of Straus Hall. But there had been a disturbance in Massachusetts Hall back in 1972, when a rowdy bunch of students had occupied the building, and after that the old windows had been replaced with imitations in aluminum and impregnable plastic. No callow young barbarians would smash those windows in.

Idly James Cheever watched the late-morning sun strike through the plastic panes and move across the floor, picking out the soft colors of the old Caucasian rug. Moment by moment the patch of sunshine crept closer to the glass case containing the Great Salt, that precious piece of seventeenth-century silver that had been placed before him at the time of his installation as president, along with the silver keys and the seal and the charter of 1650. Soon the sunlight would touch those curving silver surfaces and scatter a brilliant pattern of light on the north wall. It happened every morning. In the five years since he had been elected to the presidency by the Harvard Corporation, James Cheever never tired of savoring this small daily miracle. At such times he wondered whether his predecessor was ever homesick for this room, whether he ever regretted his elevation to the Supreme Court. President Cheever smiled, remembering that there had been those who had questioned whether it could be considered an elevation, to exchange the presidency of Harvard University for even so august a national distinction.

If only his high office carried with it the rights and privileges he had expected, to balance the cares and responsibilities that had at once descended on his shoulders! President Cheever frowned at the Great Salt, struck by the notion that ill-mannered students were not the only barbarians at Harvard. After all, a voting majority of the Harvard Corporation were no more than aesthetic philistines. Even Hemenway and Bowditch, who were themselves collectors of art objects, had joined the others in voting against his Museum of Decorative Arts. The five Fellows had opposed him unanimously. The more he had argued in its favor, explaining the long-overdue need for a small museum devoted to the university's scattered collection of small precious things, the more they had got their backs up. Bowditch, the Senior Fellow, had even taken him aside and presumed to warn him against this "very serious error of judgment." The faculty would never stand for it, Bowditch had said. Well, Bowditch was a senile old fool. Sloan Tinker had gone to bat for the project, of course, arguing the case with Bowditch, even carrying the matter to the Faculty of Arts and Sciences. But then that self-righteous young prig, the Dean of the Faculty, had responded by calling for Cheever's resignation. And there had even been murmurs of the name of the President's old enemy. "It just keeps coming up all the time," Tinker had said, "the same damn dangerous name. You'd think they'd bring up another one now and then. It looks like some kind of conspiracy."

The Corporation had voted against him. So had the faculty. Very well, then, he would take the matter to the Board of Overseers. He would go over the heads of the Harvard Corporation, or, rather, since there was nothing over the Fellows' heads but

God, he would go around and behind them and consult the larger body, the Harvard Overseers. After all, the Senior Fellow himself was always cautioning him to remember that the university was a *diversity* as well—how the man loved his pious little joke! And then old Bowditch never lost an opportunity to remind him of the broad range of needs of all the scattered professional schools, Medicine, Business, Law, Divinity, and of the requirements of all the multitudinous departments under the Faculty of Arts and Sciences, from the largest and most prestigious down to the humblest department of Sanskrit or Celtic languages. And then Bowditch would waggle his old head and talk about the students, all twenty-one thousand of them, drinking thirstily at all these fountains, and about how complex and important their wants and necessities were. Well, then, it was only proper that he should take his request to the Harvard Overseers, whose task it was to visit all of these various schools and departments. He wouldn't be acting behind the Corporation's back. In fact, he might ask the President of the Board of Overseers to do something unheard of —invite the Fellows to attend the meeting in person. The whole matter would be right out in the open. Bowditch was practically asking for it.

James Cheever sipped his coffee and lifted his eyes to the two portraits hanging on the south wall of his office. It always calmed his mind to contemplate the two paintings he had chosen from the Harvard Portrait Collection to hang in the presidential chamber. It never failed to amuse him to examine them together. The subjects of both portraits had been benefactors of Harvard College, but there the resemblance ended. The likeness of William Stoughton had been daubed by a primitive hand, and it scowled back at Cheever with all the superstitious malice of the man who had been Chief Magistrate at the witchcraft trials in Salem. Stoughton looked like a badger. The glowing face of Count Rumford, on the other hand, seemed still glistening from the brush of Gainsborough. How the lively face shone with humanity and reason! What a paradox that the dour faith of the one should have

7

resulted in a physiognomy so savage, while the love of natural science in the other had kindled a countenance so angelic!

President Cheever's door burst open.

His door never burst open. It was always opened quietly after a soft knock and his own gentle, "Yes, Mrs. Herbert?"

Mrs. Herbert was on her hands and knees. She had stumbled over the sill. "A bomb," said Mrs. Herbert. "There's been a bomb."

The President of the Board of Overseers was running around

Mrs. Herbert. "Jim, the most God-awful thing has happened," said Julia Chamberlain. "A bomb just went off in Memorial Hall."

"Oh, is that what that noise was? I thought I heard something. The window rattled." President Cheever glanced back at the Great Salt. Only another moment now.

"Somebody put a bomb under the floor. And, oh, the most terrible thing." Julia Chamberlain's voice broke.

Dazzling reflections sprayed the wall! The President smiled, then pulled his face together and turned to Mrs. Chamberlain. "You mean the building has been destroyed? Memorial Hall?"

"It's Ham. Ham Dow, the chorus conductor. He's dead. He was the best person in the whole place. All the students were crazy about him. Oh, it's absolutely ghastly."

"Good Lord. And the building?"

"Oh, the building's all right. There's a big hole in the floor, and the stained glass in the transept has been blown to bits. The Brimmer window and the one on the other end too. But all in all, it's not as bad as it might have been. I mean, at Princeton last week they blew up the entire stadium. It could have been worse. But *Ham Dow* . . ."

The President reckoned losses and gains. Of course, it was too bad about the building. Too bad it hadn't been blown up altogether, because it was a monumental eyesore. A blot on the architectural landscape of the university. One could not, of course, ever have hoped to persuade the other members of the Harvard Corporation and the Vice President for Administration that it should be torn down altogether. You couldn't deliberately tear down a building sacred to the memory of the Harvard men who had died in the Union cause in the Civil War. But if a bomb had done the work for him . . . Well, it was too bad.

But as for Ham Dow . . .

James Cheever rose from his chair. He supposed he must take command. He loathed taking command. "Ham Dow. That is a

9

loss indeed. I suppose they have called the police?" He was doing his damnedest to suppress the smile that was tugging at the muscles of his cheeks.

His enemy was dead.

The Great Salt

Chapter Four

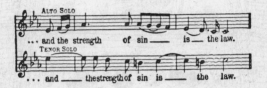

John Campbell ran down the steps to meet Captain McCurdy from the Boston Police Department Bomb Squad. McCurdy was parking a patrol car in the circular driveway on the north side of Memorial Hall.

Captain McCurdy slammed the door of his car. "Is everybody out of the building?" he said.

Campbell gestured at the crowd pressing against a rope barrier on the other side of Kirkland Street. "Oh, we cleared everybody out right away. It's a miracle nobody else was hurt. They poured out of every crack in the wall. You'd be amazed. I mean, the place always looks so empty. Well, it was chock-full. There was a big class going on in the lecture hall down at the other end, and I don't know where all the other characters came from. They kept coming out of the woodwork, and I had to keep shoving them all out."

McCurdy and Campbell hurried up the steps and through the north door, where another poster advertising the performance of Handel's *Messiah* hung flapping from one thumbtack. "See—there," said Campbell. "We left the body where it fell."

MEMORIAE · EORVM
QVI · HIS · IN ... STITVTI
MORTEM ... OPPETIERVNT
CIꝹ·DCCC ... CIꝹ·DCCC·LXV

McCurdy barely glanced at the mounded shape under the tarpaulin. He walked around the hole, stepping carefully to avoid the smears of blood and the fragments of broken marble that littered the floor. A blaze of warm October sunshine was flooding through the empty stone mullions of the rose window to the south, slanting down in dusty shafts on the clutter below. Uneasily Captain McCurdy looked at the other men in uniform milling around the lofty hall. He recognized the insignia of the police departments of Harvard University and the city of Cambridge, and there were fire fighters from across the street in rubber

12

coats and boots. "The first thing we've got to do is make sure nobody else is buried under all that fallen debris. Are all these people authorized personnel? If not, they should clear out. Who's that guy in the gray suit?"

"That's Maderna. He's the mechanical foreman for the North Yard. Harvard Buildings and Grounds. Hey, Donald, you got everything turned off now?"

"Yes," said Donald Maderna. "Heat, gas, water, electric power. If there's anything else you want us to do, just let me know. And as soon as you people are through in here we'll want a go-ahead, so we can get the building back in shape. We'll bring in steamfitters, carpenters, plumbers, everybody; get the place back in use as soon as possible."

"Right you are," said McCurdy. "Now let's get most of these people out of here. We've got to go through all this debris with a fine-tooth comb. Who's that? Oh, Frank. Come on in, Frank. Mr. Campbell, this is Frank Harvey from the U.S. Treasury Department of Alcohol, Tobacco and Firearms. Hey, Frank, you think this is some more work by that crazy Nepalese Freedom Movement?"

"I wouldn't be surprised. Damn fools. I suppose they'll call up sooner or later and take the credit."

"Well, let's get started. We've got to sift through all this wreckage. And then we'll have to go over the entire building to make sure there aren't any more explosive devices hidden anyplace."

Someone else was elbowing his way into the conversation. "But, my God, man, that will take a year."

McCurdy and Campbell and Harvey looked up in surprise at the tall man with the bushy head of hair. "Look," said John Campbell, "I already told you, the building is closed to unauthorized personnel. Nobody from outside is supposed to be in here."

But instead of explaining himself, the big man in the mismatched coat and pants was rumbling on in a kind of excited babble. "You can't search every nook and cranny in this place in less than a year. The building is as convoluted as the human brain. There are a hundred rooms in the basement alone. I know that for a fact. Why, you can't even get from one floor of the building to the other. It's different universes. Whole different geometrical nonconnected dimensions. It's like trying to take off your vest without removing your coat. And the tower. Just think of the tower. And the big spaces between the wooden vaults and the roof. My God, man, just think. Say, listen—oh, please, Chief, could I come along when you go up there? I mean, I'm really crazy about towers. If there's one thing in this life I'm really crazy about, it's crawling around on the tops of vaults."

They were looking at him vacantly.

The man smiled at John Campbell. "I'm sorry. I should explain myself. Visiting professor. My wife and I, we've got this one-year appointment. I was teaching in the lecture hall over down yonder when the thing went off. It was my first day of teaching, you see, because Mary had the class the first few weeks. What I'm trying to tell you is that before I was a student of American literature and all that sort of thing, I was an assistant to the District Attorney over there in East Cambridge. I was a lieutenant detective in Middlesex County before I retired to a bookish and sedentary life in Concord. My name's Kelly. How do you do."

"Kelly? You're not *Homer* Kelly?" John Campbell stared. "Well, no kidding. So you're Homer Kelly. Well, sure, I guess you can come along. But we won't search the rest of the building until we've got all this debris cleared out, and make sure nobody else is buried down there. So if you'd just step outside for now, Mr. Kelly, and stand across the street, I'll send for you when we get around to looking at the tower."

Homer Kelly beamed and shook everybody's hand. He stepped over the broken door in the north entry and started down the steps outside.

A hearse was turning into the circular driveway from Kirkland Street. The driver pulled quickly to a stop and leaned out and shouted at Homer.

"What did you say?" said Homer, bending down politely to the car window.

"I said, is there anything left of the guy? My name's Ratchit. North Cambridge Funeral Parlor. I mean, sometimes, when you get a bomb, there's nothing left but pieces all over. You've got to mop them up in a bucket."

"Oh, well," said Homer mournfully. "It was pretty bad." He shook his head and stood back as Ratchit bounced out of the hearse and ran around the front of the car.

John Campbell was there to meet him. "Hello, Ratchit," he said. "You're early. They're not through taking pictures yet. You want to come back this afternoon?"

"No, it's all right. I'll wait." Ratchit had a small sharp face. He bounded ahead of John Campbell up the stairs, snapping under his feet glass fragments bearing the names of the virtues, fallen from the rose window high above: *Fortitudo, Disciplina, Prudentia, Patientia.*

Chapter Five

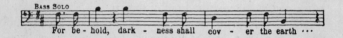

He was back in New Jersey. Although he didn't know how he knew it was New Jersey, because all the lights were out. But it must be New Jersey, because his great-aunts were lined up in a row beside him, singing. Oh, they were terrible. Oh, why didn't they stop? Oh, Christ, it hurt his head to listen. He had thought at first they were angels, only angels wouldn't sing like that, and when he had got a look at them by the light of the candles in their hands, he could see immediately that they were his old great-aunts, the ones in the picture on the bureau, back home in New Jersey. He had never met them in real life, because they had all died before he was born, but now they were all lined up just like in the picture, with their fuzzy hair and their shirtwaists and high collars and their staring faces, singing *ROCK OF AGES, CLEFT! FOR MEEEEEEE! LET ME HIIIIIIIIDE MYSELF IN THEEEEEEEEE!* Oh, God, why didn't they stop?

Chapter Six

TENOR SOLO

Com-fort ye, com - - - fort ye ____ my peo-ple …

From the sidewalk on the other side of Kirkland Street, Homer Kelly looked up solemnly at the sunless north façade of Memorial Hall. The building rose above him like a cliff face, mass piled upon mass, ten thousand of brick laid upon ten thousand. It was ugly. Majestically ugly. Augustly, monumentally ugly. It was a red-brick Notre Dame, a bastard Chartres, punctured with stained-glass windows, ribboned around with lofty sentiments in Latin, finialed with metallic crests and pennants, knobbed with the heads of orators, crowned with a bell tower and four giant clocks. Homer knew that the colossal edifice contained a theatre and a great hall and a memorial transept and a lecture room and a radio station and a lot of small offices and classrooms, but now in its gloomy grandeur it was a gigantic mausoleum as well. When it had been erected in the 1870s it had been intended as a half-secular, half-sacred memorial to young graduates who had died in the Union cause in the Civil War. Now it was an actual coffin.

Some of the people on the sidewalk had stopped to stare across the street because they were merely curious, glad of some excitement between a class in Nat Sci 4 and another in Soc Sci 2. But most of the people pressed up against the rope barrier were mourners. Homer listened while Ham Dow's students and choris-

17

ters and friends murmured bitterly among themselves. A large woman in a red dress was weeping, clutching two fat boys in her arms. Mr. Crawley, the custodian of the building, was repeating his impressions of the morning over and over again. "Jeez, you should of seen him. His head was blowed right off. Blood running out of him down the hole. You should of been there."

A short girl standing in front of Homer gave Crawley a savage look. "Oh, shut up, Crawley."

But he gabbled on. "Hey, lookit. See that big car? That's Cheever, President Cheever. He was here yesterday. Jeez, if they'd of blown up the place yesterday they'd of blown up Cheever. You see that other guy with him? That's whooseywhatsis. Tinker. Sloan Tinker. Vice President or something. Excuse me, I think they're going to need me over there. It's all right, officer, I'm the super. I got all the keys. They can't unlock nothing without the keys."

"Oh, Homer, there you are." Homer's wife was reaching

around shoulders and over heads, touching his arm. He took her hand and squeezed it. Someone was trailing after Mary, hanging on to her. Homer recognized the girl who had arrived on the scene of the disaster just as he was rushing upon it himself. And he had talked to her, he remembered now, before his class had even begun. Earlier this morning she had been a thin, handsome girl with long hair pouring over her shoulders in a violent mass of red. Now she was tear-stained, rumpled and pale, her hair hanging in lank dripping strands over her shirt.

"Homer, this is Vick Van Horn," said Mary. "She was Ham Dow's assistant. She's really pretty shaken up."

"Well, hello again," said Homer. "I know Vick. She found my classroom for me this morning. Here, just let me speak to Officer Corcoran, so he'll know where I am. Come on, we'll find someplace to sit down."

There was a bench in the garden of the Busch-Reisinger Museum. The three of them sat down, with Vick stiffly erect in the middle. "Oh, it's so terrible," she said, thumping one skinny fist into the other hand. "Oh, of all the people in the world. Ham was one of the few people in the *whole world* who were doing anything good for anybody else. He meant so much to so many people —with his music, I mean. He was the best. He really was. And now he's gone. Oh, I can't stand it. I just can't stand it."

Homer didn't know what to say. "There now," he said, "don't cry. There now."

"Oh, Homer, don't be an idiot," said Mary. "Of course she should cry. And she's right. She really is. Even I could see that. I'd only been singing with him twice, at my audition and then this morning, but I could tell he was just what Vick says. He was one of those people who are just born to teach. He was—well, he was just great. Well, I'm going to bawl a little myself." Mary put her arms around Vick, and Homer sat helplessly while the two women leaned on each other and sobbed. But then Vick stopped crying and jumped up and began gesticulating with her thin, freckled arms. "I mean, it wasn't just the music. It was the way he was so, you know, kind to everybody. Once—you won't believe this—once I found him leaning down over a manhole in the street, and there was this man with his head sticking up out of the manhole, and they were singing this really corny old song, 'Silver Threads Among the Gold,' only it was beautiful, it really was. Funny and beautiful. They were both throwing themselves into it. It was just the way he was. He couldn't even be mean enough to turn anybody down who wanted to sing. He was always getting himself in trouble by letting some really *strange* people into the chorus. He was just so *kind.*"

"That's right," said Mary. "He let me in, and I was surprised. I mean, I'm just a visiting teacher, really old, compared to the rest of you. And I don't even sing all that well. I didn't think I'd pass the test. But he said it was all right. Of course, there are still the quartet trials to get through. I may not get in after all."

"Well, everybody would get in, if we left it up to Ham. So the quartet trials have to be taken care of by other people. I do some and Jack Fox does the rest. He's the accompanist and the manager. Even so, Ham slips some really weird people in behind our backs. Oh, excuse me, I didn't mean you. Oh, damn. Oh, excuse me. Oh, God, I just can't believe it. To think we were working in there, all together, just an hour ago, in Sanders Theatre, and Ham was making a joke about my shirt."

"Your shirt?" said Homer.

"It's got stripes, you see?" Vick threw out her arms to display her shirt. "And he said, 'What a nice shirt,' and then he sang the first line of that chorus from *Messiah*, you know—"

"And with his stripes"—Mary laughed—*"we are healed."*

"Right. That's right. I mean, he was just so . . . Who would want to hurt him? A man like that?"

"Oh, my dear Vick," said Homer, "it probably didn't have anything to do with Ham Dow himself. It was just some crazy fool, some terrorist. It was probably that Nepalese Freedom Movement. Ham just happened to be standing at the wrong place at the wrong time." Homer stood up and took Vick by the shoulders and gently shoved her down on the bench. "Now look here, girl, tell me what happened this morning. Everything you saw. I mean, the police are going to want to talk to you anyway. And I used to be in the District Attorney's office for Middlesex County, so I'd kind of like to understand the whole thing myself. Just begin at the beginning."

Vick hunched her shoulders and plunged her hands between her knees. Her face was a narrow white cleaver between the fiery masses of her hair, which was beginning to spring away from her head as it dried in the sun. "Well, I came early. I had a schedule. Chorus rehearsal was to be at ten o'clock from now on, every Monday and Wednesday, only I was coming an hour early to make sure everything was all set up and ready. I mean, Mr. Crawley's supposed to do it, but he's kind of—well, you know, he's not very sharp. He's really different from Michael Lane, who was there before. Only they promoted Michael, so now we're stuck with Crawley. So I have to check up on him, you see. But the real reason I came a whole hour early was to practice. Oh, God." Vick put her hand on her mouth. "I forgot my cello. I left it there, where it fell on its face. Oh, the heck with my cello. Where was I? I came an hour early to practice. You see, I just store my cello there in the instrument storage closet under the stairs. I've got my own key now." Vick jerked a string from under her shirt and showed them the key hanging around her neck. "I take these lessons from Ham. Oh, I mean, I *was* taking lessons from Ham. He was a cellist himself, you see. That was his instrument. And he's good, really good. Oh, I mean he *was* good. Oh, what a waste, what a waste." Vick's eyes filled again, but she shook herself and glared at Homer. "It must have been about nine o'clock when I got to Memorial Hall, walking over from Winthrop House, where I live, over there by the river. The bell was ringing, the new bell in the tower of Memorial Hall. I had the new posters about the concert under my arm. I tacked one of them up on the south door as I went in. . . ."

Chapter Seven

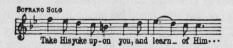

SOPRANO SOLO

Take His yoke up-on you, and learn_ of Him...

Vick stuck her box of thumbtacks in her pocket and stood back to look at the poster.

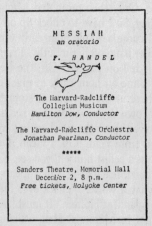

MESSIAH
an oratorio

G.   F.   H A N D E L

The Harvard-Radcliffe
Collegium Musicum
Hamilton Dow, Conductor

The Harvard-Radcliffe Orchestra
Jonathan Pearlman, Conductor

*****

Sanders Theatre, Memorial Hall
December 2, 8 p.m.
Free tickets, Holyoke Center

Free tickets. Free tickets again. That was Ham's doing. Of course, it was crazy, just crazy. Because Ham would be handing out tickets too, and he'd lose track, and too many people would show up, and they'd be hanging from the rafters and crowded in the aisles, just the way they were last year. That was the way Ham wanted it. Let everybody in. Admission free for all. Well, that was what some people called it, a free-for-all. All that noise and confusion. But somehow Ham always seemed to make it work, and when they came to the end of *Messiah*, Part Two, he'd let everybody in Sanders stand up and sing the "Hallelujah Chorus" at the top of their lungs, and when the concert was over they'd all go home glad and satisfied. A concert with Ham Dow was always a lot more than just a musical experience. It would be like that again.

Vick pulled the door open, but the wind sucked through the enormous dark chamber on the other side and blew the door wide, slamming it against the side of the stone portal. She reached for the handle and tugged the door shut behind her and walked into the memorial transept. Morning light was slanting through the rose window, casting colored splotches on the wooden timbers that rose to the ribs of the pointed vault high over her head. The vaults themselves were almost invisible in the gloom. It was as if sheets of night sky were hung, pitchy black, down the length of the high corridor. Vick knew the building was supposed to be sort of medieval, but in her opinion it felt more like her great-grandfather's house in Illinois, which had been built during the presidency of Ulysses S. Grant. The dark volumes of musty air had the fragrance of that house in Illinois, with the dim shadowy parlor and the laundry with the set tubs and the high varnished pantry. Vick's footsteps were sharp chips of sound as she walked past the pale marble memorial tablets glimmering along the walls.

HENRY LIVERMORE ABBOTT. 6, MAY, 1864. WILDERNESS

JOHN LYMAN FENTON. 28, JULY, 1863. GETTYSBURG

She knocked on Mr. Crawley's door.

Mr. Crawley looked out, his face vague under his duck-billed hat. "Oh, hi, there. You want something?"

"Oh, Mr. Crawley, did you remember to set up the chairs in

Sanders? You know, for our special rehearsal with the orchestra. It's a big special get-acquainted rehearsal of the Collegium and orchestra together, just for today. After today it will be the chorus at ten and the orchestra at eleven, every Monday and Wednesday. Remember? I mean, today is Wednesday."

"Oh, Wednesday. Jeez, I thought it was Tuesday. Besides, I got like this acid stomach. Heartburn, you know?" Mr. Crawley belched stupendously and pressed a pitiful hand on his chest.

"Oh. Well, all right. I guess I can set them up myself. If I could just borrow the key."

"Here, take it. It's all yours. No, that's all right. Keep it. I got lots of keys. Be my guest." Then Mr. Crawley shut the door and withdrew into his cozy chamber, where Vick knew he had a nice leather sofa for snoozing. She hung the key on its long loop of string around her neck, crossed the hall, opened the instrument storage closet under the stairs, and took out her cello.

Then a long bar of sunlight fell on the floor from the door that opened on Cambridge Street, and she looked up in surprise. A very large angry man was standing over her, shouting. "Where in the name of God is Memorial Hall 201? I've been all over this place from top to bottom. I've turned it inside out, and I can't find that sly, skulking lecture hall. I mean, Christ almighty, the building is so colossal, you'd think it would be bristling with lecture halls, but all I can find is vast caverns and long lonely corridors intertwining underground. Where in the hell is it *at?* I have given up all hope

Vick laughed. The man was pretending to be furious, but he was sort of crazy at the same time, and he looked so really incredibly tall and funny, with that shock of hair standing up all over his head. "Mem Hall 201? Oh, it's way around the other end. You have to go out and come in again. It's way down at that end, only on the other side."

"Thank you," growled the man. He disappeared, and Vick drew her music stand out of the closet, locked the closet, and unlocked the door to Sanders Theatre. She climbed the stairs to

the stage and began moving chairs, hauling them from the back of the stage to the front. Sanders was empty, except for the stained-glass lady in the window at the back of the balcony, who was hanging a piece of crepe on a column, and the marble statues of Otis and Quincy, who were posturing at either side of the stage, and the foxy wooden faces of animals on the ends of the beams overhead. Would there be enough chairs? The chorus would be sitting on the benches out front, too swollen with hopeful candidates to fit on the stage with the orchestra. Ham would have to conduct in all directions at once.

The man came back.

He stood on the floor in front of Ham's music stand and thundered at her. "No, it's *not*, by God. I'll be damned if I can find anything but a bloody copy center. I mean, how in the hell do the students find it? I'll bet there are students wandering like lost souls around the city of Cambridge looking for Memorial Hall 201. I'll bet they've got into another time frame entirely, and they'll never get back into this world until another age dawns and judgment day bursts upon us all, and the architects who designed this building get their just deserts. I mean, why didn't they make a Greek temple or something good-looking like that? Well, actually"—the man stopped his tirade and looked around and smiled —"actually, I like it, I mean, all this. It's nice." He waved his arm at the surrounding forest of timber in Sanders Theatre. "The light in here. It's like amber. You can almost feel the flies stuck in it. You know. Ladies in long skirts. Gentlemen in frock coats. I'll bet when you sit down you can feel their plump ancestral undergirding knees." The man sat down promptly on the front bench and leaned back and grinned at Vick. "Really comfortable. The cozy ample laps of the forefathers. Now, where was I?" He stood up. "I got carried away."

"You were looking for Mem Hall 201," said Vick. "Come on. I'll take you there myself. Just follow me."

"You see, my wife had the course the first two weeks. She's a specialist in the Boston abolitionists and Harriet Beecher Stowe

26

and so on. It's this course we're teaching, 'The Great Cloud Darkening the Land.' That's a quote from Walt Whitman, you see, that famous poem about Lincoln's funeral train. It's what we call it, you see, the course. I mean, it's the literature of abolition and the Civil War, and Mary and I teach it together. Thoreau, Whitman, Parkman, Garrison, Phillips, Melville, Lowell. People like that. Great stuff. Except for the fact that my wife—good grief, you know what she did? She palmed Louisa May Alcott off on me. How do you like that?"

"Gee, it sounds like a great course. I wish I could take it instead of Chem 2. I'm over my head already in Chem 2. Look, you see that door? You just go in that door and up the stairs instead of down."

"Well, so that's where it is. Well, thank heaven. And thank you, Ms. . . . ?"

"Van Horn. Vick Van Horn. I'm Ham Dow's assistant conductor for the Collegium Musicum. That's the mixed chorus. That is, I am until I flunk Chem 2."

"Kelly here. Homer Kelly. You'll be seeing my wife, Mary, at ten o'clock. She's going to sing in your chorus, the Collegium Whatchamacallit, this fall. I mean, it's so handy, because the rehearsals are at ten and our class meets in the same building at eleven. Well, so long, Vick. You've been a friend in need."

Vick ran back to Sanders and sat down with her cello and spent the next half hour practicing double stops in thirds. They were a brand-new exercise. Ham had assigned them at her lesson the day before. They were gruesome. Vick spraddled her left hand over the G and C strings at once and tried to get the major thirds on pitch. When Ham came in at quarter of ten with Jonathan Pearlman, she shouted at him, "Don't listen."

"Who wants to?" said Ham. He grinned at her and thumped his big *Messiah* score on the edge of the stage, while Jonathan began fussing with the chairs for the orchestra, shifting them a few inches this way and that. More people trickled in, greeting Ham with glad handshakes because they hadn't seen him since last June. The trickle became a flood. Old and new members of the Collegium and the orchestra were thronging in the doors. The music librarian for the chorus moved back and forth, slapping down music folders on benches in alphabetical order, shouting, "A through H, pay your music deposit here." A hundred pieces of music snapped into a hundred folders with sharp popping noises like scattered firecrackers. Ham stood at one side, his huge stomach thrust forward, his great bearded head turning, his big laugh breaking out. Something came sailing through the air, and Ham reached up calmly and caught it and threw it back. It was the Esterhazy boys, Siegfried and Putzi Esterhazy, throwing a Frisbee. They were running around the balcony, and up and down the stairs. Vick laughed. Why weren't those little kids in school? Mrs. Esterhazy was terrible about making her children go to school. Then Mrs. Esterhazy herself steamed in, wearing a red fat-lady's dress that nearly swept the floor. "Darling Veectoria," boomed Mrs. Esterhazy. She was carrying a basket. She was passing out homemade candy. Vick took a piece. Rosie Bell, first trumpet, took another. Rosie was a star, a famous economist, and you'd think she'd be too busy to play in the orchestra, but Rosie was a good sport, and she never missed a rehearsal. She took her trumpet out of its case. The trumpet glittered in the sunlight. Rosy blew warm air into it and sat down and flapped through her music and let go with her solo from the end of *Messiah.* It was Rosie's big moment. *TahDAH, dadidadiDAH, dadidadidadidadi-DAH, DAH DAH DAHdida,* blared Rosie, her trills rippling like water. And then Mr. Proctor unbuttoned his sweater and swelled his barrel chest and closed his eyes and sang the words that went with Rosie's fanfare: *The trumpet shall sound and the dead shall be raised, the dead shall be raised incorruptible.*

"I won't stand for it." Jonathan Pearlman was shaking Vick's arm. "She's back. That crazy old lady. You know, the one Ham squeezed into my second-violin section last year. I tell you, I won't take it lying down. Not again."

"Oh, no, not Miss Plankton?" Vick looked around in dismay.

There she was, Jane Plankton, that funny little old lady, pulling her fiddle out of its scuffed case, her hair ribbon bobbing, her cheeks bright pink. Oh, it was incredible. Ham had *sworn* he would get rid of her. Because the poor dear could hardly play at all, and she was always downbow when everybody else was upbow. She had no business being in the orchestra anyway, even if she was an old 'Cliffie of the class of aught nine or something. What was the matter with Ham? Why didn't he *do* something?

And then Vick saw Jennifer Sullivan. She ran up to Jennifer and took her by the shoulders and stared at her in mock horror. "Jennifer, I didn't know." Because Jennifer was pregnant, really bulging.

"Oh, never mind," said Jennifer. "Just never mind. I don't want to even talk about it. And if you want to know who the father was, it was just some guy I know, I mean I don't care, I mean it doesn't make any difference. I'm staying with Ham. I mean, they wouldn't let me have a baby in the dorm, so Ham said I could have it there at his house on Martin Street. So shut up. Just tell me where you want the sopranos. Over there? Hey, Betsy, the sopranos are over there."

But Betsy wasn't listening. Betsy Pickett was riding around on the back of Jack Fox, screaming to be let down, and the new people in the chorus who didn't know Betsy were staring at her. You'd never think Betsy was a prize-winning student in the Classics Department, you'd just never believe she was writing an honors thesis on some old Roman poet. Betsy's boyfriend, Tim Swegle, was dragging at her from the rear. Tim had a firm grip under Betsy's fat shoulders, but Betsy was hanging on to Jack's neck with her little hiking boots and shrieking with rapture, and Jack was choking and clawing at his throat. Vick smiled and sat down with the cellos, then looked up as a tall big-boned woman bent down to speak to her. "Where do you want the altos?" said the woman. "I'm new. My name's Mary Kelly."

"Oh, hi, there, Mrs. Kelly," said Vick, beaming at her. "The altos are over there on the left side. And, say, I just met your husband. He's really great. I sure wish I could take your course."

Ham was on the podium, tapping his music stand. Instantly disorder became order. Betsy was in her place with the sopranos. Jack Fox struck a note on the harpsichord. A threadlike piercing A escaped from the oboe. The orchestra tuned up, and then Ham pulled something out of his pocket and waved it in the air. "Peanut brittle," he said. "Did everybody get some of Mrs. Esterhazy's peanut brittle?" Mrs. Esterhazy's basket was passed around once more. Then Ham stepped aside and Jack Fox, the manager of the chorus, talked about the quartet trials that were still to come. Newcomers who had passed their preliminary auditions trembled. Jack talked about attendance. Ham stepped back on the podium and talked about the music, turning slowly to face the orchestra on the stage and the chorus on the benches.

"There are some things I'd like to say about Handel's *Messiah* before we begin. As usual we will be performing it at Christmastime. But it was never intended solely as a Christmas piece. The text is concerned not only with the birth of Christ, but with his suffering, death, and resurrection, and the resulting redemption of all mankind. It could just as well be a Good Friday or an Easter piece. Handel himself first performed it in Dublin on Good Friday. Now, the soloists will as usual be drawn from our own forces. Mrs. Esterhazy, of course, will sing the contralto arias." (Cheers for Mrs. Esterhazy.) "Mr. Proctor will be our bass." (Cheers for Mr. Proctor.) "The tenor part will be sung by our own Tim Swegle." (Whistles of amazement for Tim, whose voice was still a little thin and shaky.) "And last but not least, our soprano soloist will be Betsy Pickett." (Applause mingled with insane shrieks from Betsy.) "Now, before we begin, I have a poem I would like to read." (Shouts: "Oh, no, spare us!") Ham took a piece of paper out of his pocket and read aloud.

> "There once was a young girl named Vick,
> Whose favorite expression was 'Ick.'
> Whenever you kissed her,

She said, 'Listen, mister,
Don't touch me, you make me feel sick.' "

Vick reached out past her cello with her foot and kicked Ham in the shin, and the chorus and the orchestra laughed loudly, even the newcomers who didn't know who Vick was. Ham said *"Ow"* and rubbed his leg, and then he made a joke about Vick's striped shirt, and lifted his stick at last.

The noise died down. The thick volumes of music were riffled open. "All right now, you good Rats," said Ham, "let's begin from the beginning with the overture. The chorus can just sit there and enjoy it. We'll get to them in a minute. We'll do as much of Part One as we can get through this morning, but we've got to finish up right on time. I've got to meet somebody promptly at eleven-

Sandino Theatre

thirty." He stroked a great upbeat, and the orchestra struck the E-minor chord and sailed serenely up, the violins trilling mournfully on D sharp and then landing on the G for three solemn dotted notes. "Upbow, Miss Plankton," shouted Ham.

Vick's music was part of the bass-line carried by the harpsichord. Moving her bow across the D string, drawing from it steadily the half note on E from which the voices of the other instruments sprang, she smiled up at Ham. It was good to be starting again. He knew what she meant, and smiled back.

"He had to meet somebody at eleven-thirty," said Vick. "Isn't that right, Mary? He said he had to meet somebody."

"He did say 'somebody'?" said Homer. "Not 'I have to meet a man,' or 'I have to meet a woman,' or 'some people'?"

Vick and Mary shook their heads. "No," said Mary. "He said, 'We've got to finish on time, because I have to meet somebody at eleven-thirty.' "

"And the bomb went off at eleven thirty-five," said Homer. "I know, because I'd just made a joke, and the students all laughed, and I began to relax for the first time, and I wasn't scared of all those kids any more, only I was horrified to discover that I had less than half an hour to cover nine-tenths of the lecture. And then there was this big noise and the whole room shook and everybody started yelling and I ordered everybody to go outside."

"And then, you big dumbhead, instead of running outside with the rest of us, you disappeared completely," said Mary. "You really gave me a turn."

"Well, I was looking for a shortcut. I got lost in the basement for a while, and then I found a little secret stairway and it took me up into that enormous cavern of a room, and from there I could cut right through into that big memorial hallway where the bomb went off. What about you, Vick—where were you?"

"Still in Sanders. I did some more practicing, and then I had to put away all the chairs again. I mean, Mr. Crawley is supposed to do it, but, well, I told you, he's pretty hopeless. So I was hauling chairs to the back of the stage, one by one, when there was this big boom, and it sounded sort of dull but tremendous, and I was lifted a couple of feet in the air, and I fell into the chairs, and I didn't even feel anything, I was so astonished. And the first thing I thought of was my cello, because it had fallen on its face on the floor, but I just lay there in the middle of the chairs for a minute, trying to get myself together. I mean, I could hear all the glass crashing outside, and huge noises as if the whole place were falling down. And I got scared and thought maybe it might all fall down on top of me, so I picked myself up and stumbled out into the hall, and it was raining out there, and I saw the firemen, and I saw you, Mr. Kelly, and—"

"Homer. Call me Homer."

"And I saw the sole of somebody's shoe and this big shape on the floor with just black shreds of clothes, and I went to look, and it was—" Vick's face began to come apart again.

"Now, look here," said Mary Kelly, taking her firmly by the hand. "I'm absolutely starved. I'll bet you are too. You're going to come home with me right now and have lunch. I made some soup with the last of the vegetables we grew back home in Concord last summer. You just come on home with me. We've got a nice apartment on Huron Avenue. It's the top deck of one of those big comfortable three-deckers, all lace curtains and over-stuffed upholstery and a nice view of the back yard and the laundry hanging out on the back porches next door. You'll like it."

"Mr. Kelly?" An officer wearing the insignia of the Harvard Police was beckoning at Homer. "They're going to search the tower now."

"Oh, good," said Homer. "Listen, you two, save me some soup."

Chapter Eight

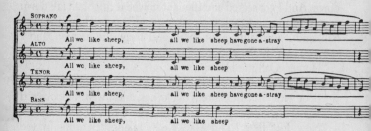

SOPRANO — All we like sheep, all we like sheep have gone a-stray
ALTO — All we like sheep, all we like sheep
TENOR — All we like sheep, all we like sheep have gone a-stray
BASS — All we like sheep, all we like sheep

Homer walked into the memorial corridor by way of the north entry and stopped beside the hole in the floor. It didn't seem possible that a gap in the flooring only fifteen or twenty feet wide could have dropped that much debris into the basement. But of course the explosion had blown out all those walls downstairs too. That would account for some of the mountains of plaster dust and shattered marble and broken timbers, and all the rubble of brick and concrete block. Jerry Crawley, the building superintendent, was blundering around in the hole, wearing a hard hat, getting in the way of Captain McCurdy and one of McCurdy's men from the Bomb Squad.

"I see you're hard at work with that fine-tooth comb of yours, Captain McCurdy," said Homer.

McCurdy looked up, his face gray with plaster dust. "That's right. Tom and I just have to make sure there isn't anybody else buried down here in all this mess. And then Frank Harvey will take over. He'll sift through everything, see if he can find pieces of the explosive device. So far we think it's just dynamite. Tom found a piece of the cap. Fulminate of mercury. Just a bundle of dynamite, that's all it was, with a fulminate of mercury cap."

"Sort of run-of-the-mill, eh? No imagination? No creative spark? Ha ha, no joke intended."

"You should of seen President Cheever," said Crawley, looking up at Homer, his rheumy eyes alight. "He was sick to his stomach. Honest, I thought he was going to throw up. They didn't clean up the blood yet, you know? It was laying all over the place, and he slipped in the blood. Had to hang on to that other guy. Tinker. You know."

"Tinker?"

"Some big guy way high up. Sloan Tinker. I don't know who the hell he is. Cheever had to go in my office and lay down. I got this sofa in there. President Cheever almost threw up on my sofa."

"Well, congratulations. That would have been an honor indeed for your sofa." Homer moved rapidly away from Crawley and climbed over the remnants of the shattered door to the great hall.

"Whatsamatter with him?" said Crawley. "Queasy, I guess. Some people got no stomach. Can't stand the sight of blood. Me, it never bothered me none." He picked up a brick from one pile of rubbish and moved it slowly to another. "Like once I saw this accident. There was four, five people laying all over the road. I pulled my car over to the side—"

"Hey, Crawley," said Captain McCurdy, "have you got the key to that room there? Room 196? It's the only one down here that didn't get its door blown off. We've got to get in there and look inside. You've got the master key?"

"Right, you bet I do," said Crawley. He felt around his neck for the key on the string. It wasn't there. He patted his shirt pocket. "I got it right here someplace."

A head appeared at the edge of the hole and said hello to Captain McCurdy. "Oh, Bert, there you are," said McCurdy.

"Good. You can take over now. Tom hasn't had any lunch and I've got to go up in the tower with Maderna from Buildings and Grounds. Now look here, Bert. Take it slow and easy. And that room there, with the locked door—take a good look in there. Crawley, here, he's got the key." McCurdy climbed up the ladder, followed by Tom, and Bert climbed down.

Mr. Crawley was feeling cheated out of his story about the bodies on the highway. "I was just telling those guys about this terrible accident I saw on Route 128. There were these people all over the road, dead bodies."

Bert looked at the door of Room 196. "You've got the key to this room here?" he said to Crawley.

"Jeez, it's on me someplace," said Crawley. "I know I got it here someplace." He felt feebly in his pants pockets. Then he looked at the locked door of Room 196. "Oh, 196," he said. "That's right; 196 is okay anyways. I already looked in 196. Now, as I was saying, there was all these corpses—"

"You already looked in there?" said Bert. "You mean, it's all cleared out in there? What's that sign mean on the door: *Ethiopian Literacy?* What the heck is that?"

"Damned if I know. They got all these organizations here downcellar. Yeah, I already looked in there. See, that room isn't even under the hole. The ceiling didn't even get blowed off."

Bert shrugged his shoulders and began shoveling plaster dust and brick rubble out of Room 197, which had once housed the Harvard Sci-Fi Comics Library.

"Hey, look at that, will you," said Mr. Crawley. He reached over and picked a dusty comic book out of Bert's shovel. "An old Flash Gordon comic. What do you know?"

Bert dumped his shovelful of plaster dust against the door of 196. "You swear you looked in here?" said Bert.

Jerry Crawley leaned against the ladder and turned the pages of his comic book. "Oh, sure, I swear," he said. He sealed his oath with a mighty belch.

Chapter Nine

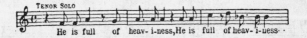

TENOR SOLO

He is full of heav-i-ness, He is full of heav-i-ness ·

His great-aunts were gone, but the pain in his head was still there. He could feel it pulsing and throbbing in the dark. Why he should be on shipboard he didn't know, but there he was. It was a small creaking wooden ship, some explorer's ancient sailing vessel, trying to find North America, wallowing uneasily around in a heaving sea in the middle of the night, and he was wedged in the hold like a piece of cargo, and far over his head he could hear the distant shouts of the seamen on deck. He wanted to tell them they were off the coast of New Jersey, because after all he came from New Jersey, and he knew the coast of New Jersey like the back of his hand. He could even smell the wild grapes on the shore and hear the shore birds cry. But the damnfool captain was yelling, "Port! Port your helm!" and the ship was coming about. They were missing the mainland altogether, heading in their doomed boat back out to sea.

Chapter Ten

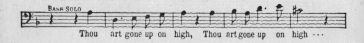

Thou art gone up on high, Thou art gone up on high ···

It was an expeditionary force that assembled on the second balcony above the great hall. Fire Chief Campbell was there, and Frank Harvey from Alcohol, Tobacco and Firearms, and Oliphant from the Cambridge Police, and Peter Marley, Chief of the Harvard Police, and Donald Maderna, the mechanical foreman from the Buildings and Grounds Department for the North Yard, and a swarm of men from Captain McCurdy's department in Boston. Then McCurdy himself came puffing up the second flight of stairs.

"We found a belt buckle," he said, "and some melted plastic credit cards, and a fulminate of mercury detonating cap. That's all so far."

Donald Maderna led the way up the third flight of stairs to the door at the summit of the ceiling, where the arching hammer beams met nearly a hundred feet above the floor. Homer climbed the last stairway slowly, looking down, feeling a pleasant sense of vertigo, enjoying the panorama of the colossal chamber. It had once been a dining hall, he knew that, but now it was more like an empty unused attic or lumber room on a stupendous scale. The wooden walls were a clutter of dusty hangings, marble busts, painted portraits of officers in the Union Army, electric fans, old

radiators, and wires meandering from here to there. Shriveled balloons hung from the ridgepole, left over from a freshman mixer. The room was as long as a football field, a cavernous, yawning, empty space. The stairway led to a series of empty rooms, one above another, in the turret at one side of the north entry. There was a mattress on the floor of the uppermost chamber. "What's that doing here?" said McCurdy.

"Maybe somebody used to live here once," said Homer. "Nice room. Great stained-glass windows. Terrific view. All the colors of the rainbow."

Oliphant kicked the mattress. Dust flew out of it. "Not lately. Nobody's slept here lately. Who would have a key to these rooms up here anyway?"

"Oh, of course nobody's supposed to have keys unless they're issued by the university," said Donald Maderna. "But after the keys get out of our hands, we can't really guarantee what happens to them."

"They have to change the locks all the time," explained Marley of Harvard Police. "We get a hundred break-and-enter complaints a year around here. I mean, let's face it, this is a high-crime area." He turned to Homer Kelly. "You should have seen all those little rooms in the basement. Crazy mess of offices and organizations they've got down there. And the whole place was full of cots and blankets and sleeping bags and illegal hot plates. Makes you wonder what the hell's going on."

"Not like that in my time," said Frank Harvey darkly. "Back in the fifties. Not so many fruit cakes around here then. Whole Boston area's gone to hell."

Donald Maderna opened another door. "Careful now," he said. "From here on it's all catwalks and ladders." He climbed a narrow stair and led them crouching under a low-hanging jungle of ventilating ducts and pipes. "Your people will have their work cut out for them up here, Mr. McCurdy. It's like this under the roof all over the building. Look, here we are at last." Mr. Maderna's voice turned thin and flat, its reverberations lost in the great empty spaces of the tower. "We're right above the memorial corridor now. The trap door to the bell deck is way up there over our heads."

They had emerged from the jungle of pipes to find themselves suspended on a narrow wooden catwalk over a void. For a moment they were silent, looking up at the high brick walls rising around them, up and up to the floor of the belfry, and down and down to the curving surfaces of the wooden vaults below. The space contained within the four lofty walls had never been intended for human use. Most of it was filled with another vast system of galvanized iron air-conditioning and ventilating ducts, some of them glittering with silver padding.

Until now Homer had been silently bringing up the rear, feeling like an Indian in the midst of all the chiefs. But now he was enchanted, and he spoke up. "Oh, isn't this staggering. Look at those vaults from up here. Wastebaskets! Don't they look like giant wastebaskets?"

"Wastebaskets?" said Frank Harvey.

"Look. See the way they taper down to a point at the bottom, like a container? See those paper cups and lunch bags down there? People working up here have thrown things over the railing. See there: popcorn boxes. Beer cans. Look at all that trash." Homer threw back his head and laughed, while the others peered solemnly down. "I mean, when you're standing on the floor of the memorial transept, or whatever you call it, I mean down below, looking up at the vaults, you see all these rising ribs and pointed arches, and you're filled with religious awe and inspiration, right? When really, just look at that, they're just a lot of big wastebaskets for old cigarette packages and beer cans." Homer clutched the railing and the catwalk bounced with his laughter, as the others hung on and tried to see what was funny. "I mean, the way they look like those complicated, mathematical, three-dimensional curves. You know, hyperbolas and parabolas, only all meeting at infinity, you know, those beautiful three-dimensional geometrical constructions with grids making hills and valleys. Oh, noble. You know, now that I really take a look at this building I can see its charm. It's the sublime and the ridiculous all mixed up together. Grotesquely noble. Nobly grotesque. And what could be more charming than those two things together? I ask you." The chiefs looked at one another silently and began moving slowly along the catwalk again, while Homer trailed after them, chuckling to himself, shaking his head. "Inside-out vaults. I'm just crazy about upside-down inside-out vaults."

Afterwards he tried to explain to Mary and Vick what it had been like. He sat at the kitchen table in the flat on Huron Avenue, eating his third bowl of vegetable soup, describing the open bell chamber at the top of the tower. "There wasn't any railing, you see, and the asphalt sort of sloped down in the direction of the open arcades all the way around, and it was all slippery with pigeon droppings. Some of McCurdy's boys were climbing past us into the tower roof to look around up there, and then the bell rang. The clock was striking the hour, and we all nearly fell over the edge with shock and plummeted to our doom. But I hung on to Harvey, and he hung on to Maderna, and Maderna hung on to Oliphant, and Oliphant hung on to Marley, and Marley hung on to Campbell, and Campbell hung on to the corner of a brick with his little finger, so we're all still here."

"Oh, Homer, my God," said Vick.

"Oh, don't worry about Homer," said Mary. "Don't believe a single word he says."

"Well, it was really great up there," said Homer. "You could see all over. The river and all the bridges and Harvard Yard. And Donald Maderna showed me all the sights of Harvard, you know, all those nice blue and gold domes. But in the meantime I was looking eastward, straining my eyes for a glimpse of the dear old Middlesex County Courthouse, over there in East Cambridge, where I used to hang out with the District Attorney. Of course, Maderna didn't know anything about East Cambridge, and neither did the federal guy, Harvey. All they could see was Dunster House and Eliot and Mather, and all those other places with

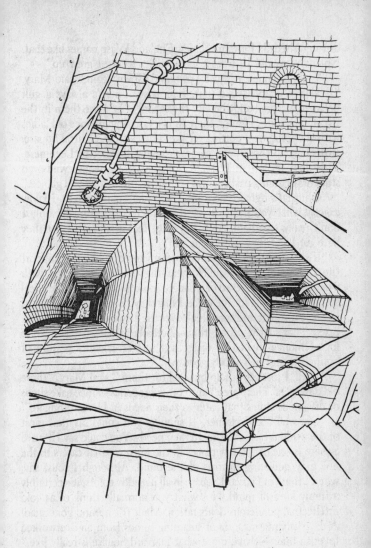

distinguished old Puritanical New England Wasp names like that. Not crummy old Irish East Cambridge, where I grew up."

"Well, of course it's just Town and Gown again," said Mary. "It always happens like that, I suppose. There's always a gulf between a school and the city the school is in. I see them in the street, you know, Homer, there in Harvard Square, nice old ladies with shopping bags getting off the subway from Central Square, struggling up those cruel steps, or taking the bus to Lechmere. They look so lost in Harvard Square, with all those wild-eyed students charging past them, never giving them a second glance."

"Oh, that's right," said Vick. "You're absolutely right. I know exactly what you mean. I see them there in the square, only I don't really *see* them. And they must feel it, sort of. I bet they hate us. I bet they just loathe us."

"It's too bad the citizens of New England don't have to support the college any more," said Homer, "the way they did at first, with a peck of wheat or a cord of wood, or something. Then they'd feel sort of responsible for the place. Now they're just mad at Harvard because it squats and sprawls all over the city and doesn't pay any taxes. That's what people think. Actually, it does pay the city a lot of money in lieu of taxes as a sort of friendly gesture of bonhomie and neighborly good will."

"Well, I just can't help but feel for them," said Mary, "those old dowagers. There aren't any corner groceries or nice cake shops or dry-goods stores that cater to their needs in Harvard Square."

"Oh, well," said Homer, "I suppose you could say that most of the world is busy catering to their needs. You could say Harvard Square is one of the few places in the universe that caters to the raw gray quivering furrows of the mind. Although I must say, when I think of Harvard Square in all its giddy colors, it's certainly a funny kind of mind. Not what you normally think of as cold intellectual ponderous deliberation. Mad! It's a mind gone mad! A dizzy phantasmagoria of steaming fumes from an overworked feverish brain—that's more what Harvard Square is really like." Then Homer looked thoughtfully at Vick's outfit, which was a

44

purple vest over an orange striped blouse that hung loose over her tattered scarlet skirt. "Well, when you get right down to it, it's just youth, really. It's just the delirium of being young. That's what it is, really."

Huron Avenue

Chapter Eleven

Homer had another look at Harvard Square the next morning, when he stopped at the newsstand on the corner for a copy of the *Crimson.* The full surge of the square flowed around him, collecting in pulses at the crossing and then streaming forward, trucks thundering and squealing around the corner of Mass Av and Brattle, pedestrians seething on the curb beside the clock, the pavement trembling with the vibration of trains passing through dark tunnels underground. Homer had once supervised the throbbing tides of traffic from a kind of lighthouse on the curb across the street, but now the lighthouse was gone, and the traffic lights alone held sway over the square. STOP, they commanded. GO. WALK. DONT WALK.

He looked at the spot on the sidewalk where his tiny house had stood, and remembered the occasional resentment that had risen in his breast as he had watched his peers shoulder their way across the street. They had seemed to him in those days insolent with privilege. It had been a judgment tainted with envy. Night school at Northeastern had not gilded his head with the kind of light that fell on these students now, as they ran boldly across Mass Av to the Yard against the oncoming traffic as if by a kind of divine right. Harvard, after all, was a kind of religion. One said the word with reverence, or ironic awe: *Haaaarvard.* Strait was the gate and narrow the way that led through the admissions office into the sanctified inner spaces of the Yard. And that was why, when old Dr. Summer had asked Mary if the two Kellys would teach a course in the Department of English and American Literature and Language, there had been on Homer's part a small unspoken sense of triumph. Not for Mary. For Mary it was home ground anyway. She had gone to school here herself, and most of her male ancestors had come to Cambridge for their higher education. Modest Concord farmers they had been for generations back, riding in on the cars with the Concord sons of bankers and senators and railroad men. Hoars and Keyeses and even Emersons. And of course Henry Thoreau had gone to Harvard, walking from the country into town sometimes, or picking up the coach at the Middlesex Hotel before the railroad had pushed west through Concord to Fitchburg.

Homer wormed his way into the crowded newsstand and paid for his *Crimson* and a copy of the *Globe*.

HAM DOW DIES IN MEM HALL BOMBING

ran the banner at the top of the *Crimson*'s front page. Halfway down there was another headline:

U.S. UNCONCERNED WITH PLIGHT OF NEPALESE

The *Globe* had a feature on Ham Dow:

BOMBING VICTIM HARVARD FAVORITE

Outside the Harvard Coop two girls were hawking the *Boston Phoenix* and the *Real Paper*.

FRUSTRATED NEPALESE STRIKE AGAIN?

suggested the *Phoenix*.

HARVARD GOES BOOM!

said the *Real Paper*.

"Homer, for heaven's *sake*."

"What? Mary, dear, what are you doing here?"

Mary Kelly was shaking him, her big breast heaving. "Didn't you hear me shouting? I've been chasing you ever since you left the house. Screeching at you, making a fool of myself."

"Good God, no. What's happened?"

"The President of the Overseers, she called you. The Harvard *Overseers*. Julia Chamberlain, her name is. I didn't know how I was ever going to reach you in Memorial Hall. So I raced down two flights of stairs and I've been galumphing across half of Cambridge trying to catch up."

Homer looked around vaguely. "Telephone. Where's a telephone?"

"There's a pay phone in front of the movie. I've got the number in my pocket. Here, dear, here's a dime."

"Mrs. Chamberlain?" said Homer, staring into the dark cave of the entrance to the Harvard Square Theatre. "This is Homer Kelly."

"Oh, Mr. Kelly, thank you for calling me back. I've just got a couple of things to ask you. It's about this horrible thing at Memorial Hall. We're all just miserable about Ham Dow. I just can't believe he's not going to be around any more. I mean, he was the best-loved person in this whole place. It just makes you want to— Well, I don't know why those crazy Nepalese couldn't have blown up somebody else. Ham probably *agreed* with them, for heaven's sake. Well, we're all just sick."

"Yes," murmured Homer, "I get that from every side. I understand he was a good man."

"Well, I'll stop complaining and come to the point. Peter Marley of the Harvard Police tells me you have a background with the forces of law and order here in Cambridge, as well as being on the faculty, and he says you were almost a witness to the disaster. So I wonder if you'd be willing to help us out with a couple of things."

"Well, certainly, Mrs. Chamberlain. I'll do anything I can."

"Well, first of all, there's the funeral. There's going to be a big funeral service for Ham in the church here in the Yard on Sunday afternoon. The students are in charge. They've just taken over the whole thing. Ham didn't have any near relations, so the kids were insisting on doing it themselves, and nobody could think of any reason why not. They're going to sing their hearts out, naturally. You know, things from that oratorio they were all doing together, Handel's *Messiah*. Ham's assistant is going to be in charge of the music, a girl named Victoria Van Horn."

"Oh, yes. I know Vick."

"Well, I understand the chairman of the Music Department has appointed her to be chorus director pro tem in Ham's place. I mean, she's just a senior, but everybody seems to think she's the one Ham would have picked himself. And Charley Flynn's going to give the eulogy. Young chemistry professor, Ham's closest friend on the faculty. Well, we've had some trouble about that. He's the faculty radical. But he's the one the students wanted. And after all, they're in charge. That's what I said to President Cheever and Sloan Tinker. I mean, they were raising serious questions. I think they thought he might blow up the church."

"Was Ham pretty far to the left himself? I mean, it just occurs to me to wonder whether he was or not."

"Ham? Oh, I suppose so. Well, really, I don't know if he was a political radical or not. The way he lived was certainly unconventional. But he didn't upset people the way Charley Flynn does. You know, I sometimes wonder if Charley is related to Errol Flynn, that movie star from way back. Remember those old pirate movies? The way he was always jumping on board some ship with his cloak flying behind him and a knife between his teeth? Really refreshing. Well, Charley's like that. Oh, I know he wants us all to walk the plank, I mean all of us in the Harvard establishment, but God knows he's probably right most of the time. We need people like that desperately, believe me."

Homer found himself warming to the President of the Overseers. "Just what is it you want me to do, Mrs. Chamberlain?"

"Oh, sorry; back to the point. You see, I volunteered to help out in any way I could, so Vick asked me to take care of the grim practical side of things. So I need to know about the body. Where is it? And can we have it in the church for the service on Sunday? And there's a lot of sentiment about a plain pine box; in fact, the students are really *fierce* on the subject, and they don't want any embalming or anything like that. They just want to let nature take its course. You know the kind of thing. They want a real funeral, with the body right there in the church, not just a polite memorial service. Everybody facing up to death, and so on."

"I see, Mrs. Chamberlain. You want me to make the necessary arrangements to get the body released for burial. I'll be glad to."

"Well, that's great. Now, the other thing is this. Could you come to the meeting of the Board of Overseers next week and report to us about the whole miserable bombing episode? I mean, the Overseers will be coming to the meeting from all over the place, and they'll be worried. They'll be wondering if the place is safe for the students. Well, of course, Buildings and Grounds has already given the all clear on the use of Memorial Hall. That man from the Bomb Squad said he was satisfied there weren't any more bombs in there anywhere, and Donald Maderna's got the hole in the floor all fenced in and that part of the basement boarded up, and the poor old rose windows are boarded up too. They're going to seal up the floor and put down fresh cement, but they're going to leave all the debris in the basement till next spring. Next April sometime they're going to gut that whole part of the basement and turn it into new office space. That Donald Maderna works fast. He had people in there all night long, getting the place ready for public use once again."

"That was quick work, all right. You mean I can use my classroom again tomorrow? Say, that's great. Now, just tell me where and when the Overseers meet."

"University Hall, right there behind the statue of John Harvard in the old Yard, the Faculty Room on the second floor. Monday morning. Now, the question is, what time? Usually the Overseers don't get together until two, but President Cheever is calling for a joint session with the Corporation, so we're starting early so we can go on with the reports of the Visiting Committees later on. You'll be present at a historic occasion, I guess, Mr. Kelly, a joint session of both groups. I mean, I never heard of them meeting together before. But President Cheever has a building project he wants to bring up before everybody at the same time. I gather the Corporation already turned it down, but I guess in the President's opinion that didn't exactly settle the matter. In fact, I understand it came up before the faculty last week. Anyway, our meeting is supposed to begin at nine-thirty, but I think if you came along about ten o'clock, we could squeeze you into the agenda. Is that all right with you?"

"That's fine. I'll be there. And I'll see about the funeral. I'll call you back this afternoon, Mrs. Chamberlain."

"Well, good for you. You're a peach."

NORTH CAMBRIDGE FUNERAL PARLOR

Dignified Personal Service

FINEST FACILITIES

Centrally Air-Conditioned

PRE-NEED PLANNING

Air-conditioned, noted Homer. That was important. You wouldn't want the body of your loved one to smell on a hot day. Pre-need planning was probably a good thing too. More efficient. Pre-griefstricken folks could make plans to get their nearest and dearest into the ground a lot faster when the sad moment finally arrived.

Homer poked around the building and found Mr. Ratchit in a small office at the back.

"Oh, sure," said Mr. Ratchit. "He's all yours. We've got the permit from the Board of Health. The Medical Examiner saw him at the place where he was blown up, Whatchacallit Hall, that big church there. And they had the autopsy already."

"Memorial Hall. It's not a church. It's a Civil War memorial."

"Well, it looks like a church. Say, you know, that individual was obese. I mean, he was heavy."

"Well, he was pretty tall too, right? I never met the man," said Homer gloomily. "I mean, when he was alive."

"Tall, oh, sure, he was tall. But flabby. I mean, he was flabby. Well, you know, really repulsive. I look at it this way. God gives you a magnificent body, right?" Mr. Ratchit arched his narrow chest and spread his scrawny arms. "So you ought to take care of it, right? But look what some people do with it."

"Well, yes, I suppose so."

"You should of seen his hands. I mean, like I'm really interested in hands. Well, this guy's hands were soft. White and flabby. Pudgy, really soft. The hands of an extremely obese individual. Take a look at my hands, for instance. No, go ahead, feel. Feel those calluses? That's work, man. Hard work. With a spade, with a hoe. Hard physical work. I mean, I really believe in good hard physical exercise. You take your average sedentary person, they've got hands like bread dough. Sitting there at a desk all day."

Homer shrank down in his chair and sat on his hands, feeling his stomach brim over his belt buckle. "Well, actually, I don't think Ham Dow sat at a desk all day, exactly. But I suppose he didn't go in much for real exercise. Now, there's another thing, Mr. Ratchit. All we want is a simple pine box."

"A pine box? Oh, no, you don't want a pine box for a VIP like that. I suggest this casket here. Solid walnut. Solid brass handles." Mr. Ratchit handed Homer a pamphlet. "After that you go into your metal caskets. Light gauge. Heavy gauge. Solid copper. I mean, I understand from the papers he was really an important member of the university personnel."

"No," said Homer, closing his eyes and speaking through his teeth. "We want a plain old-fashioned ordinary box. A plain pine box. And then there's the matter of the embalming. There's to be no embalming."

"No embalming? They must be out of their mind! It'll swell up! It'll stink! Well, we've got it in the fridge. Maybe it'll keep. Let's hope it's cool on Sunday." Mr. Ratchit reached over and poked Homer in the chest. "You know, you're not in such great shape yourself, friend. Three-quarters of an inch of blubber there. Maybe an inch. You ought to get out in the open more, you know?"

Chapter Twelve

Homer and Mary Kelly came to the church early because Mary was going to sing with the chorus. Mary dodged around to the back, and Homer started for the front, but early as he was, he suspected he might be too late to get a seat. People were streaming into the building from every direction, crowding on the stairs, pressing thickly into the doorway. Most of them were students, or people the same age as the students. Some of them looked bizarre to Homer's innocent eye, a motley lot, a little odd and wild, dressed in the fantastic plumage of street people selling bangles or handing out religious pamphlets in the square.

Homer waited patiently on the stairs, moving slowly upward one step at a time. To amuse himself he studied the delicate white spire, floating above the roof like a piece of intricately cut and folded paper. The spire was too light for the monumental pillars of the porches, he decided, but the building itself was in keeping with the other buildings in the Yard. It was better matched to the local architecture than was Memorial Hall, over there across Cambridge Street. But this church was a war memorial too, he knew that. When he squeezed through the vestry into the main body of the church, he saw the tablets on the high south wall, recording in gold letters the names of the Harvard dead in World War II. World War I had a room to itself, off to the side. He could see it through an open door, all polished marble and solemn inscriptions and flags.

The church was nearly full. The ushers were seating people in the rear seats under the balcony. Homer sat down in the last row and took off his coat and looked around. The place was luminous and white. Through the tall windows light flooded the high ceiling and the massive white columns and the rows and rows of white-painted pews. Hot air warmed the church, blowing out of the registers under the windows, and the great space was comfortable with red cushions and red carpets. Not dark and drafty like Memorial Hall, where there was nothing to sit down on while you contemplated the martial sacrifice of those who had gone before. But this building seemed to expect a well-groomed sort of mourner. It wasn't a primitive holy place like Memorial Hall, where some remnant of the bloody superstitions of the Middle Ages seemed to stain the dark tracery of the woodwork, matching the carnage of the battles in which those young Union soldiers had died. Of course, the two world wars had been worse, if anything. But the polite perfection and bright light of this handsome building gave no hint that mankind could ever under any circumstances be anything but reasonable and heedful of the requirements of etiquette. It wasn't like Memorial Hall, where the air was thick with myths of death and resurrection.

Homer stared at his big right shoe, which was skewed sideways against the back of the pew in front of him. He wondered if anyone had erected a memorial to the Harvard men who had died in Vietnam. Probably not. Altogether too controversial and nasty a little war. Too sticky a little problem. For the Civil War you got a building. For World Wars I and II you got a building. For

Vietnam you got a dean carried *out* of a building. Heads busted in by the cops.

"Excuse me." The usher was squeezing a crowd of people into Homer's pew. Homer looked up and moved over, and then he saw the Vietnam memorial. It was a small plaque on the north wall. Beside it hung another small tablet for the dead of the Korean War. "Sorry," said the girl sitting next to Homer. She glanced at him apologetically and socked him in the hip with her bony little haunch. The usher was wedging still one more friend and admirer of Hamilton Dow's into the pew.

The ushers had their work cut out for them. The church was full. Homer looked over his shoulder and saw large jowly faces jammed in the doorway, raising their eyebrows at Homer's usher. And now the usher was looking across the rows of seated bodies, searching for somebody expendable. He was walking forward, bending over the scruffy boy in front of Homer, murmuring something about prominent alumni.

The student didn't move a whisker. He spoke up clearly. "Fuck the alumni." A fleeting expression of pleasure bloomed on the bland face of the usher, who then softly withdrew and approached the prominent alumni, shaking his head.

Something was going on up front. Homer craned his neck to see past the frowsy head in front of him. A mighty woman in a black pyramidal veil was creating a disturbance. She looked gigantic and monumental like the Great Sphinx, only all in motion. It was the woman Homer had seen on the sidewalk outside Memorial Hall. Her two tubby little boys were behind her now, forming a phalanx. She was hissing at the usher, jabbing her finger at an empty pew in the front row. And now the usher was hastening to the back of the church to consult with Homer's usher. "But it's the President's pew. It's all I've got left. I can't put her in the President's pew. I've already got to get all the pallbearers in there. She can't sit in his pew. But what am I going to do with her? She says she's Ham's mistress, for Christ's sake."

"Oh, God, it's Mrs. Esterhazy. She's not his mistress. I mean, good God, just look at her. Go ahead, put her in there. She's going to start swinging in a minute. The hell with President Cheever."

The organ began filling the church with sound, and there were trumpeters, too, behind the choir screen, and then Vick's chorus began to sing, massive and serene.

James Cheever was doing his best to control himself. He had been chivvied about in the crowd, and pushed aside to make room for the casket, and then prodded to walk directly behind the pallbearers. Now he was walking slowly, holding back, because he was afraid the pallbearers weren't going to make it, they were having such a struggle with the coffin, they were so burdened by the weight of the gluttonous body within. The idea of bringing the casket into the church at all was grotesque. A memorial service would have been in better taste. And the choice of music, good lord. "Worthy Is the Lamb That Was Slain." As if Dow were some sort of latter-day Jesus Christ. Then the President of Harvard stopped short beside his customary pew and gazed thunderstruck at Mrs. Esterhazy and her two sons. The woman gazed fiercely back at him, streams of water pouring down her cheeks from eyes that were black blotches of mascara.

President Cheever turned boiled eyes on the usher. "I can't sit here," he said.

"I'm sorry, sir. It's all there is left. Now, if you'll all just push over as far as you can, the pallbearers will just squeeze in here alongside."

One of the pallbearers was a young red-headed boy with a big nose. The President of Harvard recognized him immediately, because he often saw him in Massachusetts Hall, washing windows and emptying wastebaskets. The whole thing was a plot, a conspiracy to make the President of Harvard look ridiculous, squeezing him into his own pew in the front of the church between a janitor and a prostitute. It was just one more example of the way everything connected with Ham Dow had brought him bad fortune from the beginning. Well, it was the last time.

From now on the pew would be his alone. The white Corinthian columns with the rams' heads and the four signs of the gospels and the doves of the holy spirit, they would be his too, in a manner of speaking, and the fanciful pulpit, and the serene classical spaces filled with music. No longer would he have to share them with Hamilton Dow.

James Cheever folded his arms on his chest and glanced to the side and nodded across the aisle at Julia Chamberlain. Julia was sitting beside Sloan Tinker, looming above Tinker and the whole row of gray-headed faculty, looking as usual like one of the caryatids on the Acropolis. Julia was blowing her nose dolefully. It passed through President Cheever's mind to wonder if she would grieve for him, if it were his own funeral rather than Dow's. Because it had come down to that, very nearly. A choice. Oh, Julia had pretended to be impartial. But her bias showed through. Her true feelings were perfectly clear.

Who was that climbing into the pulpit? Oh, good lord, not Charley Flynn? Wouldn't you just know. James Cheever fixed his eyes on the choir screen, refusing to look at the idiot as he put his hand in the pocket of his blue jeans and began the eulogy. But, in all the pews to left and right, people were sniffing, sobbing, breaking down. The President of Harvard reached into his breast pocket for his handkerchief and passed it across his nose. It should not be said of him that he was lacking in feeling.

"Homer, here we are." Mary was beside him in the crowded vestry, coming up from the locker room downstairs with Vick.

Vick's fingers pierced Homer's coat sleeve. "Homer," said Vick.

"Well, now, Vick," said Homer, patting her on the back, "the music was magnificent. You did him proud."

Vick's hair had been twisted into thick pigtails and pinned up at the back of her head, but now the pressure inside her skull burst the pins. Her pigtails sprang loose and one braid came apart, its three rivers of red hair untwisting in one flood. "Yes," said Vick. "I think he would have liked it. Nobody was allowed to cry. I mean, until we were all through. Then we cried buckets. Now listen, Homer, what are you going to do about it? I mean, it's your turn now."

"What do you mean, what am I going to do?" Homer stepped out of doors onto the porch, urged along by the throng pressing up against his back. "My dear girl, I'm no longer an official member of any law-enforcing body. I can't—"

"But don't you *care?*" Vick hung on to Homer and pounded his arm. "Oh, I know you didn't really know him, or anything like that, but just the same. Mary, he's got to do something, doesn't he?"

"Homer, dear," began Mary, "I really think—"

"Now look here," said Homer. "There are at least four or five different outfits already involved in this investigation: the Boston Police Department, the Cambridge Police Department, the

Cambridge Fire Department, the Harvard Police, and the United States Treasury Department of Alcohol, Tobacco and Firearms. Not to mention the FBI. So what possible reason could there be for me . . . ?"

"But they don't have the personal sort of close-up, you know, relationship," said Vick.

"My dear Vick, I never met the man." Homer stumbled, and almost lost his footing.

"Oh, Homer, watch out, you poor great ox," said Mary. "Now just be careful. The steps begin right here. She's right, you know, Homer. Vick's right. You can't just stand there. You've got to do something."

"I'm not just standing here. I'm falling downstairs." Wedged in by a thick crush of human bodies pouring inexorably forward, Homer bungled the top step and sent a wave of imbalance reeling forward among deans, professors, students, Overseers, and miscellaneous nonacademic types from Harvard Square and the back streets of Cambridge. "Oh, God," said Homer, throwing his arms around the great bosom of a matron at the bottom of the stairs' "I don't know. I just don't know."

Chapter Thirteen

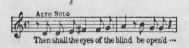

Then shall the eyes of the blind be open'd ···

Ham opened his eyes. His tongue was thick in his mouth and his head throbbed. It was the middle of the night, pitch black. He closed his eyes and drifted off again into painful dreams. Some time later he became conscious that his face was resting on something uncomfortable. He tried to roll over, but he couldn't move. Something was weighing down heavily on his back. His head was pounding. His body ached in every limb. He turned his head to one side and tried to spit out the grit that was pressing into his mouth, and then, straining to lift his head, he stared into the darkness.

Where was he? Where, in the name of God?

Chapter Fourteen

Homer was supposed to appear at the meeting of the Harvard Overseers at ten. He had allowed himself an extra hour to spend with the Harvard Police Chief. He galloped across Mass Av, panted for a moment on the cement island where a green statue of Charles Sumner gazed vaguely down on the raging traffic, and then plunged across the rest of the avenue and entered the Yard. Beside the old brick front of Harvard Hall he stopped to look at his map. Homer was not yet at home with the lay of the land. He knew a lot more about the place from books than he did from experience. Of course, he had long been familiar with the vast staircase of Widener Library, and the layers of stacks and the call desk and the card catalogue, where he hardly needed to glance at the signs to know on which side of the aisle to find T for Thoreau or V for Jones Very or C for Christopher Pearse Cranch. But he knew the rest of the buildings and their history only from book learning. He knew, for example, that Henry Thoreau's grandfather (A.B. 1767) had led a student rebellion against the quality of the college butter. He knew that Henry himself had lived in Hollis Hall. He knew that President Dunster had been forced to resign in 1654 because he didn't believe in infant baptism. Homer knew which of his favorite abolitionists had been to Harvard. He knew Theodore Parker had run into a tree while reading a book and knocked himself out; he knew Oliver Wendell Holmes (a latecomer to the cause of emancipation) had assisted in the dismissal of three black students from the medical school. Wendell Phillips and Thomas Wentworth Higginson had graduated from

Harvard. Longfellow and James Russell Lowell had taught here. Homer knew all these things, but he didn't know where Grays Hall was. He squinted at the map and batted it to keep it open in the wind. Oh, there was Grays, way off to the right.

Homer pocketed his map and turned south. He was moving through the oldest part of the Yard. Some of these buildings had been here practically forever, solid hulks of brick. Homer looked at the men and women walking past him now, heading for Holyoke to study Celtic, or Mallinckrodt for a class in biochem or Sever Hall for Afro-American Studies, and they began to turn a little filmy and dim and transparent. Homer couldn't help but see them in a kind of stop-motion movie; they were racing by, their legs twittering along the path. He speeded up the film still more, and now they were merely pale mothlike figures, streaks of color, whizzing back and forth, class after class, generation after generation, century after century, while the massive houses stood fixed and permanent, their brick chimneys poking through time. Homer wondered pompously to himself whether the fleeting streaks of color were of any use or value at all, those moths existing but for a day, dashing themselves headlong at the flickering lamp of learning. He didn't know. He couldn't swear to it. He felt a little dim and uncertain himself, fumbling around the corner of Grays Hall, looking for the office of the Harvard Police.

He was just going to get a report on things from Harvard Police, and pass it along to the Overseers. That was all he would do. Because it really wasn't his responsibility in any way. He was really out of it. He would just get a general picture of the overall situation and pass it along to Mrs. Chamberlain and the rest of them at ten o'clock in University Hall.

It was clear that the incident was over. Except for the awful fact of the death of Ham Dow, the bomb had hardly disturbed the calm of the university. Donald Maderna's crew had cleaned things up and opened the building, and they were beginning to rebuild the floor. Professor Parker's immense classes in The Great Age of Athens had been forced across the street to the Lowell Lecture Hall only once. Students were taking shortcuts through Memorial Hall once again, dodging around Maderna's sawhorses, finding their way in the dim light of the chandeliers even in the daytime, because the windows were darkened with huge sheets of plywood. Things were pretty much back to normal.

The door to the Harvard Police Department was down a flight of basement stairs. Homer opened the door, trying to remember the name of the man in charge. It was something Dickensian. Marley, that was it. Like Marley's ghost, clanking his chain up the steps to Scrooge's bedchamber, crying, *Ebeneeeezer, Ebeneeeezer.*

The girl at the counter looked up at Homer. "Mr. . . . ?"

"Scrooge," said Homer. "No, no, I'm sorry. Kelly. Homer Kelly. I have an appointment with Mr. Marley."

"Oh, yes, go right in, Mr. Kelly. Mr. Marley's office is at the end of the hall to the right." The girl had to speak up over the noise of the police radio in the switchboard behind her.

Peter Marley stood up as Homer entered his office. "Come right in, Mr. Kelly. I've been wanting to tell you how glad I was to meet you last week. I mean, I read all about that case out in Concord. And that girl on Nantucket during the eclipse of the sun, the one who—"

"Oh, no, my God, never mind. I tripped all over my own big feet both times. Hideous mistakes. Ghastly errors. And I'm staying out of this one altogether. But I'm supposed to make some kind of explanation to the Overseers. Mrs. Chamberlain, she's asked me to tell them whether or not I think Harvard's going to get blown off the map."

"Oh, no, I don't think so, do you? We're not worried about it. Of course, we've had a few false alarms since last Wednesday, but they didn't amount to anything. We get them all the time. Here, take a look." Peter Marley picked up a computer printout from his desk and showed it to Homer. It was an index of police statistics for the week, and the kinds of crimes were listed separately: HOMICIDE, ASSAULT, ROBBERY, RAPE, OBSCENE CALL, BOMB THREAT, BREAK & ENTER, BUILDING TAKEOVER . . .

"Building takeover." Homer laughed. "Well, I guess you people have your own special little problems in your war against crime."

"Look here, under 'Bomb Threat,' " said Marley. "Seven of them. Of course, the one in Memorial Hall wasn't a threat, it was the real thing. But the others were just nutty calls. We get them all the time. Yes, Judy, you want something?"

A woman in a blue uniform was looking in at the door. "Excuse me, Pete. We thought you'd like to know there's been another bombing in Bridgeport. Big insurance company. And the Nepalese Freedom Movement said they did it. It was on the news just now."

"No kidding? Well, thank you, Judy. Mr. Kelly, I think they've turned their attention elsewhere. It's the banks that will be getting it next, I'll bet. They must be through with the universities. It's funny, though; they never took credit for our bombing. They usually call up some newspaper and give a speech over the phone."

"What about supporters of the movement here in Cambridge? Do you know anything about them?" said Homer. "I understand there are plenty of sympathizers with the Nepalese Freedom Movement among the student body. But I don't suppose there are any mad bombers in that lot?"

"I doubt it very much. We've talked to a bunch of them. Some of our best students are members of leftist groups of one kind or another. And of course when you say the word 'radical' around here, everybody thinks of Charley Flynn. He's an assistant professor in the Chemistry Department. But the trouble is, all these people were friends of Ham Dow. It's inconceivable any of them would have put his life in danger, let alone blow him up."

"What about people on the scene at the time? Have you got any record on them?"

"Oh, my God, there were so many of them. There was such a jumble and confusion of near-witnesses and standers-by and rushers-to-the-scene. Well, you know. You were there. At the time of the explosion the basement was full of people. They poured out of the building from every door. You know: the radio station, WHRB, the copy center, the lecture hall where you were teaching, all those little rooms and offices down there. But when we tried to pin them down—who they were, where they had been at the time, where they lived, and so on—they melted away. And the people we did manage to identify didn't seem to have the vaguest notion who any of the others might be. Tell me, have you ever heard of Ham's Rats?"

"Ham's Rats?"

"It was what they called themselves. A whole bunch of people. Mostly kids, but not all. Some of them were middle-aged, even elderly. People that hung around Ham. A lot of them weren't even students. They were people he picked up or befriended in one way or another. The trouble is, no one seems to know who they were exactly. Wait a minute, listen to this. Wait till you hear our interview with Crawley, the building superintendent. I've got a tape recording right here. Listen to this."

Homer sat back and looked at the ceiling and winced, as Mr. Crawley's whining voice began droning from the tape recorder.

"I don't know who was in the building. Damned if I know who the hell was downstairs."

"But, Mr. Crawley, whoever put that bundle of dynamite and the clock mechanism under the floor of the memorial transept must have known the building very well."

"Well, don't ask me. They were all over the place all the time, those kids. 'What the hell you doing here?' I says. 'It's a free country,' they says. So I says, 'Get the hell out.' Only, next thing you know, they're back again, all over the place downstairs. And up in the balcony."

"The balcony?"

"That balcony up there. You know. It's right up over the place where the guy got his head blown off."

"Who? Who was up in the balcony?"

"Some weirdo. I don't know. He's new. Wasn't there before."

"Well, what about the night before the bombing? Did you see anybody unusual hanging around the building the evening before? The clock mechanism would have been good for no more than twelve hours. So it was probably set the night before, around midnight."

"Jeez, I don't know. You think I want to hang around this place at night? Come five o'clock, I get out of there. Cheever was there the day before. President Cheever. There was some ceremony going on in Sanders Theatre on Tuesday. Cheever was in there giving a speech. Only, that was in the middle of the day."

"Mr. Crawley, do you know anything about Ham's Rats?"

"Well, there was this big lady—"

"Mrs. Esterhazy. Right. We know about Mrs. Esterhazy. She lived on Martin Street in Ham's house. Anybody else?"

"I don't know. I can't tell them apart. Bunch of weirdos, if you ask me."

Chapter Fifteen

The meeting of the Board of Overseers was in full swing when Homer opened the door of the Faculty Room in University Hall. No one looked up at him. They all seemed to be talking at once.

Homer was glad. It gave him a chance to get used to the room.

There wasn't anything clever or original about it. It was probably just run-of-the-mill Bulfinch. The man had probably just tossed off the design in an hour or two. He had chosen those high round-headed windows on the east side as a matter of routine. Ditto the west side. Ionic pilasters, ditto, ditto, all around the room. Classical moldings. Cut-glass chandelier. And then other people had come along, year after year, and lined the room with busts and portraits. There were presidents of Harvard all over the place. Eliot, Lowell, Conant, Pusey, Bok. It was intimidating. "Improve the shining hour," they seemed to be saying. "Expand another orbit on the great deep." Asa Gray, Louis Agassiz. Noble heads with great noses and foaming sideburns and marble muttonchop whiskers. Evangelinus Apostolides Sophocles. William James. And who was that fellow there, naked as a baby below his bushy curling beard? Longfellow, of course, Henry Wadsworth Longfellow. Longfellow looked dreamily at Homer and reminded him that *in the world's broad field of battle, in the bivouac of life,*

one should be not like dumb, driven cattle but a hero in the strife.
Homer hunched his shoulders and sat down in one of the impos-
ing chairs out of Longfellow's view. He wasn't about to be a hero.
He was just here at this meeting as a reporter in this matter, that
was all. He was just passing information along. He was merely a
conduit between the forces of law and order and the institutional
establishment of Harvard University. *Come, come, my man,* murmured Longfellow. *Lives of great men all remind us, we can make
our lives sublime; have you ever thought of that?* No, I haven't,
insisted Homer, and I'm not about to start now. He dismissed
Longfellow's nagging verses from his mind and tried to concen-
trate on the matter under discussion in the Faculty Room. It was
a heated argument. What was it all about?

There were twenty or thirty people sitting in majestic chairs
around three sides of a square, facing a table on the east side of
the room. The table was a great circle, polished and old and
venerable as the Table Round. The tall woman at the table must
be Julia Chamberlain. She was sitting at the head of the table
because she was the President of the Overseers. James Cheever
was there because he was the President of the University. One of
the others was the Treasurer. Who were the rest? Aha, the five
Fellows. The old chap who looked as if he were falling asleep must
be Shackleton Bowditch, the Senior Fellow. The Harvard Corporation was present in full strength: the President, the Treasurer
and the five Fellows, that little self-perpetuating band of men who
really ran the business of the institution. To Homer's critical eye
the five Fellows looked a little resentful and disgruntled. Mrs.
Chamberlain had said this was a rare occasion, a meeting of the
two boards in the same room at the same time. Awe-inspiring.
Homer felt duly humble, to be a witness to the secret delibera-
tions of the mighty.

Mrs. Chamberlain was looking at Homer. "Oh, Mr. Kelly,
thank you so much for coming. Would you mind waiting a moment? We'll be finished with this thing in a few minutes."

But they weren't finished in a few minutes. The matter under discussion obviously provoked strong feeling. People were shifting in their chairs, interrupting. James Cheever seemed to be standing his ground alone.

"But, Jim," said Julia Chamberlain, "it isn't just the faculty who won't stand for it. Don't forget the poor old alumni and alumnae. The money would have to come out of them. Do you remember the trouble we had getting funding for the new tower steeple on Memorial Hall, to replace the one that was burned off back in 1956? And those new clocks? The four new clocks on the steeple? It was like pulling teeth. They kept whimpering about getting blood from turnips. They couldn't see the sense in putting all that money into an unnecessary piece of architecture that didn't even add any classroom space. You know, it was just for old time's sake, just for looks. Well, it will be the same way with this. Money's too scarce. All we can think of right now is salaries. Salaries and scholarships. We can't cut back on those two things, and I doubt the old grads will hear of funding a project like your new Decorative Arts Building."

"Nobody," said President Cheever, "is suggesting for a moment that we cut back on salaries and scholarships."

"And of course, don't forget, there's the stained glass," said Julia Chamberlain, rushing forward bravely. "Did you know that, Jim? They're talking about replacing the broken stained glass in Memorial Hall."

James Cheever was obviously taken by surprise. "They're what? Oh, no. Oh, no they don't. No, sir. Why, that would cost thousands. Hundreds of thousands of dollars. You mean they're thinking of pouring more money into the restoration of a monstrous horror of a building that had the misfortune of being constructed at the very nadir of this country's architectural history? Oh, no they don't. Not while I'm President of this university."

Homer looked up at the sun-filled volume of air over the heads of the Overseers. He could almost see its clear substance thickening and hardening into clots of opposition. There was some common but unspoken solidification of opinion, of polite but stubborn separation. Some of the Overseers were sitting with folded arms, studying the floor. Others were looking steadily at Cheever, their faces blank. Most of the Overseers were prosperous-looking men in the prime of life, but a few were women. One of the women looked young enough to be a high school girl. Nearly all of them had slipped down in their chairs. They were all stretched out straight, with their ankles crossed on the floor in front of them. Homer could see why. His own great chair felt slippery and uncomfortable.

Cheever seemed to be aware of the lack of sympathy. His voice was rising, he was looking from one face to another for a support that seemed to be slow in coming. "Look here," he said. "It would be a new capital drive. It wouldn't diminish the contributions that maintain our regular programs. It would be a special extra request made only to those alumni of large means who normally contribute substantially to new undertakings in the arts. They'll be giving the money away anyhow, don't you see? To other institutions. To great museums, schools of ballet, opera houses, theatres. All we would be doing in this case would be redirecting their contributions to Harvard University. It would merely be a matter of appealing to a handful of wealthy alumni, whom I could name right now. And of course we'd ask for a few corporate gifts. Janeway and Everett, right, Tinker? Janeway and Everett have never turned down a request for support for a project of this kind, isn't that right?"

James Cheever turned around, and Homer noticed for the first time the man sitting behind him in a chair that was midway between the round table and the chairs of the Overseers in the hollow square. Sloan Tinker was the Senior Vice President, Cheever's right-hand man. Homer had seen him stepping out of a car with Cheever to visit the scene of the disaster last Wednesday.

Tinker was opening his mouth to speak, but now somebody else was bobbing up on the far side of the room. "But it isn't only the alumni and the faculty. It's the students. Don't forget the students. They'll have strong opinions on this matter too, and that's a fact."

Homer leaned forward. Who was that? It was another visitor like himself. The man was standing up, boldly interrupting. It was Charley Flynn, the assistant chemistry professor who had delivered the eulogy to Ham Dow yesterday in church. What was Charley Flynn doing here? He looked more like a buccaneer than ever, with a sort of loose open shirt displaying a triangle of hairy chest.

"Now, just a minute, Charley," said Julia Chamberlain. "Before you speak your piece, I have to introduce you and get the parliamentary business straightened out. Now, ladies and gentlemen, as some of you know, Professor Flynn is a member of the Department of Chemistry. He's here today because he wrote me a letter asking permission to attend this meeting and speak on the matter of President Cheever's Decorative Arts Building. But of course, he speaks only with the indulgence of the rest of us. Now, are there any objections?"

There were objections. President Cheever didn't see why any Tom, Dick, or Harry could attend a meeting of the Harvard Overseers and speak his mind about something that wasn't any of his business. The whole point about the Overseers was that they were an elected body of objective and disinterested people from outside the university. People from the Harvard community were by definition out of place. And therefore he, for one, was against the presence of this person as a matter of principle.

Julia Chamberlain took a vote. The Fellows cast no vote. Neither did Sloan Tinker. Tinker was probably an invited guest like the Fellows, decided Homer. He apparently tagged along wherever Cheever went.

The vote was twenty-nine to one. Only Cheever voted nay.

Charley Flynn came forward and spoke. "It's the students. You can't just pretend they're not there. And the students are just not about to take a new Decorative Arts Building sitting down. They raised a hell of a lot of trouble over the new steeple for Memorial

Hall, remember? They wanted that money to go to subsidized housing for the working people of Cambridge. I'm sure you all must know Harvard's reputation with the students, Harvard the slumlord, the parasite on the body of the city of Cambridge. Most of you people weren't in town to see it, but I can tell you what they did when that new steeple was under construction. They hung signs all over the scaffolding. They tried to talk the workmen out of working. And if it hadn't been for Ham Dow, that damned steeple might never have been put up at all, with all those expensive clocks all around it. Clocks! My God, what good is another bunch of clocks? But Ham persuaded them the steeple was providing jobs for local construction workers, and then he even gave a couple of concerts on behalf of the steeple and the clocks, and the students really knocked themselves out, playing and singing to raise money to help out. But Ham isn't around any more to lend you a hand. Look here, the new stained glass would be bad enough. They'll be plenty mad about the money that goes for that. But just wait till they hear about a new Decorative Arts Building. There'll be hell to pay. It'll be the strike all over again, like in '69, when this whole institution came apart because of the war in Vietnam and the presence of the military. Do any of you remember that? This room right here, it'll be taken over again. They'll be grinding their shoes into that antique table right there, the way they did before. I know. I was one of them. Just wait till they hear you want to put up a building full of porcelain teapots and gold salt shakers. Just wait."

Homer wanted to cheer. Oh, the gall, the mad suicidal courage. The daredevil would probably lose his job, speaking out like that against the President of the institution by which he was employed as a humble assistant professor. But Charley Flynn was not alone in his rebellion. There were sympathetic murmurs, mumbled eruptions of "Hear, hear." James Cheever had closed his eyes. The Harvard strike had happened long before his term of office, in fact it was a couple of presidents back, but Homer could see that the very thought of it was distasteful in the extreme.

The Senior Vice President was speaking up in the President's cause. "Mr. Flynn," said Sloan Tinker, "I've been a part of the administration here for a long time. I came back to Harvard to be Dean of Freshmen after World War Two. I've seen a great many students come and go. And I can tell you from my own personal experience, we've never regretted a building. Without building projects like this one—whether it was a comparable project like Houghton Library to house a priceless collection of rare books and manuscripts, or a dormitory like Mather House, or the laboratories and lecture halls of the Science Center—this university would not maintain its reputation as the most distinguished institution of higher learning in the country, with the most broadly diversified program of studies. As for the cost, my motto is simple: *Economy of means for maximum effect.* In this case, we merely approach a few donors chosen wisely from the larger body of our alumni. I regret to say that I have so far been unable to persuade the Vice Presidents for Administration and Finance and Alumni Affairs to see the merit of the scheme. But with the advocacy of this group, I am sure they would come around to our point of view. And as for the students, why, the building would be so small! Mr. Cheever has had the clever idea, you see, of building the thing in the shape of a small triumphal arch, there in the Sever Quad, so that the present path would not be obstructed. It would really be a little jewel of a building, with two exhibition rooms on either side of the arch, and a gallery across the second floor to join one side to the other. I hardly think the students would object to so small a building. *Economy of means,* you see, once again, *for maximum effect.* Do you understand, Mr. Flynn?"

"But teapots," said Charley Flynn. "And porcelain shepherdesses. Just wait till they hear what it's for. Porcelain shepherdesses. My God."

"I never said a word about porcelain shepherdesses," said President Cheever. He was looking up over Charley Flynn's head at the glittering diamond facets of the chandelier. "I was talking about Coptic glass, as a matter of fact, and Harvard's distinguished collections of silver and Wedgwood. The students would not speak of porcelain shepherdesses unless they were instructed to do so by you, sir."

"Well, see here, now," said Julia Chamberlain, her good-humored voice pouring over them like a pitcher of milk. "I suggest we put this matter aside for a minute or two and listen to what Professor Kelly has come to talk to us about. We don't want to keep him waiting any longer. Is that all right with you, Jim? We'll just let Mr. Kelly tell us what he's got to say and satisfy ourselves the whole place isn't about to be blown up. All in favor?"

Homer stood up. "This morning the Nepalese Freedom Movement detonated a bomb in the central offices of the Bridgeport Insurance Company, in Bridgeport, Connecticut."

Around the hollow square of great chairs in the Faculty Room there were small gasps of dismay. But Julia Chamberlain thumped her fist on her agenda and shouted, "Good! Good news!" Then she made a funny face of comic apology. "Well, I mean, that's a terrible thing to say, but for us I think it's good, don't you? I mean, don't you suppose it means those crazy people don't have anything personal against Harvard? What do you think, Mr. Kelly?"

Chapter Sixteen

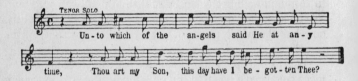

Un-to which of the an-gels said He at an-y time, Thou art my Son, this day have I be-got-ten Thee?

The Memorial Hall clock was striking eleven when Homer walked out of the wrought-iron gate on the north side of the yard. The note of the new bell was of a different pitch from that of the church in the Yard, and the two bells clashed against each other, striking together, then one at a time in a disorderly pattern, then together once again.

Homer wasn't used to seeing Memorial Hall from this direction. He was astonished once again by its bulk. *Ah, voilà quelque chose!* some Frenchman was supposed to have said, coming upon it for the first time. *Quelque chose,* indeed. What a lot of nice sweet air had been displaced by this massive tombstone! This morning the transparency of the bright October sky made it seem more than ever like a mountain of densely compacted rock. Only the new iron pinnacles silhouetted like lace along the ridge of the roof seemed delicate against the light air, providing an intermediate stage or compromise between substantiality and insubstantiality. Homer was reminded of a fragment from Handel's *Messiah* —the bass soloist had sung it at Ham's funeral: *For this corruptible must put on incorruption, this mortal must put on immortality.*

They had wanted the building to be noble. An inspiration to the young. They had mixed up architecture with morality. They had read Ruskin's *Seven Lamps of Architecture:* The Lamp of Sacrifice! The Lamp of Truth! The Lamp of Power! The Lamp of Beauty! The Lamp of Life! The Lamp of Memory! The Lamp of Obedience! They had covered the building with Latin inscriptions and painted allegorical figures all over the stained glass. The whole thing was a sort of hodgepodge of Westminster Hall in London and the Sheldonian Theatre at Oxford and the Ducal Palace in Venice and an old Navaho blanket; that was what people said. It was Picturesque Eclectic. It was awful and wonderful at the same time. And when they had finished it, they had been a little startled and taken aback. *Voilà quelque chose!*

Homer began crossing the wide paths that stretched over the sunken traffic of Cambridge Street. The wind blew unobstructed, scudding yellow leaves before it, lifting them in whirlpools, throwing them against his trouser legs. He kept his eyes fixed on the turrets and towers of Memorial Hall, where something caught his eye against the glowing brick of the south side. What was that little spot of white in one of the pointed windows of the turret beside the entry? There was something out of place on the window sill. Could it be milk? Even from this distance the white object looked suspiciously like a carton of milk. Homer remembered the musty mattress on the floor of one of the tower rooms. But that had been on the other side, way over on the Kirkland Street side of the building. Maybe there was a secret inhabitant of Memorial Hall, wandering around its upper reaches at midnight, like the hunchback of Notre Dame.

"Mr. Kelly, hey, wait a minute."

Homer swung around. It was the pirate, Charley Flynn, running through eddies and swirls of leaves, his coat flying forward around him. Homer waited for him and then they walked side by side, leaning back into the wind. "Meeting's over already, is it?" said Homer.

"Yes. Feelings were too hot. Julia Chamberlain pounded on the table and told everybody to go away and have an early lunch. They all went off to the Faculty Club. But I was satisfied. I'd said my piece."

"A triumphal arch." Homer laughed. "Harvard conquers all. You know, I thought the Board of Overseers was just a polite bunch of people who put a rubber stamp on anything the rest of the administration wanted. But those people were really making a fuss."

"This damned school. I mean, there's so much about it that's good. But you've got to keep fighting bastards like Cheever all the time. Nobody rubber-stamps anything Cheever wants. Certainly not Julia Chamberlain. Not for this President of Harvard. The trouble is, he won't take no for an answer. If he can't get anybody in the administration to agree with him, he sends out letters to the alumni, over the protests of the Vice President for Alumni Affairs. There's been a long history of this kind of double-dealing, from the very beginning, from the day he took over."

"Then he's not what you'd call a popular President of Harvard."

"Well, no, he is certainly not what you'd call popular. But I don't hold that against him. The president of a university doesn't have to be everybody's good old pal."

"I understand he's a fine speaker," said Homer encouragingly, aware of a slight sense of blood thirst.

"Well, that's right. He was a lecturer in the Fine Arts Department over there in the Fogg Museum. A pedagogue of the old school, I guess you'd say. I took his course in seventeenth-century painting when I was an undergraduate. It would all pour out of him, perfect polished sentences, a flood of information. Well, of course, he was a fine scholar, all right. Masses of small detail. And of course I know history is built up out of small things like the epitaphs and the laundry lists of the great men and women of the past. But somehow Cheever managed to miss out on the greatness. It just slipped through his fingers. I mean, after he was through with a picture it was hard to see it any more. I mean, to actually look at it and see the gods and goddesses reclining in the shade of the trees and the blue distances and the temples on the horizon—you know."

"Well, how did he get to be president of Harvard in the first place?"

"It was Tinker's doing. Of course, when Bok was appointed to the Supreme Court, they had a massive search for a new president. But Tinker had his finger on his friend Cheever from the beginning. Tinker was one of the four vice presidents then, and a member of the Search Committee. He managed to persuade the other members and the Fellows that what the university needed now was a genuine scholar of the old school, somebody who really cared about the classical definition of the educated man. Perhaps we had been so busy developing our professional schools, he said, that we had forgotten the good old humane studies that should have been our central concern. Our great heritage from the past, all that kind of thing. And Cheever can be charming when he wants to be. You know, dry little bony jokes. Learned witticisms. Quotations from Machiavelli, Voltaire. Anyway, they succumbed, and Tinker's nomination won out over all the rest. Well, of course, the first thing Cheever did was to create a new officer in his administration, a senior vice president. That was a reward for Tinker. And ever since then, they've worked together as a team. Ever since the day he was installed. You know, I decided his election was a mistake when I saw him sitting there in the Faculty Room five years ago with all that fancy silver in front of him—the keys, and so on, and the Great Salt. They haul all this ceremonial stuff out of the vault in the Pusey Library. He was enjoying it too much. It was as plain to me then as it is now that it was the trappings of the job he cared about, not the substance of the task of keeping Harvard about its proper business. Well, excuse me. I'm going the other way. I've got to get on over to Mallinckrodt and blow up my laboratory."

"Blow up your . . .?"

"Oh, don't worry. I'm just messing around with a highly unstable compound. And by the way, if I were really going to blow up something, I'd do it with equipment a lot more simple and sophisticated than dynamite and an old-fashioned alarm clock. I'd use one of those nice little remote-control devices kids use to fly model airplanes. I'd wire up the building with some kind of explosive and then just go away and blow the thing up at my own convenience with this little control panel in my pocket."

"Well, unfortunately the old-fashioned contraption seems to have worked pretty well."

"But a little explosion like that isn't typical of those Nepalese. They're professionals. They usually blow up an entire building. They could have destroyed most of Memorial Hall if they'd gone about it the right way. All they had to do was run a wire around the foundations of the tower. Then the thing would have fallen down of its own weight. Simple. Nothing to it. *Kablam*. Well, I'll be seeing you."

Homer shuddered.

The chorus was still rehearsing in Sanders Theatre when he entered the memorial corridor by way of the south door. With the rose windows boarded up at either end of the long chamber, the place was cast into a kind of perpetual midnight. It took Homer a little while to get used to the darkness. The heavy chandeliers hanging from the wooden vaults cast only a dim light. From the open doors of Sanders he could hear Vick's basses raging like the angry crowd around Pilate. *He trusted in God that He would deliver Him, let Him deliver Him, if He delight in Him.* And now the tenors were coming in, roaring the same thing. But they came in on the wrong beat, and Homer could hear them falter and stop, and then there was a loud laugh from Vick. *Ticketytack*, she was rapping on her music stand. "Now listen, men, you've got to sound mean. You've got to really sneer. This is one of those big *turba* choruses, where you're all supposed to be a big crowd. You're supposed to sound really evil, do you see? Now, once again, everybody, and this time come on, be really rotten." They were starting over.

Homer looked at his watch. It would be another twenty minutes before Mary would be released from Vick's rehearsal, before their own class would begin. He opened the door to the great hall and sat down in a folding chair beside the white marble statue of John Adams guarding the door. Looking out at the enormous space, he tried to imagine it as a dining hall. Try as he would, he couldn't picture it teeming with hungry turn-of-the-century freshmen. He couldn't hear the clashing plates and the roar of voices. It was just an oversized empty room, so colossal that the man with a broom in his hand, entering by the door at the side, looked far away and small, almost blue with distance. Was it Crawley? No, that wasn't Crawley. He was too tall for Crawley. And you never saw Jerry Crawley carrying a broom. The man began pushing his broom along the north wall, moving slowly away from Homer.

"Hey, there," said Homer. "Oh, sir!" He jumped up and began walking after the man with the broom. But the man was gone. He had opened one of the doors at the west end of the great hall and disappeared. The door led to the cloister porch, where Homer had wandered confused and lost that day last week (was it only last week?), looking for his classroom. The cloister walk was only one of the nonintersecting parts of the multitudinous separate space frames and time dimensions that were loosely called Memorial Hall. Hadn't the man heard Homer call him? Was he deaf? He hadn't quickened his pace at all; he had simply moved steadily out of sight and sound, like a playing piece on a game board, reaching the zone of safety before your own piece can catch up on the next throw of the dice.

"Oh, well, the hell with it," said Homer softly to himself. "It's not my problem, God knows." He looked up and shook his fist at the flaking blue ceiling high above, imagining God sitting on the loftiest pinnacle of the tower with his great feet spread out on the roofs to east and west. But the blue sky of the ceiling did not pulse with light, and no voice boomed down the balcony stairs its mighty official blessing on Homer's hands-off policy in this matter of the death of Ham Dow. "Vengeance is mine," God might have said, for example, or "Butt out, you big stupidhead," or something really comforting like that.

After all, it wasn't as if he didn't already have enough to do, just keeping ahead of his class. Because the class was terrifying. Sometimes he thought they didn't know anything, but then other times he was afraid they knew absolutely everything, so if he wasn't going to look like a fool he was going to have to bone up for every lecture, because he'd forgotten most of what he used to think he knew, and everything he had forgotten had to be grubbed up again from somewhere, and most of the time he'd forgotten where. And besides, he was doing something else. He was turning the course of lectures into a textbook. The two of them were taking turns, rewriting the lectures into chapters. And he couldn't even keep up with that. Mary was way ahead of him. She had finished all her chapters. She was working on the index. She was clucking at him to hurry up.

Homer looked at his watch again. There were still fifteen more minutes before the end of Mary's rehearsal. He went back to the high transept and strolled back and forth. The chorus was still pouring jugs and vats of song out of Sanders Theatre. Homer dodged around the sawhorses in the middle of the floor and looked at the flat gray sheet of cement Mr. Maderna's masons had laid across the new flooring. It was so wet he could write his name in it if he wanted to: KELLY WAS HERE. He resisted the temptation. He decided to spend the remaining minutes of the hour trying to decipher the Latin inscriptions on the wall. He threw back his head to look up. Then he blinked with surprise. The balcony over the entrance to the great hall was occupied. It was alive. There was someone on the balcony looking over the railing at him. Homer caught a momentary glimpse of a flashing pair of glasses, and something flapping and white, and then the thing was gone. What was it? Aha, the hunchback. The hunchback of Memorial Hall. Well, forget it. Homer sighed heavily. It was no business of his. He turned his mind to the problem of rendering pious Latin fragments into English. There was enough Latin glowing softly high over his head to sink a ship. Homer's high school Latin was only good enough to give him a general sense of mixed batches of the same words over and over, fine phrases about the fatherland, and courage, and honor, and eternity, and holiness, and memory everlasting. Some classical scholar had been given the job of finding lofty consolations for the bereaved friends and relations of dead student soldiers, bits and pieces from scripture and the speeches of Cicero.

O FORTUNATA MORS!

proclaimed the inscription over Mr. Crawley's door. Well, who would believe that? The death of a young man was never happy or fortunate. Useful, maybe, but not fortunate.

BREVIS A NATURA NOBIS VITA DATA EST
AT MEMORIA BENE REDDITAE VITAE SEMPITERNA . . .

Homer stared at the inscription and half closed his eyes, trying to let the meaning sink in without struggling through it word by word. It was something about the shortness of life. Nature has given us a short life—that was it—but the memory of a good life endureth forever. *Sempiterna.* A good word. It seemed to go on foreverrrrrr. *Sempiterrrrmaaaaaa.* Only, memory didn't endure forever, that was the trouble. Who gave a thought to these young soldiers now? They were just names, forgotten names on the wall. And who would remember poor old Ham Dow after a while? After this batch of students was gone? They were talking about putting up a memorial plaque for Ham, right here along with the others. But that wasn't good enough. The memory of his life was a poor substitute for a good man cut down in his prime.

The chorus was pouring out of Sanders now, hauling on jackets and knapsacks. Violinists and cellists were going the other way, carrying their instruments, butting open the doors with armfuls of books. Jonathan Pearlman bustled past Homer and nodded at him and walked into Sanders with Rosie Bell, and soon the timpani began thumping a mighty rubadub and Rosie's trumpet pealed the *Amen*.

Homer remembered a poem by Walt Whitman. *"Beat! beat! drums!—blow! bugles! blow!"* he said, as Mary ran toward him, pulling on her coat. *"Make even the trestles to shake the dead where they lie awaiting the hearses."*

And Mary grinned at him and said the rest, *"So strong you thump O terrible drums—so loud you bugles blow."*

Chapter Seventeen

He had been asleep again, but now he woke up and lifted his face from the floor and stared into the darkness, listening. Could he hear something or couldn't he? Somewhere there was a kind of rhythmic vibration. He kept feeling it in his head, and then not feeling it, and thinking it was his imagination, and then feeling it again. It was like music, like drums or brass instruments very far away. Like a marching band making threadlike sounds far away when you wait for it on the street. You hear only the thump of the drums at first, and then the toy bleating of the horns and trombones. But this was even less than that. It was only a kind of throbbing and buzzing in his temples. And now even the throbbing and buzzing had stopped.

Ham closed his eyes again and dropped his head. He was thirsty, terribly thirsty. How long had he been drifting in and out of sleep? How many hours, or days, or weeks?

Something terrible had happened. That was apparent. But what? He couldn't remember anything about it except for the stranger's face. There had been a look of surprise on someone's face, someone new to him, a stranger, he could remember that.

But nothing more. Something colossal must have happened, but he couldn't for the life of him remember what.

Something was lying heavily on his back. With an effort Ham crawled out from under it. Then he rolled over and tried to sit up. But trembling seized him. He was overcome with nausea and dizziness. He dropped down again and closed his eyes. After all, they would find him sooner or later. They must be looking for him, searching everywhere. Surely they would be digging and shoveling at the outer edges of his darkness, right now. He could trust them to keep trying. They wouldn't let him down. He would just drowse off and leave it up to them. They were his good Rats.

Chapter Eighteen

Vick hurried out of her Corelli seminar in Paine Hall and then stopped short at the west entrance and pressed her nose against one of the oval windows in the doors, studying the rain outside. It was coming down like pitchforks, like waterfalls and cataracts. Well, never mind, she didn't have time to wait for it to stop pouring. Vick hunched her shoulders and ducked her head and clutched her books to her breast and ran down the steps. It was like going swimming with all her clothes on. Head down, she splashed in the direction of the Science Center, where she could take a shortcut to Memorial Hall. In the Science Center she took off her squelching shoes and padded barefoot along the brick corridor, shaking back her wet hair. The corridor was dry, but in the Science Center Vick couldn't help thinking of her Chem 2 class, which met in the building twice a week, and she winced.

She had been an idiot to sign up for Chem 2. She should have known better. The *Confidential Guide* had given her fair warning. "Chem 2 is extremely competitive and covers almost all areas of chemistry in agonizing depth at withering speed." And it was true. She was already way behind, less than a month into the term. And it was probably too late to drop the damned thing and sign up for that gut course her roommate was taking, Nat Sci 112, which was supposed to be just one big slide lecture on the history of science, Galileo and his telescope, and so on.

Well, she could probably slog through Chem 2 somehow or other. She had always been able to get a course together sooner or later. *Victoria is highly motivated to succeed academically.* But of course it wasn't so much a matter of brains and motivation and success and all that claptrap. It was the way time presented itself to her every day as something to be carved up into pieces, like a pine board. Fiercely she hewed it into hours and minutes. It was a useful material, not to be wasted. Even the scraps could be whacked together into something. The vibration of the wheezing, jerking saw jiggled in every nerve in Vick's thin body, swiveling her head in rapid darting glances as she hurried along the sidewalk, heading for Memorial Hall. Impatiently she leaned forward.

staring eagerly through her wet eyelashes at the massive building that blocked out the whole sky.

She still wasn't sure she could do it. When Mrs. Krapotkin and Professor Howard had told her to take over for Ham, she had said, "Oh, no, no, I can't. I really can't." But they had been firm. They had insisted. Vick had walked out of Mrs. Krapotkin's office in a dazzled terrified trance. She had run upstairs to the library in Paine Hall and snatched up everything she could find about Handel's *Messiah*. Mrs. Krapotkin seemed to think Vick could just take over the whole thing because she had done so well in Ham's conducting course last year, and he had entrusted her with some of the rehearsals for last year's Christmas performance. But to take on the whole thing! To weld it all together! To nag the chorus until they could sing the long passages of sixteenth notes to perfection, to work with the soloists, to try to keep Mrs. Esterhazy calmed down, because she got so swoopy when she was excited, to take over the orchestra from Jonathan Pearlman, and on top of everything else, to give lessons to Miss Plankton! Oh, Miss Plankton, what to do about Miss Plankton! Jon Pearlman had thrown up his hands and sworn he wouldn't put up with Miss Plankton. But Vick had persuaded him to let her stay. Miss Plankton was in. She was in for good. If Jane Plankton was good enough for Ham Dow, she was good enough for Jon Pearlman and Vick Van Horn. Vick had promised to give her private lessons, free of charge.

But of course it wasn't just a matter of getting the parts right. The whole thing had to be not only note perfect, it had to be one whole, musically and meaningfully. *Christ was born and died for our sins and rose from the dead to prove that we too can be saved.* That was what the music was about. It was an exalted statement of Christian belief, whether one agreed with it or not. But how could she get it all together, unskilled as she was, so that the music really said that, *For as in Adam all die, even so in Christ shall all be made alive?* It had to be more than a collection of familiar tunes. Vick remembered Ham's cautionary joke about the man who dreamt he was playing the violin in a performance of Handel's *Messiah,* and woke up to find he really was. That was the trouble. Everybody took it for granted. They had to feel it, the whole chorus, the whole orchestra; they had to understand it and sing it and play it as if they did, as if they really cared, as if they saw the heavens open up before them to reveal the great God himself, the way Handel said he did.

She still had so much to learn. She had buried herself in the score. She had driven her roommate half crazy by playing the tape recording of last year's performance over and over and over. She had drenched herself in Handel's *Messiah.* She breathed it, ate it, drank it, dreamt it. She woke up at night with her teeth tapping the rhythm of the "Hallelujah Chorus." There was no other piece of music in the world but *Messiah.* She couldn't understand how her classmates in Paine Hall could be bothered with Corelli or anybody else but George Frederick Handel. She was temporarily insane, out of her head, a monomaniac, she knew that. But how was she ever going to get all the beat patterns straight, and the cues, and remember which arias were da capo, and master all the swift changes from one part to another? There was the place where the lilting allegro moderato of the chorus *All we like sheep have gone astray* turned into a ponderous adagio—*And the Lord hath laid on Him the iniquity of us all.* The whole thing was full of tricky transitions like that. She had to know it all by heart.

Vick sloshed up the steps of the north entry of Memorial Hall and ran barefoot into Sanders, leaving a dripping trail from her heavy wet skirt on the marble floor of the memorial corridor.

The thing was, it was all for Ham. It was his concert. He was as alive as ever in Vick's head. She would make him come alive for everybody else, just one more time.

Chapter Nineteen

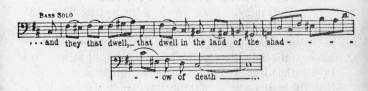

...and they that dwell,— that dwell in the land of the shad- - - -ow of death _____...

Ham woke to a feverish thirst. He rolled over, hunched himself up on his hands and knees, and began crawling in the dark. He was dizzy, but instinctively he kept his eyes closed. His head pounded, but he hardly felt it. All he could think of was his thirst. He must find water.

The surface over which he was dragging himself forward was lumpy with gravel and rock, but he persevered, making a slow journey over small sharp hills and valleys, until he was brought up short. His head cracked against a barrier. Falling back on his heels, Ham opened his mouth in a soundless cry. Then his shoulders sagged and he breathed heavily, recovering from the blow. The air in his mouth tasted of plaster dust. He closed his mouth and breathed through his nose, and the darkness around him smelled dank and wet. Reaching out with his hands, he felt the barrier. It was a flat wall with a painted surface. Slowly he lurched forward again, keeping his left shoulder against the wall. Soon the dry grit under his hands and knees gave way to a bare floor, seamless and smooth like linoleum. One of his hands slipped. The floor was wet. Ham put his wet palm to his parched lips, and then, panting with eagerness, he lumbered forward, groping for the source of the moisture. His shoulder ran into something, and he stopped and explored it with his hands.

The obstruction was a pipe, running up the wall over his head. His trembling fingers tried to follow it down to the floor, but the lower end of the pipe was broken. A slight trickle of moisture seeped from the broken rim.

It was water. Plain cold water. The wetness on Ham's fingers tasted slightly metallic, but otherwise it had no taste. The trickle was hardly more than a drop or two coalescing on the metal rim, but it was continuous. Painfully Ham got down on his elbows and lapped at the end of the pipe. He lapped and lapped, then sat back to rest, then lapped again. Ham lapped up the water trickling from the broken pipe like a thirsty dog until the fiery need of his body was a little abated, and then he stretched out on the floor and put his aching head on his arm once again and went to sleep.

Chapter Twenty

Homer told himself it wasn't inconsistent. It wasn't a positive action on his part to call up Marley. It was just curiosity. There was no harm in finding out how things were going. "I just wondered what's happening," he said to Peter Marley.

And then Peter told him about Ham's appointment book. It had turned up in Ham's house. They had searched Ham's house on Martin Street from top to bottom and found the appointment book. "And the appointment for eleven-thirty, October sixteenth, was in there. On the page for October sixteenth there's an entry, '11:30, J.C.' "

"J.C.? Who did Ham know with the initials J.C.?"

"Lots of people. After all, half the people in the world are named John or Jack or Jean or Joan or Jim, or something like that, and you'd be surprised how many of them have surnames beginning with C. Of course, we looked for an address book too, to find out who he did know, but so far we haven't turned up anybody at all likely."

"I know somebody with the initials J.C.," said Homer.

"Jesus Christ."

"No. James Cheever."

"President Cheever? Oh, wow."

"Why don't you take a look at Cheever's appointment book for October sixteenth? Maybe it says, '11:30, Ham Dow.' "

"Oh, no. Not me." There was a small silence. "Well, of course, Ham did know Cheever. They were classmates. I know that for a fact. Only I doubt they had much in common."

"Except for Harvard. The welfare of this vast educational slaughterhouse, if you'll forgive a scholarly quotation. I'll tell you what. I'll do it for you." Homer could feel his big nose twitching with eagerness to violate Cheever's sanctuary in Massachusetts Hall. "I'll just barge in on Cheever and see what happens. All he can do is throw me out."

"Good. Only leave me out of it. Whatever you do, don't mention my name."

OFFICE OF THE PRESIDENT

was written in white paint across the lintel of the door of Massachusetts Hall. Homer admired the small neat letters. They had been executed by a skillful hand. The O's were round, the spacing ample. You didn't need a big gold sign if you were the President of Harvard.

The receptionist wasn't at all sure Mr. Cheever would be free to see Mr. Kelly. She passed him down the hall to Mrs. Herbert. Mrs. Herbert wasn't at all sure either, but she said she'd find out. She knocked on the door at one side of her office and poked her head into the next room, while Homer stood modestly waiting, studying the patterns in Mrs. Herbert's rug.

"Who is it, Mrs. Herbert?" said James Cheever. "Tinker and I still have a good deal to talk over this morning. I'm not at all sure—"

"It's Professor Kelly. He's teaching in the English Department. He says it's urgent."

"Oh, yes. Kelly." Cheever made a gesture of impatience and glanced at Sloan Tinker. "He was the one who gave that report at the Overseers' meeting the other day. What do you think?"

Tinker got up from the sofa and stood by the fireplace. "Better find out what the man is up to," he said.

"Well, then, send him in. You'd think he would have the courtesy to make an appointment." A sense of what was due to his dignity rose up in the breast of the President of Harvard, and when his visitor walked into the room, James Cheever did not offer him a chair. "How do you do, Professor Kelly," he said, looking intently at the grumpy portrait of William Stoughton on the wall. "I think you know Mr. Tinker. Now, what exactly is it you want to see me about?"

The man was so thick-skinned he didn't know he had transgressed in any way. He was grinning at Tinker, walking over to shake his hand, pulling up a chair on his own initiative and sitting down. The chair happened to be a particularly fine nineteenth-century chair with a needlepoint cushion. It had once belonged to President Pusey's mother-in-law. Kelly was tipping it back on its rear legs. Next thing you knew, he would be putting his feet on the desk. The man was preposterous. Now look at the fool; he was jumping up and peering into the glass case at the Great Salt.

"Good heavens, what's that thing? Some sort of silver spittoon? Haven't you got it upside down?"

President Cheever shivered with loathing. "No, I haven't got it upside down. Those prongs on top were meant to hold a napkin.

It happens to be part of the Harvard silver collection, a rather precious seventeenth-century saltcellar."

"Oh, right, right. I see how it works. The salt goes in that little hole in the top. Funniest-looking damn thing I ever saw."

Homer sat down again, and smiled at the man on the other side of the table. All at once he saw him for what he was, and for the first time he felt a pang of sympathy for the President of Harvard. Cheever was a beleaguered scholar who had been promoted by the Peter Principle beyond the utmost reach of his capacity, when he should have been left to browse in the field of his own competency as a professor of fine arts, over there in the Fogg Museum on the other side of Quincy Street. He should never have been raised to a position of authority over living men and women who refused to stay poised like Homeric figures on a vase or icons from Byzantium in the perfection of eternity. Here he was, the poor fool, enthroned at a handsome old table upon which was dumped every day an untidy sack, tumbling and squirming with human problems. The poor man had to put his shrinking hand into it every single day and get his fingers bitten off. A good chap on the whole. A scholar. You had to have scholars. Homer was a scholar himself, after a fashion.

"I just wanted to talk to you about the death of Hamilton Dow," said Homer. "And I'm glad Mr. Tinker is here. I'd like to get your perspective on the matter, see things from your two points of view. I mean, I understand, sir, you were one of Mr. Dow's oldest acquaintances. I'm told you were members of the same class here at Harvard."

"Yes, we were," said James Cheever. "But, I must say, I hardly knew the man. I mean, we always moved in different spheres."

"Would I be wrong in thinking that it was fundamentally a matter of educational philosophy?" said Homer, not having the least idea what he meant at all. "The two of you had rather different outlooks on the whole?"

He was blundering around in the dark, but to his amazement, his fumbling finger had touched a vital nerve at the first try.

"Radically different," said President Cheever firmly.

"Different persuasions altogether." Sloan Tinker moved away from the fireplace and sat down at the table that had been the desk of Harvard presidents since President Eliot's day. "In fact, I think I can say frankly that it is no secret that President Cheever was responsible for denying academic tenure to Hamilton Dow."

"Tenure? You denied him tenure?" Homer stared at Cheever. "But that's the first time I've heard anything but enthusiasm for the man. He seems to have been so universally popular."

"Popular," said Tinker, with a dry laugh. "Oh, yes, he was popular."

"He certainly was," said President Cheever bitterly. "He was the kind of man who never went anywhere without his little band of disciples. I think he had some romantic notion of himself as a sort of beggar king, with a ragged band of lackeys, vassals, and cupbearers dragging along behind him like some sort of patchwork cloak." The President of Harvard made an elaborate sweeping gesture in the air.

"The man had a messiah complex," said Tinker. "It's as simple as that."

Homer studied the emptiness behind the President's chair, where Cheever had been flapping his arm. It contained no disciples of any kind. "No one would ever accuse you, sir," he said, "of being a messiah."

Warmed by this compliment, Cheever expanded. "When I think of the influence for good the man might have been, with that mob of supporters he swept up from the streets of Cambridge. But instead—oh, I know one should not speak ill of the dead, but so much sheer foolishness has been spoken about Ham Dow, Mr. Kelly, it's about time somebody revealed the truth. After all, facts are facts. Did you ever see the man in the flesh?"

Homer shook his head. He had lost his tongue. He was astounded. The two of them were letting themselves go. They were enjoying themselves, digging their spoons feverishly into a blood pudding. He sat back, trying not to let his jaw drop too far, and let the repast go on.

"Tell me, Mr. Kelly," said James Cheever, "did you ever read Pico della Mirandola's *Oration on the Dignity of Man?*"

Homer shook his head dumbly from side to side.

"Well, it's simply the old universal chain of being again, only Pico was a child of the Renaissance, and he had an extraordinary view of the chain of being. Man alone of all created things, he said, has the power to move freely on the chain, to fall by his own free choice to the level of beasts or even to the condition of vegetable life, or to rise to the heights, to become an angel, or even to ascend to the very summit to become one with God himself. A noble view of the creation, I've always thought. Well, Dow was one of the beasts. Whenever I think of Pico's great chain of being, I see Dow groveling at the bottom of the ladder of human possibility."

"Well, I guess I see what you mean," said Homer. "He was somewhat lower than the angels, as people say. Is that it?"

Sloan Tinker made a hooting noise in his throat. "Lower than the angels. I should think he was. He was a slobbering pig of a man. Not exactly what one would like to see as an example for the young men and women in this institution. Think of the gluttony! To have become so obese!"

It was a shame Ratchit wasn't here, thought Homer. Ratchit could have made some remark about the magnificent human body God had given you, so you ought to take care of it, right? But then he forgot about Ratchit, because Cheever was talking again about Pico della Mirandola, and it was clear to Homer that he was witnessing James Cheever at his best, warming to a subject in which he was at home.

"You know, Mr. Kelly, when I read the *Oration on the Dignity of Man,* I often think of Harvard University. Pico speaks of the friendship through which all rational souls shall come into harmony in the one mind which is above all minds, how they shall in some ineffable way become altogether one. I think of this university as Pico speaks of the soul, that it may be adorned with manifold philosophy as with the splendor of a courtier, surrounded by a varied throng of sciences, to become the bride of the King of Glory. Of course, in my opinion what Pico meant by the King of Glory was simply those things that are of eternal value —truth, beauty, justice—all that I hope we cherish in this university. I mean in the fundamental sense. Our ultimate purpose as educators here."

"Well, yes," murmured Homer, who was becoming more and more befuddled. "You mean, like *veritas* and all that sort of thing."

Sloan Tinker leaned forward. "The point is, Mr. Kelly, some of us think of this university as setting a standard. Our students, after all, are the most sifted of the sifted, the best the nation has to offer. And therefore we owe them something rather out of the ordinary. And one man's truth can be another man's poison. We must choose what we offer them very carefully."

"There is only one thing we *must* offer them, on pain of failing our stewardship," said James Cheever. "One precious thing. The little flame of scholarship. It's all we have. So we must do our best to guard it, to keep its flickering light from going out. For example, consider the pressure from the state. Harvard receives seventy million dollars a year from the federal government, a relationship that calls for a certain wariness—not altogether unlike that of our Harvard forebears Mather and Brattle and Leverett, when Massachusetts Bay lost her Royal Charter, and Sir Edmund Andros landed in Boston in 1686 with a commission as Governor from the Crown. We must hoard our precious inheritance and keep it sacred, and pass it along. There are only a few of us in every generation. A little band of scholars down through the years. A saving remnant. That's all Harvard is. Nothing more."

"But what does all this have to do with Ham Dow?" said Homer, trying to bring the conversation back down to earth. "He was one of the barbarians, you mean? The Visigoth, sweeping down on the monastery? You mean his one hot breath could snuff that candle out?"

Sloan Tinker chuckled. "That's about it. Personally, I think what bothered me most was his lack of professional decorum. There is ideally a certain distance between a professor and his students. Dow paid no attention to this delicate boundary. And you know, Mr. Kelly, even in the Music Department there was some question about his professional competence. I don't know whether you were aware of that or not."

"There was?" Homer lifted his eyebrows in surprise.

"You should talk to one or two of his peers in Paine Hall. You'd be interested, I'm sure, to learn that his taste was rather too catholic to suit some of the more discriminating members of the music faculty. And there was some question, too, about the standard of musical judgment exhibited at his performance of Handel's *Messiah* every year."

"Some question? What do you mean?"

"It was just a little too much of a circus, if you see what I mean. For instance, just as an example, there was the way he encouraged the audience to join in singing the "Hallelujah Chorus." In the middle of the concert he would turn around and conduct the entire audience in a gigantic sing-along. Now, I hardly think a community sing is what Handel had in mind, do you? That is, I've heard some repercussions from people of unquestioned musical taste whose opinion I trust."

"Again," said James Cheever, "it gets down to standards. The man had no standards. He didn't know the wheat from the chaff. He had as many outsiders among his friends and supporters as he did students. Some very peculiar people indeed. And what about those women who were living in his house? One of them is pregnant, I understand. Well, you can draw your own conclusions. I mean, all questions of professional excellence aside, as a moral example to the student body the man was dangerous. His ego seemed to demand that he become a kind of Pied Piper. I think a man of that type is a menace in any institution of higher learning. Don't forget, Mr. Kelly, not only did the Pied Piper charm the rats; he charmed the children too, and led them astray forever."

Rats. The word was well chosen. In Ham's case the rats and the children had been one and the same. Innocently Homer let his gaze rove the ceiling. "You don't suppose it was merely kindness on his part? You don't suppose it was simple kindness?"

"Oh, rot," said Sloan Tinker.

"Oh, well," said James Cheever. His face, which had been alight with malice, turned bland once more. He stood up. The audience was over.

But Homer wasn't finished. He hadn't yet asked his question. He couldn't think of any polite way to insert it harmlessly into the conversation, so he let it fall from his lips *crash-smash*. "I don't suppose, sir, you had an appointment with Ham Dow on the sixteenth, did you? His appointment book has turned up, and it shows that the person he was to meet at eleven-thirty had the initials J.C., like J.C. for James Cheever."

Tinker made a contemptuous noise in his throat. But Cheever merely blinked at Homer and then leaned to one side and called Mrs. Herbert. Mrs. Herbert bobbed into the room. She was instructed to show Mr. Kelly the President's appointments for October sixteenth. Mrs. Herbert went back into her office and returned with a big loose-leaf notebook, and held it up for Homer to see.

"I see an entry for eleven o'clock," said Homer. "See there? '11 A.M. Memorial Hall.'"

"Oh, no, that wasn't Wednesday," said Mrs. Herbert. "That was Tuesday, the day before. Mr. Cheever took part in a ceremony in Sanders Theatre on Tuesday to start the clocks."

"The clocks?" said Homer.

"The four new clocks on the new tower steeple," said James Cheever. "I pushed a button precisely at noon and the clocks chimed twelve and began running for the first time. A terrible waste of money, if you ask me. An utterly useless new steeple on that hideous tower, and a set of four fabulously expensive clocks made in Germany. At any rate, that ceremony was the day before. As you can see, there is no appointment for Wednesday other than the two-o'clock meeting with George Croft, the Vice President for Administration. It was right here in my office. Thank you, Mrs. Herbert. That will be all."

"What about you, Mr. Tinker?" said Homer, firing off a careless shot in another direction. "Have you got one of these little black appointment books on you anywhere?"

Sloan Tinker reddened, but then he drew something out of the inside pocket of his coat. It was his little black book. He flipped the pages silently, then held the book forward under Homer's nose. "Two P.M., Croft," he said.

"Ah, yes, but eleven-thirty has been written in and circled on that date," said Homer, pouncing. "What does the circle mean?"

Tinker looked again at his little black book, then closed it and tucked it back in his pocket. "I really cannot say."

But Cheever tapped on the table. "It was going to be at eleven-thirty that day, remember, Tinker? The meeting with George. And then it was changed to two o'clock. That must be why you circled eleven-thirty."

"Oh, yes, I had forgotten."

Homer stood up at last and said thank you. He shook hands with the two of them and left the room. As he closed the door behind him he looked back for a moment and saw them silhouetted against the dappled light pouring into the window behind them. They might have looked the same fifty years ago. A hundred. Maybe they were what kept a place like this going, decided Homer gloomily. Stalwart Yankee bastions of conservatism. Harvard past, Harvard present, Harvard sempiterna. A little band of scholars. A saving remnant. "Remnants are okay," said Homer, speaking up cheerfully to Mrs. Herbert. "But no rags or patches, please. Let's not have any of those."

"Right you are," said Mrs. Herbert gamely. "As a matter of

fact, I'm going out this afternoon and buy myself a new dress. Something absolutely smashing."

Homer beamed at Mrs. Herbert. She was a woman after his own heart. It might be worth his while to test her out. "Do you know offhand, Mrs. Herbert, why the meeting with Mr. Croft last Wednesday was changed from eleven-thirty in the morning to two in the afternoon?"

"Changed?" said Mrs. Herbert. "It wasn't changed. I arranged the two o'clock meeting at the request of Mr. Tinker."

"Mr. Tinker? Oh, well, then, I misunderstood."

Homer walked out of Massachusetts Hall and looked around for a moment to get his bearings. He gazed for a moment at the Johnston Gate, an elaborate barrier of brick and wrought iron that separated Massachusetts Hall and Harvard Yard from the traffic in the square. For James Cheever the iron gate was something that contained, guarding and protecting the Yard from the teeming street outside. Whereas Ham Dow had tried to throw open all the gates, to expose the narrow space within the brick walls to the wide world. Well, that was a sentimental notion perhaps. It sounded generous and fine, but what did it really mean? Maybe the man had been a corrupting influence, the way Cheever had said, snuffling around there at the bottom of the great chain of being.

"Oink," said Homer aloud. "Oink, oink," and a couple of women students going the other way looked at him and laughed.

Chapter Twenty-one

Ham spoke up. Why hadn't he tried it before? Why was it taking him so long to get his wits together? He was still so dizzy, that was why. Merely turning his head from side to side was enough to send him off into a spinning sickness. But the water in the pipe was helping. He had been waking up and lapping at the pipe and drowsing off again, and waking up to drink once more. This time he felt less ill. His mouth still tasted foul, and he wished he could brush his teeth, but his head felt perceptibly better. Ham hunched his shoulders up off the floor and coughed and said, "Hey, there," in a hoarse whisper. Then he cleared his throat and tried again. "Hey, out there."

He held his head still and listened.

There was no answer. He dropped his head back on the floor. He would keep it up. He would call out every now and then, in case somebody happened to come within earshot. Because this place might be some broom closet in an inhabited building, next to a passage that went somewhere. All he had to do was keep calling out, and they'd hear him eventually, people going by. They would stop and listen, and then they would call back, and pretty soon they'd open the door and say, "Well, for God's sake, so that's where you've been. We've been looking for you all over the place."

"Hey, hey, help, help."

It hurt his head to shout. But he called out a few more times anyway, cocking his head up, staring into the darkness. Then he lay back and listened once again.

There was no response. There was nothing in his ears but the echo of his own voice. And there was something dread about the way it battered back at him, as though the noise were not getting out at all. There was something ominous in the silence. It wasn't the temporary quiet of some useful chamber with a door giving on the outside world. It was the silence of—well, go ahead—it was the silence of the grave.

For the first time since he had begun waking up and going back to sleep, Ham permitted himself to wonder whether he might not have been buried alive underground. Or walled up alive like the man in Poe's story. At least he wasn't stretched out on some undertaker's cushion in a coffin that had been locked over his still-breathing body and lowered into the ground too soon. This hard littered surface was no coffin. That much was sure. But there was still the poor bricked-up wretch in "The Cask of Amontillado." That man's fate wasn't out of the question yet.

With a groan Ham sat up, and then struggled to his feet. Instantly his head began to throb. He was aching in every limb. He held his head with one hand, stretched the other in front of him, and began shuffling one foot in front of the other. This vault or hole or cave or subterranean chamber was small in size, he was sure of that. The echoes of his voice had rebounded too quickly. The room was very small. He had measured the size of the chamber with his ears, like a bat.

His shuffling feet nudged an obstruction. Ham stooped and felt it. The obstacle was a great beam of wood, slanted up off the floor. He had crawled out from under it. He could remember doing that. Following the beam with his fingers, Ham found the wall against which it leaned. Then, to his satisfaction, his groping hands discovered hinges, a doorknob. The beam of wood was leaning against a door. If he could move the beam aside, he might be able to open the door.

Gasping, he tried to push the high end of the beam to one side. But it was wedged against the door. He would have to raise it first. Lift now, lift, lift. There. Ham shuffled his toes backward, as the beam dropped and thudded heavily to the floor. Then he sagged to his hands and knees and leaned his whole weight against it, trying to shove it out of the way. Grudgingly it grated on the littered floor and slid sideways. Ham lay flat and rested for a few minutes. The effort had exhausted him. Then he stood up once again and felt his way to the door. He found the doorknob with his fingers. It refused to turn. It was locked. The door was locked. Discouraged, his strength giving out altogether, Ham sank to his knees and leaned his head against the door. "Hey, out there," he whispered again. "Hey, hey."

Chapter Twenty-two

ALTO SOLO

Be - hold_ your God!_ be - hold_ your God!

The place was beginning to get a grip on Homer. Every time he opened the battered door and stepped into the high windy space that ran through the middle of the building, the lofty corridor with its banging doors at both ends and its population of students taking shortcuts from classrooms and laboratories along Oxford Street to Quincy Street and the Yard, he felt pulled farther in, as though Memorial Hall were a kind of labyrinth of varnished wood. There was a spacious compartmented melancholy about it that peculiarly attracted him. Trying to put his finger on it, all he could think of was—of all the idiotic things—old lithographs by Currier and Ives, those jolly Currier and Ives calendar pictures of farmyard scenes, or sleighs dashing out of forests. Only it wasn't the hearty farmer and his wife or the fashionable lady and gentleman in the sleigh that were like the building. It was the woods in the background of all the pictures. All those Currier and Ives calendar pictures had the same thick woods, the same dark tangle of winter branches, or the same dense summer shade of trees in the woodlot, growing darker and darker as one looked deeper and deeper in.

It was the forest into which the farmer and his wife and the lady and gentleman would one day disappear. One by one they would slip into the dark woods. The gentleman in his frock coat and the lady in her thick skirt would move around the trunks of the trees and vanish. This building with its forest of varnished lumber reminded Homer of the woods. Only that moment the dead soldiers whose names lined the walls had slipped through the door into the great hall, or they were ascending or descending a staircase, or hovering in the shadows at the top of the balcony in Sanders Theatre, or moving slowly from level to level in the dim spaces of the tower, or occupying the dusty rooms in the turrets at either side, like the hunchback of Notre Dame.

But the soldiers were not real. Homer wasn't about to frighten himself with a population of ghosts from the Union Army. It was only the hunchback who turned out to exist, after all.

It was Tuesday morning. Tuesday wasn't ordinarily a class day,

but Mary was busy with students just the same, making herself available, helping them choose topics for the first paper of the semester. She would be through at twelve o'clock. Homer looked at his watch. He was early. He could hear music in Sanders Theatre. He poked his head in the door to see what was going on, and found Vick Van Horn working with a couple of her soloists. He walked into the amber light and sat down on one of the benches at the side.

Betsy Pickett was standing at the front of the stage. Tim Swegle, the tenor, was waiting his turn. Jack Fox was accompanying Betsy at the harpsichord. *"I know that my Redeemer liveth,"* sang Betsy, *"and that He shall stand at the latter day upon the earth."* Vick was brooding at the back of the hall, staring at Betsy, her elbows on the back of the bench in front of her, her chin in her hands. Betsy's thin trembling voice was a silver wire, a floating spun-glass thread. She was lost in her own miracle. Her seamless outpouring flowed around Homer. He could feel the ethereal spirals of her aria curling around the little iron pillars that supported the balcony, wreathing the rising rows of benches, billowing over the white marble statues of Josiah Quincy and James Otis, filling all the spaces and interstices of the forest of Sanders Theatre. Even the wooden volutes above the stage seemed ready to spring open and flower lush oaken blossoms in celebration of Betsy's faith in the risen Christ, in all things of the spirit, in everything true and—

"Oh, shit," said Betsy, breaking off in midflight. "I forgot the worms."

"It's all right," said Vick. "Just start over. And this time don't come down so hard on the appoggiatura. Just let it happen by itself. Did you want something, Homer?"

"Oh, no. Excuse me, I was just listening." Homer stood up and grinned and waved his hand and went out, as Betsy put her hands in her back pockets, threw her head back and began lobbing clear notes into the vault high over her head again. *"And though worms destroy this body, yet in my flesh shall I see God."*

Her voice flowed after Homer out of the hall in a cascading waterfall. He was still half transported. So it didn't surprise him at all to see the golden vision of the crucified Christ on the little balcony above the entrance to the great hall. In fact, it took him a full three seconds to realize that the little balcony did not usually support a vision, that Handel's *Messiah* was not usually accompanied by visual effects in pantomime. But there it was, a living picture. Someone was standing on the balcony in a white robe with his arms outspread in the attitude of the cross, his hair puffed out around his head. He was staring through a pair of thick glasses at the opposite wall.

"Jesus," gasped Homer. "Jesus X. Christ."

Homer didn't mean anything in particular by this exclamation, but instantly a spasm shook the body of the vision on the balcony, and it turned its head to look down at Homer tenderly. "I am," said the vision in a gentle voice. "You see, I am."

"Say, listen here," said Homer. "I saw you there before. How did you get there? Oh, I know. It's that staircase on the other side, isn't it? One of those stairways to the balconies in the great hall, right?"

The smile on the face of the vision faded. He picked up his white skirts and scuttled through the door at the back of the shallow balcony.

He couldn't go far. Homer ran across the creamy new cement of the floor under the balcony, just as the bell in the tower began to chime for noon. The bell sent hollow spheres of sound clanging throughout the building, declaring the end of class all up and down Oxford Street. Homer could imagine professors picking up their briefcases while their students billowed up the stairs of the amphitheaters in the Science Center and down the stairs in the Lowell Lecture Hall, tugging on coats and jackets against the early November chill, pouring along the sidewalks in the direction of the Student Union or Elsie's or the Wursthaus or other eating places around Harvard Square, or heading for dining halls in the river houses or the dorms in the Radcliffe Quad. Homer felt a pang in his own insides. He was starving. Mary would be there to meet him in a minute, and then they'd walk the long mile home for lunch. He really didn't have time to pursue this fool. But he ran into the great hall anyway, and looked around. The enormous room was empty, but he could hear a pattering scramble on the balcony over his head, then the sound of something falling over, and then silence.

Homer galloped up the stairs. The first balcony was a dusty place, cluttered with broken chairs. The Jesus vision was nowhere in sight, but the chair he had knocked over was lying on its side. The door to the tiny balcony over the memorial corridor was ajar. Homer wandered out onto it and looked down at students coming and going on the floor below. There was very little room on the balcony, only enough space for an orator making a speech, or a row of trumpeters blowing ruffles and flourishes. In Homer's brief acquaintance with Memorial Hall the little balcony had so far been unoccupied. He turned to go, but then he noticed something wedged in the shadows in the corner. It was a shoe. A man's shoe. Big and black with a buckle on its side. The Jesus vision had rushed away like Cinderella, leaving his glass slipper behind him. Well, he couldn't have rushed far.

Homer carried the shoe back out onto the big balcony over the great hall and looked left and right. Then he remembered the turret rooms at either side. He moved softly into the alcove at one side of the balcony and peered into its hollow depths. At the other end of the little hall there was a door, and through the stained glass in the window of the door shone the light of day.

Homer rattled the knob. The door was locked. "Hello, in there," he said loudly. Immediately he heard a *bump* on the other side of the door and then a scurrying noise like a mouse in the wall. Then silence.

"Hey, in there, open up." Homer shook the door handle. Then he noticed a white card on the door frame.

113

said the white card.

"Hey, open up in there," thundered Homer, knocking on the glass. "I require administrative assistance."

There was more scuffling. Then more silence. Then a shape loomed up in the glass and opened the door slowly. A frowzy head looked out, the wispy strands of hair around it catching the sunlight like an aureole. The thick glasses peered out into the dim corridor. The narrow face was in shadow. "May I help you?" said the administrative assistant, speaking softly through the crack.

Homer waggled the big black shoe at him and said the first thing that came into his head. "I am—ah—looking for assistance from the curriculum committee of the university faculty of general education and the fellowship for undergraduate health services," he said, letting his eyes rove from the pale face downward to the too-large sweater and the trousers, which were strangely wadded and bulging. The corner of a white sheet trailed from one pant leg. The orange sneakers were very small. The big glass slipper would never fit those tiny feet. This was not Cinderella, after all. Homer stuck the big shoe back under his arm.

"Oh, of course," said Jesus. "You want Bellweather Hall. The second floor. Room 242." He was nodding his head up and down in the kindliest way.

"I've already been there," said Homer. "They told me to come here." Behind the frowzy head he could see an untidy sleeping bag on the floor. An open can of SpaghettiOs stood on a large box trunk. One of the windows was propped open with a stick, and on the sill stood (aha!) a carton of milk.

"Oh, so many people make that mistake." Jesus smiled. "But we don't take care of that kind of thing in here any more. Perhaps it is Muggleby Hall now. Muggleby, you see. Not Memorial Hall." He pointed vaguely over Homer's shoulder in the direction of a possible Muggleby Hall, and began closing the door. "I

114

remember now. There was some talk of moving that committee from Bellweather to Muggleby. Yes, I feel sure that must be the case. Just proceed down Oxford Street. You'll find Muggleby on the left-hand side. A big yellow-brick building." He was nodding through the crack. The door was closing. "You can't miss it." The door clicked shut.

Homer was enchanted. He stood staring at the blurry shape of Jesus as it faded away from the door on the other side of the glass. The man was living there. He had found a home complete with heat and light and a magnificent view of Harvard Yard and the traffic swarming around Cambridge Common. Free, free! But the question was, had he been manufacturing bombs in there in his spare time? Had he blown up a chunk of Memorial Hall as a portent of the wrath to come? Homer rapped on the door again. "Now look here, friend. No nonsense, now. Open up."

Once more the door opened. Again the round glasses blinked amiably at Homer.

"I want to know what you think you're up to. What were you doing out there on the balcony? Just what the hell is going on?"

"But you heard."

"I heard? What did I hear? Go ahead. Tell me what I heard."

"You know. The music. What they were singing."

"Singing? You mean in Sanders Theatre? You mean, the *Messiah?* Handel's *Messiah?*"

Jesus smiled modestly. "Exactly. You see, I was handing out pamphlets out there on the street one day last week, and I heard them singing. So I came in to listen. Because, you see, I am. I told you."

"You said that before. You am. You mean, you *personally* am? You am what?"

"The Messiah. Reborn into this generation. Come back to earth. I am only awaiting the moment. The right moment to announce my return."

"Oh, go on," said Homer. "You don't really mean it."

"Why, certainly. Certainly I do. You see, the Messiah is reborn into every generation. It is a fact. There have been others. Many others. But in this generation—"

"In this generation it just happens to be you, is that it? Oh, look here, now," said Homer, "that's the nuttiest thing I ever—"

"Listen. Listen to the music!"

Faintly from Sanders Theatre the voice of the tenor soloist wavered upward: *Behold and see if there be any sorrow like unto His sorrow.* The wispy-haired Messiah lifted his arms to right and left and stood in the position of the cross, beaming at Homer, the ragged edges of his hair and the fluffy sleeves of his sweater and the knobby silhouette of his trousers outlined in the yellow light of broad noonday. Homer was appalled. Between them as they stood staring at one another floated the melancholy rising sevenths and the lost bereft dyings away of the tenor aria, casting into outrageous perspective the callow posturings of the self-styled Messiah of Memorial Hall.

Homer closed his eyes. "Oh, no. Oh, no, I can't stand it. Oh, Jesus Christ."

The Messiah smiled and laid his hand on Homer's arm in a gesture of gentle blessing. "He stands before you."

Mr. Crawley came out of his office just as Homer lifted his hand to knock on his door. "Sorry. Gotta go. In a hurry," said Mr. Crawley.

"Oh, Mr. Crawley, I just wanted to ask you if you know anything about that guy who lives upstairs."

"Upstairs? There ain't nobody living upstairs."

"Haven't you seen that character in the white sheet who stands up there on the balcony sometimes?"

"Oh, you mean that weirdo."

"Well, could you tell me how he might have acquired a key to the room above your office, right upstairs?"

"Upstairs? I don't know about no rooms upstairs. It's all them little rooms in the basement. Dow, he had a master key. You know, the guy that got his head blowed off. He let them practice all over the basement. There was all this noise coming out all over. Terrible. You couldn't hardly hear yourself think. Go ahead. Go on down there. See for yourself. Whole place, full of them, like rats in the wall. Coming out of the woodwork." Crawley pulled his hat down further over his face and shambled off in the direction of the south entry, where he nearly ran into Mary Kelly, who was hurrying in from out of doors.

"Oh, hello, there." Mary smiled at Mr. Crawley. "Oh, Homer, I'm sorry to be late. Those kids, I don't know where they all come from. There's more of them every day."

"Coming out of the woodwork, right?"

"Exactly. And they all want to talk. They cluster around. They're all eating *lunch* down there now. It's like a picnic. It's really nice. Oh, Vick, dear, hello."

"What's that?" said Vick. She was standing stock-still, her arms full of music, staring at the shoe under Homer's arm.

"What's what?" said Homer. "Oh, this? It's a glass slipper. Cinderella's glass slipper. No, no. It's somebody's shoe. I found it on the balcony up there. I'll bet it's Ham Dow's shoe, blown off his left foot."

"That's not Ham's shoe. Ham would never have worn a shoe like that."

"He wouldn't?"

"No. He wore thick laced-up boots. Or sneakers. Not the yachting kind of sneakers. The cheap kind that lace above the ankle. You know, the kind that say 'Coach.' We used to kid him about being the coach."

"Well, what kind was he wearing the day he died?"

"I'm not sure. I don't remember. But not anything like that one there. He would never have worn anything so sort of yukky and disgusting as that shoe there. Never. Never in a million years."

"Hello, Mr. Ratchit? This is Homer Kelly. You remember me. I came to see you about the bombing victim at Harvard."

"Oh, yeah. Sure, sure. I remember you. What's on your mind?"

"Can you tell me if the man still had both shoes on his feet? I know most of his clothing was blown off or burned in the explosion, but I wondered if his shoes . . .?"

"Sure, sure, I remember his shoe. He only had the one shoe. The other one was gone. You mean, you got the other shoe? Big shoe, black, with like a buckle on the side? Left shoe? That's right. That's it. The right shoe was almost burnt to a crisp, but you could see what it was. Where'd it turn up?"

"On the balcony. It must have blown right up in the air and landed on the floor of the balcony."

"It's all run down on the outside, right? That's it. You get a really overweight individual, they wear their shoes down fast on the side."

"Well, thanks, Mr. Ratchit. That's fine. You're a big help. Thank you very much."

Women, thought Homer, putting down the phone. They were supposed to be so observant of small detail. Well, this time they hadn't been. Vick was wrong. Yukky and disgusting or not, the big black shoe with the silver buckle had once belonged to Hamilton Dow.

Homer tapped the shoe on the palm of his hand thoughtfully. There was something else he ought to do. Just out of curiosity. He should explore the basement. He should take a look at the basement and see what the woodwork was like—the woodwork from which the rats were so abundantly pouring.

Chapter Twenty-three

Lying flat on his back on the floor gazing upward, it occurred to Ham to wonder if he were blind. It was stupid of him not to have thought of it before. Perhaps the reason he couldn't see his hand in front of his face was not because there was no light, but because he had lost his sight. But if this accident or disaster, whatever it was, had blinded him, then why was there no great pain in his eyes? His eyes felt all right. At least they didn't hurt any more than any other part of him hurt. It was his head that bothered him most. The knobs on the back of his head. But even his head was feeling a little better. The great lumps were subsiding. They were less like huge swollen eggs. He must have had a concussion of some sort, perhaps even a fractured skull. There had been some kind of disaster or explosion. It must have been an explosion, to have created so much havoc around him, the fallen beam and the litter of brick and the chunks of concrete block, the bits and pieces of rock, the drifts of gritty plaster dust.

Maybe there had been an explosion in the gas line. Maybe all of Cambridge had gone up in smoke, or in some gigantic atomic blast. Maybe the whole city was buried in ruins. Otherwise you would think he'd be hearing picks and shovels, the bangings and hammerings of a rescue party, all his old friends and students digging out their old professor. Even if they thought he was dead, you'd think they'd be trying to remove his body from the rubble.

Well, give them time. Ham wasn't about to panic. He was going to get out of this somehow. After all, he hadn't really tried to free himself yet by his own wits. He had found the door, and the door had refused to open, and he had given up in exhaustion. But now he was feeling a little stronger. Ham breathed in great chestfuls of air, and pulled himself to a sitting position. Then he stood up shakily, reached out for the wall, and leaned against it. How long had he been without food? His trousers were hanging slack. He was feeling too ill to be hungry—still, it had been a long time. It occurred to him to wonder what was in his pockets. Maybe there was something useful in his pants pockets, something he could use to open the lock of the door. Carefully he removed the contents of his back pockets. He found his wallet. He put it away again. He found a folded piece of paper. He couldn't remember what was written on the paper, but as he unfolded it, a picture floated out of the folds and appeared before him in the dark. It was the face of Vick Van Horn. Vick was looking at him in sharp concern. The image was so bright and clear, her glance so full of dread, Ham grunted with surprise. He folded the paper and put it away again. Then he turned his attention to one of his front pockets and found a big lump. What on earth was that? The lump had a crinkled metallic surface. Aha, aha! Ham felt his face stretching in a smile. It was aluminum foil wrapped around a great chunk of Emma Esterhazy's peanut brittle. God bless the good Esterhazy! Ham broke off a tiny chunk of the peanut brittle and ate it slowly, savoring the sweet salt juices trickling down his throat. Then he reached out for the pipe, knelt down beside it, ran his finger around the broken rim and washed his brief dinner down. Then he finished off the first meal in his dark prison by wetting his hands and washing his face.

His spirits rose. His mind cleared, and something else occurred to him. Not only did the pipe supply him with fresh water, it might be good for something else. Where did it go? Ham crouched beside it until his ear was pressed against the open end. He could hear faint windy sighings in the pipe, slight tringlings and distant thrumming noises. He turned his head and put his mouth against it. "Hello," he shouted. "Helloooooo, out there. Can you heeeeeaaaar meeeeee?"

He took his mouth away and turned his head so that his ear was pressed up against the pipe. Again he could hear the windy whistling, the thrumming—but nothing more.

He sat back on his heels and thought about the pipe. Where did it go?

Suppose he were buried somewhere under Memorial Hall. Just suppose. Because the last thing he could remember (except for the insistent picture of the stranger's face with its look of surprise —and Ham was beginning to think he must have dreamt the stranger's face, along with all those other crazy things)—the last real thing he could remember was the rehearsal in Sanders Theatre. So perhaps he was walled up in one of those little rooms in the basement. There was no other place he could possibly be. Although for the life of him he couldn't understand why he didn't hear people going and coming in the hall outside, if that was where he was. (For the life of him. Well, that was some kind of joke.)

Well, then, if he was under Memorial Hall somewhere, then

the pipe could go in any one of ten million directions. It would be part of the enormous interconnecting plumbing system. It might even pass through rooms and passages and corridors where people were actually passing by. By calling through the pipe over and over again, he might eventually be heard.

No, no, that was wrong. It wouldn't do any good to call through the pipe. It was a matter of simple physics. It wouldn't do any good to make standing waves of air inside the pipe unless by some wild stroke of luck the pipe came to an end against somebody's ear. But if the pipe *itself* were vibrating, then the noise would be heard all along its whole length, not just at the end.

Ham got up off his knees and kicked his way slowly along the floor until he found a brick. Then he knelt down and hit the pipe with it. BANG BANG. He put his ear to the pipe and struck it again. The blow rang in the metal. It sounded musical and loud.

He began with the call for help in Morse code.

bingbingbing BANGBANGBANG bingbingbing
bingbingbing BANGBANGBANG bingbingbing . . .

Chapter Twenty-four

bingbingbing BANGBANGBANG bingbingbing
bingbingbing BANGBANGBANG bingbingbing

Jerry Crawley woke up. He turned over on his side on the sofa, lifted his head, and stared at the pipe rising from floor to ceiling in the corner of the room. Jeez, the thing was making a hell of a racket. Mr. Crawley pulled his hat down over one ear and huddled his head down in the crevice of the sofa again.

bingbingbing BANGBANGBANG bingbingbing
bingbingbing BANGBANGBANG bingbingbing

Christ, you didn't get no peace. He got up off the sofa, took his coat from the hook on the door, settled down on the sofa again with the coat over his head, and went back to sleep.

BANG bingbangbing! BANG bingbangbing!
bingbingBANGbing! bingbingBANGbing!
bingBANGbingBAAANG BANG

In the room above Mr. Crawley's office, the Messiah of Memorial Hall paid no attention to the rhythm of the "Hallelujah Chorus" thundering in the pipe in the corner of his room. His attention was elsewhere. He was squatting naked on his sleeping bag reading the Book of Revelation.

He who testifies to these things says,
"Surely I am coming soon." Amen. Come, Lord Jesus!

Basement entry
Memorial Hall

Chapter Twenty-five

SOPRANO SOLO

Come un - to Him, all ye that la - bour, come un - to Him, ye that are heav-y la - den, and He will give you rest.

The building was a dark mountain blotting out the night sky.

"Look," said Homer. "There's a light in that room right over Crawley's office. That's where Jesus lives. He's got a really cozy little apartment."

"And, Homer, look up there. Way at the top. Jack-o'-lanterns. Two of them. Somebody's hung a couple of pumpkins up there at the top of the tower." Mary Kelly pointed upward.

Homer looked up too and saw the grinning faces glowing orange at the corners of the bell chamber. "Wow, they must be a hundred and fifty feet up. Hanging on those gargoyles that stick out up there. Halloween was two weeks ago. You'd think they'd rot and fall down."

"What a crazy thing to do," said Mary. "They might have broken their necks, climbing up there. Crazy kids."

"How do you know it was kids?"

"Well, who else would do a dangerous charming thing like that? Oh, don't they look marvelous."

"How did they get up in the tower at all? That's the question," said Homer. "More crazy people are running around with keys to every nook and cranny in Memorial Hall."

There was a concert in Sanders Theatre. From the memorial transept Homer and Mary could hear the plangent chords of a harpsichord, and through the windows in the doors they could see the audience listening solemnly on the benches at the side. In the corridor a girl was selling tickets at a small table, almost lost in the dim vastness of the long dark hall. "You want to hear the second half?" she said. "I'll sell you a couple of tickets half-price."

"No, thank you," said Mary. "We're just trying to get into the basement. I guess we'll have to go in by way of the service entrance on the other side. Right?"

"I'm afraid so. The great hall is all locked up."

A delivery ramp was mounted beside the stairway in the service entrance. "Look at that," said Homer. "They must have had one like that in the old days. When the old kitchen was down here. Imagine the sides of beef coming in, the cases of milk bottles, the barrels of apples."

The door to the basement corridor at the bottom of the stairs was open. A light glimmered around a corner to the left. "Listen," said Mary, taking Homer's arm. "You can't actually hear anything, but the place is alive. It hums. I can almost feel it."

"Feel what?"

"People. It just feels inhabited. And look at the way the light flickers and changes down there at the end of the hall. Something's going on down there. Listen! Did you hear that? Somebody laughed."

"Oh, go on. That was outside."

"No, I could swear it was down this hallway." Mary walked to the corner. "Right about here."

"Nobody here now." Homer took a flashlight out of his coat and looked at the closed doors lining the corridor on either side. "This place is just one little cubbyhole after another. Ecology Action Committee. The Worshipful Companie of Freemen of the Shire. What on earth is that?"

"Tolkien." Mary laughed. "It must be a bunch of Hobbits."

"Christian Science Youth. Harvard-Radcliffe Gay Students Organization. You know what it's like? A huge hotel. My father's house hath many mansions. Well, not mansions exactly. These little rooms must be about the size of closets."

"Listen," said Mary. "I hear flute music. Back there where we came in."

"It must be from the concert upstairs." Homer cocked his head. "No, no, you're right. You couldn't hear anything from upstairs down here in the basement. It's somebody playing a flute down here." They stood still and listened to the thin silvery sound of flute music purling down a scale, then breaking off.

"They know we're here. Somebody's spread the word," said Mary. "I can feel it. They're everywhere. Behind all these doors. Waiting for us to go away. Where are we now? I'm lost."

"We must be under the corridor upstairs. You know, the memorial part, the transept, that big hall that runs all the way through the building. Look, there's where the bomb went off."

"Where? You mean where those boards are nailed up?"

"That's right. They boarded it all up. They dumped all the debris back in the hole and boarded it up down here at both ends. Maderna told me they're going to clear it out in the spring and turn it into a new office. They're going to open up all the little rooms into one big space. Harvard's always looking for more room. Institutional elephantiasis."

Mary plucked Homer's sleeve. "I saw somebody. A man with a broom. He saw us, and then he just faded away."

"It wasn't Crawley?"

"No, no. He was taller than Crawley."

"Must be the nighttime custodian," said Homer. "A tall bald guy? I think I know who you mean. I saw him once upstairs, only in the daytime."

They explored the basement of Memorial Hall for half an hour, wandering up and down the corridors from the curtained windows of the radio station at one end to the shuttered counter of the copy center at the other. The locked doors of WHRB to the east and the Harvard Personnel Office to the west looked businesslike and uninhabited, but everywhere else there were snatches of music, voices, laughter. Doors closed ahead of them at the ends of narrow vistas. Lights flickered and went out. There were warm fragrances of coffee and cigarettes. The spaces behind the doors thrummed with life, with breath that seemed to be held as they moved past, and then exhaled again.

At last they found their way back to the service entrance on the north side. Homer opened the door and followed Mary up the stairs. "It's true, then," he said, "about the woodwork. People coming out of the woodwork. I mean, it isn't just that Jesus freak who's found a free place to live up there over Mr. Crawley's office."

"No," said Mary, "it's Ham's Rats. Dozens of them. They're all over Memorial Hall."

"They're living here. It's a bloody orphan asylum. They've got the run of the whole place, from the cellar to the tower. It's a kind of enormous apartment house for squatters, and Ham was its mad landlord. No, no, it's more like Sherwood Forest, and Ham was Robin Hood. Everybody was invited to move in and settle down with the rest of his raffish band of outcasts, debtors, excommunicants, and thieves." Then Homer staggered and threw up his hands and clutched the back of his head. "Good God, what was that? An arrow! You see, I was right!"

"Oh, Homer, you poor dear." Mary turned back and picked up the object that had come hurtling through the open door behind them to strike its target straight and true. It was a blue plastic Frisbee.

Chapter Twenty-six

TENOR SOLO

...the Lord shall have them in de-ri-sion.

Homer sat at his desk beside a sunny window in the bedroom of the flat on Huron Avenue and called Peter Marley. "It's just a failing in my education, you see, Peter. I don't know enough about criminal psychosis. I mean, I don't have the faintest idea how it's related to other kinds of insanity. Delusions, for instance. What do you call it when people think they're somebody else? You know, like Napoleon Bonaparte? Would somebody like that be harmless, or would he be a dangerous lunatic and try to take over East Cambridge by force of arms? What I'm leading up to is this character I ran across in Memorial Hall the other day. He thinks he's Jesus Christ in the flesh. You're laughing. It's not funny. Listen, Marley. Well, I admit in a way it's kind of funny, but in another way—"

"Listen, Homer, we know all about him. He's a well-known Cambridge fruit cake."

"No kidding."

"Freddy Fulsom. Harmless as the day is long."

"Freddy Fulsom? He's not one of the Boston Fulsoms?"

"Oh, yes, he certainly is. Fine old Boston family. His mother came and got him. She swept in there and took him by the ear and cleared him out and took him home to Mount Vernon Street.

129

She said she worried about his laundry more than anything else, and whether or not he was keeping himself sanitary. I wonder about that myself. The nearest bathroom must have been ten miles away. She brought him down here and told me all about it. Made him promise me he wouldn't be naughty any more. As a matter of fact, she said his psychiatrist is quite pleased with this new phase of Freddy's. I mean, apparently Freddy used to think he was some kind of little nocturnal animal that lives in trees. A potto, or something like that. So it's a step up for Freddy to think he's Jesus Christ. I mean, at least he's not sitting on top of the bureau any more."

"A step up." Homer laughed. "I'll say it's a step up. It's President Cheever's great chain of being again. Good for Freddy! He shot from the bottom to the top in one lifetime. You know, Peter, he was living in there. Right up there over Crawley's office. That little balcony over the transept was his front porch. How do we know he didn't blow the place up?"

"Oh, no, not Freddy. He doesn't have the wit or the know-how."

"Well, I suppose he was just another one of Ham's Rats. Ham must have felt sorry for him and found a place in the building where he could stay."

"No, I don't think so, Homer. He didn't know Ham Dow. I don't think he really focuses on people at all. He's up in the clouds all the time. You know what I mean."

"Well, then, maybe it's true that he came in because of the music, the way he says. Maybe he did just move in a couple of weeks ago. He heard the music and decided it was all in his honor, and he just moved right in on his own. A long time after the bombing. So I guess he didn't have a bomb factory in that big trunk of his. We don't have to go in there and look around."

"I'll tell you the place I'd like to turn inside out," said Marley. "Cheever's office. If I had the gall, I'd do it this weekend, because Cheever's going to be away. I'd just go in there and take a look. Because I'm still curious about why he and Tinker lied to you that

130

day. But of course that's just an insane notion on my part. It's not something you do behind the back of the President of Harvard."

"Cheever's going away?"

"Yes, he's going to Chicago with Tinker. It's some conference of college presidents. They're off for the weekend. Say, listen, Homer, there's another thing. Something else has turned up. You'll be amused to learn that Ham Dow left a funny will. It turned up in his house. Pasted to the refrigerator. He added new beneficiaries every day."

"He did? What kind of a crazy will is that? Did he have a lot of property to bestow? I suppose he must have had a pretty good salary, being an associate professor at Harvard University. Right?"

"Well, maybe he did, but I don't think there was much of anything left for anybody to inherit. He was always spreading it around all over the place. I think it was just a few personal possessions and the house itself. It's true, he owned the house free and clear."

"His house is on Martin Street? Could I go there? I mean, I admit, I'm just curious. I can't help it. The man intrigues me."

"Well, I don't see why not. Of course, his estate is in probate court, I understand, but I think one of the kids is still living there. Why don't you just knock on the door and see what happens? Sixty Martin Street."

"Well, maybe I will."

Homer hung up and tried to get back to work. He was supposed to be finishing the last chapter of the textbook, *The Great Cloud Darkening the Land*, which was growing out of the course of lectures. But he was bored with the last chapter. It was the index that really captured his interest. The index was going to be the best part. It was going to be the most informative, garrulous, cross-indexed index there ever was. A magnificent index. At the moment the index was only a crawling swarm of three-by-five cards, proliferating all over the table. Homer put his hand into the pile at random and plucked out a single card. The telephone rang.

It was Julia Chamberlain. "Hello, Homer? I hope it's all right to call you Homer? And please, for heaven's sake, call me Julia. I loathe being called Mrs. Chamberlain. Homer, I wonder if you and your wife would like to come to the cocktail party in the ballroom at 17 Quincy Street as my guests after the game tomorrow."

"The game? There's some sort of game tomorrow?"

"Some sort of— Listen, you ninny, it's the Harvard-Yale game. Didn't you know that? Homer Kelly, you amaze me. I'm really surprised. Anyway, how about it? It's a sort of big ceremonial party for all the bigwigs who come up from Yale for the game. I want to introduce you to Jim Cheever. I mean, I think it's important for him to get to know new members of the faculty, especially really refreshing ones like you, Homer. And I'm eager to meet your wife. I understand she's a peach too."

"Well, of course, we'd love to come. But President Cheever is going to be away. Peter Marley just told me on the phone, there's a conference of college presidents in Chicago this weekend. Cheever's going to be there, and so is Tinker."

"They are?" There was a pause. "Well," said Julia Chamberlain.

"So maybe you'd rather withdraw your invitation," said Homer. "Mary and I would be glad to be sociable another time."

There was another pause. "Oh, yes. Well, maybe. Well, yes, I guess, as a matter of fact, I will. I mean, if Jim isn't going to be there, I may not go myself."

"Very good, then," said Homer politely, and then he waited for Julia to begin the little ceremonial exchanges of courtesy required for a telephone farewell.

But instead there was an awkward pause. The conversation seemed to have come to a dead halt. Homer sensed that the woman on the other end of the line was staring into space. Sportingly he pitched in, casting about for something to say. He brought up the stained glass. He wondered how that campaign was going. He hoped they'd find enough money somewhere to replace the stained glass in Memorial Hall.

132

Then Julia Chamberlain laughed and came back to life. "Oh, good Lord, who knows what will happen about the stained glass? The only progress so far is an estimate from Connick Associates in Boston. If you could call that progress. Because it will be two hundred dollars a square foot. Do you know how much that comes to altogether? Three hundred thousand dollars."

"Three hundred thousand—my God."

"The entire building only cost four hundred thousand, back in the 1870s. I haven't dared mention it to anybody yet. Certainly not to Jim Cheever. He'll have a fit. You say he's going to be away? How long? Did Peter say how long?"

"All he said was they'd be away for the weekend."

"Mmmmmm. Well, so long, Homer. I'll be calling you and your wife pretty soon about something friendly. Good-bye."

Homer put the telephone down, picked up a handful of index cards, and began sorting them by color. The colors stood for chapters. He spread them fanwise in his hand and began plucking them out one at a time, a pink one, a pink one, a blue one, a green one. Then he pulled out too many at once, and the entire fistful of cards slithered to the floor. Homer cursed and got down on his hands and knees and scrabbled them together and slapped them on the table. Then he snatched up his coat and went out, persuading himself that what he needed most right now was a breath of fresh air. A brisk walk. A nice hike over to Martin Street. He glanced at the map of Cambridge before he burst out the door, and was surprised to discover that Martin Street wasn't one of the polite streets of large houses running off Brattle Street, where any right-thinking Harvard professor would want to live. It was way the hell and gone out Mass Av on the way to Porter Square. But it wasn't so far from Huron Avenue. He could make a shortcut past the Radcliffe Quad.

Ten minutes later Homer turned into Martin Street and made his way to number 60. It was a small wooden-frame building with a narrow porch close to the sidewalk. Homer guessed it belonged to the same era as Memorial Hall.

Jennifer Sullivan opened the door. Homer remembered Jennifer. She was a member of Vick's chorus, and even in that miscellaneous collection of people she would have been hard to miss. She was a frail-looking moth of a girl in a swollen maternity jumper.

"Come in," said Jennifer. "You're Mary Kelly's husband, aren't you? A professor or something, like Mary? I mean, Mary and I are together in the chorus. We stand side by side. That is, we will be if I make it to the concert. My baby's due on Christmas day, only who knows? It might be early. What can I do for you? I mean, nobody else is here to talk to. They've all left. I'm all by myself now. And I'm getting out myself next week. The house is all mixed up in some kind of legal tangle. Probate, I guess it is. Here, I'll just move this stuff out of the way. Sit down."

Homer sat down and looked around. Ham's living room was clean, and it was plain that someone, probably Jennifer, had attempted a kind of tidiness. But beneath the superficial order a more fundamental disorder was apparent. The place was a musical jungle. A baby grand piano stuck out into the hall. A harpsichord was wedged behind the sofa. A cello case lay under the harpsichord. Stacks of music were everywhere. Scattered about the room were a pair of guitars, a banjo, a zither, a trombone, a great gold harp, and an accordion sparkling with plastic mother-of-pearl.

"Don't tell me," said Homer. "That handsaw on the mantelpiece. It's not just for cutting up firewood, right?"

"Oh, no," said Jennifer, giggling. "That's a musical saw. You bend it into a sort of double curve on your knee and play it with a bow."

"You've got enough instruments in here for a concert band," said Homer. "How many people were living here when Ham was alive?"

"Oh, wow, I don't know. They were always coming and going. There was Mrs. Esterhazy, of course. And her two kids. And Mr. Proctor. They were here all the time. But other people came and went. Like Suzie. Look here." Jennifer jumped up and snatched something off the mantel. "What am I going to do with Suzie's dollar fifty? Here, listen to this. She left a note: 'Dear Ham, This is just to thank you for letting me stay while I was so mad. I wish I could pay for all the food I ate, but this is all I've got. Maybe it will pay for the Cokes. Love, Suzie.'"

"Who was Suzie?" said Homer. "Why was she so mad?"

"Oh, she was this little kid. She ran away. She was only fourteen. Her parents had been just so incredibly disgusting. Ham talked to them, and then she went home."

"She was one of Ham's—ah—Rats, I gather?" Homer smiled ingratiatingly at Jennifer, not sure whether Rats was an outsider's or an insider's word. Maybe Jennifer would be insulted.

But she laughed. "Oh, no, not really. But the rest of us were

Rats, all right. Of course, I'm a Rat and a student too, at the same time. At least I am so far. I don't know how long it will last—being a student, I mean. They won't let you have a baby in a dorm, so Ham invited me to move in here. But now I've got to go someplace else."

"You're not married, I guess, Jennifer?"

"Oh, no."

"You can't just go home like Suzie?"

"Oh, God, no. Not home. My parents don't even know." Jennifer patted her swollen jumper. "I've got some friends. I know a place to go. Sort of a big place with a lot of extra space. I'll be all right there."

"Well, that's good. Central location?" said Homer innocently.

"Oh, yes, a really great location. You see, I'm going to keep the baby. I'm making little clothes for it and everything. I mean, you know, it's this big sort of primordial *motherhood* kind of thing. I've absolutely lost all interest in the intellectual history of the Reformation. All I can think of is, like, making little quilts for the baby, and, I mean, it's so strange, I just want to sit and sew. Isn't that strange?"

Homer remembered James Cheever's suspicions about the women in Ham's house. He wanted to ask a nosy question, but he didn't dare. But then Jennifer read his mind and she spoke up fearlessly. "And if you think Ham was the father of my child you're just stupid, that's all. Just really dumb like all the rest."

Well, it was none of Homer's business. It occurred to him that the infant might even have been immaculately conceived, if it was going to be born on Christmas Day. Oh, blasphemy. Oh, sacrilege. He screwed up his courage and asked another question. "Well, what about Ham? Did he have a girlfriend at all? Am I right in thinking Mrs. Esterhazy was . . .?"

"Oh, no, not Mrs. Esterhazy." Jennifer laughed. "I don't think he had anybody at all. Well, there was Vick, of course. He did a lot of kidding around with Vick Van Horn, only it was, you know, sort of a teacher-and-student relationship. Except, wow,

I've got three friends right now who are living with teaching fellows and section men."

"So teachers do still have affairs with students," murmured Homer. "Like good old Abélard and Héloïse."

"Oh, right. Of course, plenty of people had a thing about Ham Dow. I mean, they would have given their eyeteeth! But I think he was just too sort of, you know, *honorable* to take advantage of anybody. He was just really so kind. I mean, look at the way he took me in. That's the way he was with everybody. Look at Mrs. Esterhazy. He invited her to live in his house, and of course he invited her kids too. Mrs. Esterhazy was having a hard time, I guess, trying to earn enough money singing, and she said she was too proud to live on welfare, so he took her in, and he was getting voice students for her too." Jennifer jumped up. "I vass alone in da vorld," she said, rolling her eyes like Mrs. Esterhazy. "My hozband, *poof!* he ron avay vit anozzer vooman. My cheeldren, zey vere *starving!*"

"Starving? Those enormous little cherubs, surely they weren't starving?"

"Well, they certainly weren't starving while they were living here. Ham was a really good cook. He'd whip up a big vat of something every night, and of course we all helped, and people would, you know, drop in. It was just really so much fun. Sometimes it was string quartets, and we'd all sit around on the floor and listen, and sometimes it would be folk singing, and we'd all sing. Or there was some crazy kind of ethnic music, or bluegrass. You know. And people would bring beer, or bottles of wine. And you won't believe it, but we even did folk dancing in here. You wouldn't think there'd be enough room, but we'd just lift the sofa out of the way on the table, and everybody'd be bumping into everybody else, and there'd be the craziest people playing native instruments. And everybody came. Not just all young ones like us. Real old people too. Even Miss Plankton. Miss Plankton used to come and bring homemade cookies and get a little tipsy on a glass of wine, and say things like, 'Oh, what fun!'" Jennifer clasped her hands and beamed like a little old Cambridge lady. " 'Oh, isn't this a lark?' I mean, it was like a party here almost every night. It was all really just so great." Jennifer kicked the leg of the sofa. "You know, the funny thing is, this place belongs to me. I mean, I own one sixty-fifth of it. I suppose they'll just have an auction or something and divvy up the money."

"One sixty-fifth? Oh, that's right," said Homer. "Marley told me there were a lot of beneficiaries to Ham's will."

"It was just a joke, you see," said Jennifer. "His will was just a big joke. He started making it last summer, when some guy from the Law School was here, and this guy told him he ought to make a will. So Ham took a scrap of paper and scribbled something on it, and the Law School guy signed it, and then Ham kept this crazy piece of paper taped up on the refrigerator, and every time anybody new came along he'd add their name to his will. It was just a big joke."

"But it was legal, I suppose?" said Homer.

"Oh, right. He always put down the date and got witnesses to sign it. But it was just a sort of running joke. It was just for fun."

Homer said good-bye to Jennifer and walked home again. There was an odd sensation in his breast, and it took him a moment to identify the feeling. He had often been aware of the same thing, reading Henry Thoreau. He had felt it again, just the other day, looking again at Melville's delirious letters to Hawthorne—a sense of affection and loss. He wanted to know them in the flesh. But Thoreau and Melville were dead, irretrievably dead and gone. It was the same with Ham Dow. The more Homer learned about Ham, the more he felt the man had been a force for something which he did not hesitate to call good. Little by little Ham's death had become more than an interesting professional problem. It had been transformed for Homer into what it was for nearly everyone else, a personal disaster. Walking home to Huron Avenue from Ham's house, he was overcome by a foolish and impossible desire to meet and know the man alive.

Chapter Twenty-seven

... and the rul — ers take coun — sel to-geth — er,

... a-gainst the Lord and His an —

oint — ed.

Saturday was mild for the middle of November. Homer and Mary took a walk along the Charles after lunch, and then Mary turned around to go home to work on her half of the index, with which she was as infatuated as Homer. "Now listen, Homer, don't forget to stop at the grocery store when you're through at Widener. Have you got the list?"

"Right here," said Homer. "The trouble is, I've got two lists. One of them is the references I've got to check, and what I'm afraid I'll do is march up to the call desk in Widener and pound on the counter and demand a dozen tortillas and a can of enchilada sauce."

"Well, just be sure you don't hand me twelve volumes of the *Proceedings of the Massachusetts Historical Society* and expect me to turn them into a Mexican dinner. Oh, Homer, look at the traffic up there on the bridge. It's a good thing you're on foot. What a snarl! Look, it's backed up as far as the eye can see."

But when Homer made his way to the congested corner of

Boylston Street and Memorial Drive, he found the walking almost as bad as the driving. Turning up Boylston in the direction of Harvard Square, he was immediately buffeted by a thick flood of pedestrians moving the other way. What was happening? Where were all these people going? They were like lemmings, pouring toward the river.

"Whoops! Oh, excuse me. Oh, Homer Kelly, isn't this awful?" Somebody else was trying to move in the direction of the square, struggling against the tide. It was Julia Chamberlain. "Oh, Lord, why didn't I go around by way of Dunster Street? I should have known better. Oh, excuse me, ma'am, I'm *terribly* sorry."

"Well, what the hell is it?" Homer had to roar because all the cars on the street were blowing their horns at once. "Where's everybody going?"

Julia Chamberlain looked at him and screeched, "I just can't believe it. What a nitwit you are, Homer Kelly. I told you on the

phone yesterday. It's the Harvard-Yale game. Look, here comes the band."

"Oh, *football*. Is that it." Homer couldn't make himself heard above the blare of the trumpets and sousaphones and the thump of the drums. A lot of people in crimson jackets were turning into Boylston Street from the square, while the traffic came to a full stop and the drivers all gave up and leaned out their car windows and the sky lavished sunshine on the dazzling sousaphones and flashing trombones and glittering flutes and glockenspiels. Homer's entire understanding of sporting life at Harvard was limited to a song by Tom Lehrer, "Fight Fiercely, Harvard! Demonstrate Your Prowess, Do!" He was about to quote this in Julia Chamberlain's ear, but then she stopped to buy a Harvard pennant and began waving it over her head, and he decided to forbear.

"You know, it's all I can do not to turn around and follow the band," shouted Julia. "The fever, it's really catching. But I'd never get into the stadium. You have to get your ticket way ahead. I gave mine to my nephew this morning."

"But why aren't you going? I should think a loyal member of the Harvard administration like you would be front and center on the fifty-yard line."

"Oh, I've got a meeting. One of those everlasting meetings. You know how it is."

"You mean somebody arranged a meeting for the same time as the Harvard-Yale game? What kind of a sour puckered-up heartless old creep would do a thing like that?"

"Well, Homer, dear, I'm afraid it was me, as a matter of fact."

"But what was so important that you had to call a meeting for a time like this?"

Homer's face was very close to Julia Chamberlain's. He had a tight grip around her waist as they rammed their way across Mass Av in a kind of flying wedge, and therefore he could clearly see that something was troubling her. She was incapable of lying, that was it. She was one of those staunch Yankees who would rather throw up their lunch than let a false word cross their lips. Homer knew the breed well. The Puritan Ethic and the stern New England conscience were the glue that held Julia Chamberlain together.

"Well, you know, Homer, you can't always talk about these things, what with one thing and another. Emergencies come up."

"Touchdown!" cried Homer, and he landed the two of them on the sidewalk in front of the entrance to the Yard. Then they had to force their way through the narrow gate, because a crush of football fans was squeezing through it in the other direction. The gate was a mean little entry, a gift to the school from the class of 1875. It was a clumsy piece of architectural braggadocio, all scrolls and pediments and little concrete pineapples, and the message it proclaimed on a marble tablet had irritated Homer in the days of his youth when he had directed traffic at the crossing:

OPEN YE THE GATES THAT THE RIGHTEOUS NATION
WHICH KEEPETH THE TRUTH MAY ENTER IN

The inscription still gave him a pain. He nudged Mrs. Chamberlain and pointed at it. "Arrogance," he said.

"Oh, I know. Isn't it disgusting. I mean, it's the whole trouble. Look at those alumni, will you? Don't some of the alumni look positively frightening? Sometimes it makes you wonder. It just makes you wonder if the whole thing is worthwhile after all."

At University Hall she said good-bye. "I'm going in here, Homer, dear. Thank you for running interference for me like that. I really appreciate it."

Homer asked a polite farewell question about the game. "Who do you think will win this afternoon?" he said, his mind already running through the list of references he wanted to lay his hands on in the library.

But to his surprise Julia Chamberlain grasped him by the coat collar and tapped him on the chest with the end of her pennant. "Yale," she said. "Fourteen to seven. You see, Homer, it's Goober. Oh, I know, we've got a terrific offense and a couple of really great fullbacks, Puffer and Halloran. But they've got Goober. Their defense is terrible, but with a forward pass like Goober's, there's absolutely no hope." Julia shook her head earnestly at Homer and started up the steps of University Hall.

The woman was as transparent as a pane of glass. Homer thought about it as he turned away. She should have been going to the game. She was dying to go to the game. Why had she called a meeting for the same time as the game?

Homer walked slowly up the gigantic staircase of Widener

Library, and puffed his way up another grandiose set of marble stairs, and gasped his way into the catalogue room and approached the call desk. But then he stopped short, turned around, ran headlong down the two great staircases and loped in the direction of University Hall. As he rounded the corner of the building he slowed down and craned his neck to see what he could see.

Yes, there was Julia, standing on the porch, talking to a couple of men who looked faintly familiar to Homer. They were Overseers. He had seen them before in the Faculty Room, along with President Cheever and Senior Vice President Sloan Tinker and the five Fellows. This must be another meeting of the Board. But this time Cheever and Tinker would not be there, because they were away in Chicago. Who was that? That old gentleman wasn't an Overseer. That was Shackleton Bowditch, the Senior Fellow. Were the Fellows and the Overseers meeting together again? Maybe the thing had become a habit. But surely you would think they could contain their enthusiasm for each other's company until after the Harvard-Yale game?

Something was up. Another huddle of Overseers was hurrying in the direction of University Hall. Some of them were carrying suitcases. They had come from far away. Homer suspected they had come in a hurry. He leaned his back against the monumental base of the statue of John Harvard and pretended to examine the roof of Massachusetts Hall, as the newcomers lugged their suitcases up the stairs. One of them was the girl who had looked so young among the gray-headed men and women sitting in all those tall uncomfortable chairs upstairs a few weeks ago. Why were they meeting so soon again? Weren't their regular meetings supposed to happen only every couple of months? "Emergencies come up," Mrs. Chamberlain had said. Well, what emergency was it this time?

"I dropped everything," said the girl who looked too young to be an Overseer, struggling with the heavy door. "I had to get a baby-sitter only six months older than Bobby. She's only about two feet tall, but she can twist Bobby around her little finger."

The Overseers disappeared inside. Another bunch of them came pouring up the stairs. Homer idled around the outside of the building for five more minutes, and then he couldn't stand it any more. He went inside and climbed the stairs to the second floor. The door to the Faculty Room was open. Homer didn't see any reason why he couldn't just saunter casually by the door as if he were on his way to somewhere else. Slowly he ambled past the door and glanced inside.

They were all there. The meeting had been called in a hurry, but the great square of stately chairs was packed. The President himself was missing, and so was Senior Vice President Sloan Tinker. But Julia Chamberlain was not alone at King Arthur's table. The Treasurer and all five Fellows sat on either side of her central chair.

Once again Homer stared inquisitively at the Harvard Corporation. It was a little band possessed of fabled power, he knew that, chosen from hand to hand, its members touching one another on the shoulder down through the generations, going back in time to the year 1650, when Harvard College had been little more than a scrap of ground with two or three drafty buildings and a handful of shivering students, back during the presidency of Dunster, who had been forced to resign because he was an Antipedobaptist. A pretty shocking thing to be. Everyone had been scandalized by a president who didn't believe in infant baptism. Homer suspected the Corporation had always been a conservative body. After all, they were Fellows for life, the five of them. They must grow old and crusty on the job. Surely they were a force for the status quo. No radicals or Antipedobaptists in that bunch.

Homer leaned against the wall, out of sight, and cocked his ears in the direction of the open door. The Overseers and Fellows were still shifting about in their chairs and exchanging the time of day. They were noisy, excited, positively effervescent. Something of an unusual nature must be in the wind. Could it be the stained glass in Memorial Hall? Mrs. Chamberlain had talked about the stained glass on the phone yesterday. But Homer couldn't believe she would have dragged all these people here to talk about the cost of the new stained glass.

Her strong voice was rising above the tumult, calling the meeting to order. Immediately the room quieted down.

"Well, now," said Julia comfortably, her voice level in the silence, "let's have the reports of the Visiting Committees."

It was a joke. It must be a joke. They were all laughing. Laughing and laughing. And it wasn't ordinary laughter. Homer leaned against the wall and shook his head in wonder. There was a slightly hysterical note in the laughter, something explosive. They were laughing with the kind of abandon that comes with the release of tension bottled up for a long time.

"We can't go on this way much longer," said Mrs. Chamberlain. "The time has come."

"Hear, hear. Right you are." There was a general murmur of approval and thumps on the table and shuffling of feet. Homer could imagine backbones bracing themselves staunchly against the rock-ribbed backs of chairs.

Someone else spoke up. "We've waited far too long already. We should have done it last year."

"That's right. You know, I just can't help but wonder"— Homer could picture Julia Chamberlain's strong honest face leaning forward over the table—"whether if we had had the courage of our convictions two years ago, if we Overseers had encouraged you people in the Corporation to do what had to be done, then this awful thing might never have happened. Ham might no longer have been a professor at Harvard University. He wouldn't have been in Memorial Hall at all. He might never have been blown up."

"Oh, Julia, don't torture yourself like that. The question is, what to do now?"

"Well, then, let me put the question to the lot of you in an informal way. Now, remember, nobody's committing himself or herself to anything. It's just a sense of the meeting. This is not a formal meeting. No minutes are being recorded. *The question*

146

is not what to do, but when and how. Is that right? Look at all those hands. Does anyone disagree? Now, don't be afraid to hold up your hand and speak your piece. How about it? What, nobody? Not a soul? You mean, we all agree? Well, I'll be a monkey's uncle."

There was another explosion of laughter. People were roaring, gasping for breath. They were slapping their knees. Someone started clapping. They were all clapping. Prolonged applause. General rapture.

Homer inched his back along the wall closer to the door. Mrs. Chamberlain was speaking again, but she had lowered her voice. She was talking quietly in the midst of an attentive silence. What was she saying? Something about Cheever?

Homer was as close to the door as it was possible to be without being seen, but now he craned his head so that his left ear was closer still, and shifted more of his weight onto his left foot. But then the polished floor undid him. His left foot slid out from under him and he fell down heavily on his left side, sprawling full length across the sill of the open door. "Oh, ouch," said Homer. He sat up, his face blazing. There were shocked exclamations and scraping back of chairs. The youngest Overseer jumped up and strode firmly across the floor to shut the door. Homer got to his feet and glanced guiltily at Julia Chamberlain, who was staring at him with her mouth open. He grinned at her with all his teeth, feeling like the world's fool. The door closed in his face.

Oh, well, hell. Homer looked at the door. Shamelessly he put his ear against it. But he could hear nothing more. The voices in the Faculty Room were a subdued murmur. Homer gave up. He rubbed his sore shoulder and went downstairs and out of doors, heading once again for the call desk in Widener, mulling over in his mind the fragments of the emergency meeting he had been privileged to overhear.

They had been going to fire Ham Dow. Two years ago they had been about to fire Ham Dow, only they had changed their minds, and then he had been killed. Why had they wanted to get rid of

Ham? Because he was a corrupting influence on the students, the way Cheever said? Had Cheever talked them into it?

But what difference did that make now? Ham was dead and gone. And what did the firing of Ham Dow have to do with President Cheever? Why had they been so eager to meet behind Cheever's back? Julia Chamberlain had been delighted to hear that Cheever and Tinker were going to be away. She had called the meeting at the last minute because they would be away. What were they discussing that was not suitable for Cheever's ears? *The question is not what to do, but when and how.* They had all agreed to that. Unanimously. Not a single dissenting vote. They had been eager to agree. They had been exhilarated, overjoyed.

Homer stopped with his foot on the bottom step of the tremendous staircase that led upward to the imperial colonnaded façade of Widener Library and looked back at the second-story windows of University Hall.

What if the question about which they had all been so happily unanimous was the decision to *fire* President James Cheever? Maybe he had offended them, like Dunster. Maybe in his general intransigence he was some kind of contemporary version of an Antipedobaptist. The enforced resignation of a Harvard president: that would be a crisis indeed! What a sacrifice of honor and esteem, for a president of Harvard to be canned!

The windows of the Faculty Room gave no sign of what was going on inside. Those tall round-headed windows had once shed the dim light of dawn on sleepy students attending compulsory chapel before breakfast, back in the beginning of time. Now they were transmitting the sunlight of a November afternoon on an emergency meeting of Overseers and Fellows, a meeting called hastily during one of the great sentimental events of the year, the Harvard-Yale game. The beautiful room had apparently always been a sacrificial chamber.

Chapter Twenty-eight

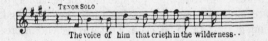

The voice of him that crieth in the wilderness··

Ham had worked out an order to his life, a sort of daily routine. Of course, it was impossible to know how long a day really was, to guess when one day ended and another began. But his waking and sleeping had taken on a pattern, and he had established a schedule for the waking hours that he now thought of as the daytime.

After all, there had been only two choices. Either he could curl up in a corner and die, or he could grasp at life by every handle he could find. Ham had simply decided that Vick would search him out sooner or later. In his mind he had settled the entire responsibility for his rescue on Vick Van Horn's young shoulders. Vick was the kind of person who wouldn't stop until she had accomplished her object, who threw herself into things with all the gristle in her body. He was putting his trust in those strong bones of hers, those long determined bones that were charged to the marrow with purpose. He would rather rely on Vick's thin fingers with their bitten fingernails to claw at the walls of his prison than depend on any number of jackhammers and power shovels to dig him out.

In the meantime there was his daily routine.

First: Hygiene. Ham had found a closet in the far corner of the room, and he had spent one entire waking day piling debris from the floor into it, picking up pieces of brick and handfuls of plaster dust, eventually getting down on all fours and sweeping the residue in the direction of the closet with his hands. Now he used the closet for a urinal.

Second: Breakfast. Cold water from the pipe. Ham had found a lump of concrete with a cavity in it, and he was using it as a catch basin under the pipe. Now he picked up the basin and tipped it carefully to his lips. Then he used the remainder to wash his face and hands, emptied the basin into the closet, and set it back under the pipe to fill again. That was the end of breakfast. Well, it didn't matter. He had long since stopped feeling hungry. His stomach often hurt him, gnawing and clenching on nothing, clapping its empty sides together, but he no longer thought about food. He was weak, he knew that, and each day was taking its toll. But he no longer felt the nausea and dizziness of those first waking hours underground. He had had a problem with his belt, because of the lack of food. He had been unable to make new holes as his body shrank, so for a while it had been a problem to keep his pants up. But now he was able to tie the ends of the belt in a sort of knot, bunching the folds of his trousers around his waist.

The next item on Ham's daily schedule had once been exercise, but it had occurred to him almost immediately that for the first time in his life the fat on his body was something to be hoarded. He must not waste it, burning it off with unnecessary movement. He would continue to keep his parts in working order, but there would be no more jogging in a circle in the middle of the floor.

Third: Music. Ham picked up his cello and his bow from the corner where he had leaned them carefully the day before. The cello was the remnant of a long piece of split wood, broken to the right size over his knee. The bow was a thick splinter about two feet long. Ham sat on a pile of bricks in the pitch dark, wedged the pointed end of his cello against another brick on the floor, grasped his bow and drew it across the cello, humming a strong A for the voice of the open string. Then he performed his usual warm-up exercises, his left hand racing down the neck of the cello, working its way through a hundred combinations of accidentals in brisk seesawing tiddle-diddles. Swiftly he ascended the scale of B-flat major, from first position to third to sixth, and then his hand rode up over the swelling curve of the body of the cello into thumb position. Humming in a higher and higher falsetto the notes that lay closer and closer to the bridge, Ham brought his fingers down *thucka-thucka-thuck.* Then he came rapidly down the scale again in double stops. It was a useful exercise of Popper's. Ham grinned in the dark, remembering how Vick had hated that one. "Oh, God," she had cried one day, shaking her fist at the ceiling. "I hope Popper fries in hell." But she had struggled through his exercises, she had whaled away at Feuillard's *Tägliche Übungen,* month in, month out. She had sunk her long healthy teeth in them like the bulldog she was, and wouldn't let go.

End of exercises. Now he had earned a little reward. Ham shifted his weight on his hard chair and lowered his head over his instrument. Then he began thumping the fingers of his left hand on the neck of his surrogate instrument in precise sixteenth notes, singing at the same time the pure patterns of the first of the Bach Suites for Unaccompanied Cello, slowing the tempo only for the rubato passages that brought the strict geometry of the music to nodes of wonder and power. He played as many of the Suites as he could remember.

Fourth: Lunch. Ham's mouth watered. He put his cello and bow away in the corner of the room and took the package of peanut brittle out of his pocket. He unwrapped what was left of it carefully and then, closing his eyes, he bit off a tiny corner. Then he sucked it for as long as there was anything left to suck, before he permitted himself to crush the salty nuts between his teeth.

Time for dessert. Ham knelt in the corner beside his concrete basin and took a drink. Then he picked up the brick that lay on the floor to begin the next task in his daily routine.

Fifth: Hit the pipe. Hit the pipe for two solid hours. (For what felt like two solid hours.) Every day Ham hit the pipe with the dots and dashes of the Morse Code SOS, in separate bursts of a hundred times. Between sessions he allowed himself daily excursions into his repertoire of rhythmical patterns, humming the tunes at the same time, or singing the words of all the songs he could remember. Right now he was running through the *Pilgrim Hymnal of the Congregational Conference of New Jersey.* A pious youth spent in a choir loft had imprinted it on Ham's mind, page by page. So far he had worked his way through all the hymns for the Beginning and Close of Worship, and for Morning and Evening, and now he had arrived at Advent—hymns for the Christmas season. Well, that was probably about the right time of year for the world outside (if there was still a world outside). Ham had tried to make a wild stab at figuring out how long he had been imprisoned in this small chamber in the dark. He had calculated so many days for this, and so many for that, and then he had divided by two, because his own days were shorter than twenty-four hours, he was sure of that. But his calculations still brought him all the way to the end of November, even into December. Six weeks. How much longer could he hold out? Well, he wouldn't think about it. Today was today. He would hit the pipe. Hit the pipe. Hit the pipe.

O Come, O come, Emmanuel, and ransom captive Israel,
That mourns in lonely exile here, until the Son of God appear.

bingbingbing BANGBANGBANG bingbingbing!
bingbingbing BANGBANGBANG bingbingbing!

Chapter Twenty-nine

Thou shalt break them, Thou shalt
break them with a rod___ of i-ron...

"Hello, is this Buildings and Grounds? Mr. Maderna? Hey, Maderna, this is Crawley. You know, Crawley at Memorial Hall?"

"Oh, yes, Mr. Crawley. Is everything all right over there now?"

"Oh, yeah, except there's this pipe. Keeps knocking."

"A knocking pipe? Is it one of those old radiators? Just where is the pipe located, Mr. Crawley?"

"Here in my office. Going half the time. You'd think it was a whole goddamn marching band. Bangs like crazy."

"You mean the radiator? Did you loosen the radiator valve?"

"Oh, sure, only I don't know if it's the radiator or not. Doesn't do no good, loosen no valve on no radiator. You just ought to hear it. Christ, it's driving me crazy."

"Well, it sounds like a simple matter. I'll send someone— Oh, just a minute, Mr. Crawley."

Mr. Crawley took the receiver away from his ear and looked at it. A high thin beep was coming over the line. It stopped, and there was silence. Then Mr. Maderna spoke up again, sounding agitated. "I'm sorry, Mr. Crawley, we've got an emergency situation in William James Hall. A pipe burst on the fifteenth floor,

153

flooding the entire building. I'll have to get back to you later on."

Mr. Crawley hung up the phone, then cocked his head, listening. There, now, wouldn't you know as soon as he hung up, the pipe would start up again? If only Buildings and Grounds could get a load of that.

bingbingbing BANGBANGBANG bingbingbing!
bingbingbing BANGBANGBANG bingbingbing!

Mr. Crawley picked up his hat and jammed it on his head and wandered out into the memorial transept, leaving the door of his office ajar. In Sanders Theatre a big class was going on. The rising tiers of seats were full of students. He crossed the hall and opened the door. Five hundred heads glanced up at him, then bent over notebooks again or looked back at the lecturer, who was reciting from Aeschylus, speaking for Orestes, who had come home to avenge his father's death.

> In there! Inside! Does anyone hear me knocking at
> the gate? I will try again. Is anyone at home?

Mr. Crawley sat down on the nearest empty bench, put his feet up on the back of the bench in front of him, tipped his hat forward over his face, and went to sleep.

In the memorial transept, a tall man with a bald head was pushing a broom slowly along the floor. When Mr. Crawley disappeared inside Sanders Theatre, the man picked up his broom, walked to the open door of the custodian's office, and went inside. Closing the door softly behind him, he let his eyes rove inquisitively over the walls and furniture. Then he pulled open the top drawer of the desk and glanced at its contents. A pipe in one corner of the room was making a tremendous noise, as if there were some kind of air lock in the radiator.

bingbingbing BANGBANGBANG bingbingbing!

went the pipe.

bingbingbing BANGBANGBANG bingbingbing!

The intruder in Mr. Crawley's office pushed the drawer shut and lifted his head. The pipe was shaking and shuddering with great crashing jolts of thunderous sound.

bingbingbing BANGBANGBANG bingbingbing!
bingbingbing BANGBANGBANG bingbingbing!

Slowly the man turned around and stared at the clattering pipe that rose from floor to ceiling in the corner of the room.

Chapter Thirty

By Ham's reckoning it was the middle of the night, but he woke up sharply and lifted his head from the floor. He had been awakened by a sound. Perhaps he had dreamt it. He had heard things before in his dreams. But this was a loud thump. An honest-to-God thump.

There! There it was again. And then there was a skreeking noise, like heavy nails screaming out of the pith of a wooden board in the teeth of a wrecking bar. And now there were more of those reverberating thumps, like blows of a sledge hammer.

Someone was coming. They had found him at last. Ham drew himself up on his knees, his head high, listening.

The shrieking and banging stopped. There was a pause, and then another kind of noise. Footsteps. Footsteps slowly descending a staircase. Ham struggled to his feet and stared in the direction of the door, his heart pounding. He ran his fingers through his hair and clawed with shaking hands at his beard. He must look like a wild man. He blinked, as something smote his eyes. There was a yellow line along the top of his door.

Ham swallowed and tried to speak up. "Hello," he said. "I'm here." His voice was hoarse and weak. "Vick, is that you?"

The footsteps stopped. In his eagerness Ham stumbled over the wooden beam that lay between him and the door, and he fell with his whole weight against the lower half of the door panel, but he hardly felt it. He leaned up against the door and hammered on it with trembling fists. "Here I am. Right here. Vick? Are you out there?"

There was no reply. Only a peculiar silence. No one shouted back at him with joyful recognition. No one thumped on the door in reassurance and glad discovery. The light flickered again at the top of the door and dimmed and disappeared.

"Hey, hey, I'm right here," cried Ham. "Open the door!"

But the steps had begun again on the stairs. Again he heard the light tread on one step after another. This time it was diminishing, going away.

And then the hammering began again. *Crash crash crash.* The vault was being sealed once again with heavy boards and long sharp nails. The coffin lid was again being fastened down. Ham could feel the blows of the hammer shivering into his own flesh.

The hammering stopped. The silence began again. This time it was unbearable. Ham began to sob. He reached his hand up toward the top of the door where he had seen a strip of light. His blood thundered in his head. He fainted, and slumped heavily to the floor.

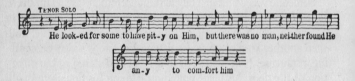

TENOR SOLO

He look-ed for some to have pit-y on Him, but there was no man, neither found He an-y to com-fort him

Chapter Thirty-one

Class was over, but it took Homer twenty minutes to work his way through the students crowding around him. He was starved, but then someone came running down the aisle with a plate of Mrs. Esterhazy's pastry, and pretty soon Homer was trying to talk and eat at the same time.

Today's lecture had been altogether too successful. It was the second half of his Abraham Lincoln chapter. Homer suspected he had made the mistake of telling one too many of Lincoln's funny stories. And perhaps there had also been just a drop too much of awe and affection, in spite of the trouble he had taken to crush any remaining illusions his students might have had about the great emancipator. The students were an unsentimental lot, on the whole, hard-boiled in the cleansing water of historical cynicism, wary with disbelief. But today they had lapped up Homer's lecture. It was the martyrdom that had finished them off. Like everybody else, they were suckers for a good martyrdom. Lincoln had been another martyred saint, like the dead Union soldiers whose praises lined the walls in the memorial transept upstairs. Abraham Lincoln should have had a tablet to himself in that wooden Valhalla. Only, of course, that would have been impossible, because the poor soul had never been to Harvard. (There was going to be another memorial. Homer had heard the rumor. The President of Harvard was going to dedicate a bronze tablet in the memorial corridor to the memory of Hamilton Dow. But then Ham had been a genuine alumnus of Harvard University, so that was all right.)

Homer accepted another piece of cake and looked around at his teeming classroom. Who were all these people? Some of them were members of Vick's choir, Homer was sure of that. He recognized Jennifer Sullivan and Tim Swegle and Mrs. Esterhazy and Betsy Pickett, and that old guy who was the bass soloist—what was his name? Mr. Proctor. Mr. Proctor came down the aisle and tapped Homer's chest and began talking about all the cities and towns in the country that had been named after Abraham Lincoln, especially Lincoln, Nebraska, which was Mr. Proctor's home town.

At last Homer was able to excuse himself. He walked out of the lecture hall and around the outside of the building and then in again by the south door to pay his daily respects to the great drafty vestibule, where he now felt so much at home. He never seemed to tire of wandering up and down the hall in the gloom, gazing up past the boarded windows at the wooden vaults rising dimly overhead. Today the memorial tablets on the walls invited reverie on the subject of martyred saints, and Homer remembered what Henry Thoreau had said about saints: that Christ was always crucified, and Copernicus and Luther forever excommunicated, human nature was so brutal and depraved.

Ham Dow was a case in point. Homer was beginning to get a sort of instinctive notion in his head, that the bombing in which Ham had lost his life had been a malicious intentional murder, rather than a random act of violence by a crowd of militant outsiders. The man had inspired too much affection for his own good. Homer looked up now at the golden shimmer of Latin words running around the high walls. They were noble sentiments, all of them. Everyone had believed in noble sentiments in those days. Nowadays if a noble sentiment stuck its head out of a foxhole, it was swiftly decapitated. That was what had happened to Ham. He had been a living, breathing noble sentiment, and maybe that was the whole trouble. He was another goddamned bleeding Messiah, cut down in the midst of his teaching.

And therefore the man from the FBI and the people at Alcohol, Tobacco and Firearms could waste all the time they wanted to, tracking down rumors about the Nepalese Freedom Movement. The Nepalese didn't have anything to do with it. Homer was more interested in someone whose initials were J.C., someone Ham had expected to meet right here on this spot at eleven-thirty on the morning of October sixteenth. Who was J.C.? If Ham's death had been accidental, if he had merely happened to be at the wrong place at the wrong time when some underground organization had exploded its Harvard bomb, what had happened to J.C.? Why had he not come forward? It looked to Homer as if someone had set the bomb to go off on Wednesday, October sixteenth, at eleven-thirty in the morning, right there in the middle of the high corridor running through the middle of Memorial Hall, and then had lured Ham to that place at that time under the pretext that J.C. would expect him there.

Query: How had the bomber known where in the basement to attach his explosive device? The basement was a rabbit warren, a complex labyrinth of little rooms and corridors. In order to determine what coincided with what, one would have to superimpose a plan of the first floor over a plan of the basement.

Who would have access to a set of plans? Where would the plans be?

Homer stood on the smooth cement that had been poured into the broken floor by Mr. Maderna's craftsmen, and listened to the bell in the tower chime a single stroke for one o'clock. Mr. Maderna would have a set of plans. Surely he would have plans for every building within his domain. Donald Maderna would know the place inside out, if anybody would.

Homer consulted his pocket map, and then he set out along Oxford Street in the direction of the Buildings and Grounds Department for the North Yard. The day was raw and cold, with a heavy mist lowering over the city of Cambridge. Halfway to his destination, Homer turned around and looked back at Memorial Hall. Shaggy clouds were dragging tattered shreds over the roof.

This time Homer saw the building as a pathetic enormous beast, some fabulous ill-assorted creature crouched warily on its haunches. Its long backbone was knobby with vertebrae. The iron finials along the ridge were like birds picking fleas from the back of a rhinoceros. It was a behemoth, a camelopard, a vast griffin of a building. The fog pressed down on the tower and the building weighed down on its foundations and the foundations crushed down into the earth so heavily that it was a wonder to Homer that the entire planet was not lurched into a lopsided orbit. Ponderous as it was, Memorial Hall seemed threatened. In his imagination Homer saw it rising gently in the air, burst asunder in some final tremendous disaster, some dreadful last day, its monstrous fragments flying skyward, then pelting down again to bury Vick and all her musicians and Handel's entire *Messiah* and all the rabble in the basement and Homer Feeble-minded Kelly in one colossal mountain of rubble. Maybe Freddy Fulsom was right. Maybe the Time was at Hand.

Homer turned around again and loped along Oxford Street. As he ran, he amused himself by imagining all the massive blocks of science buildings left and right exploding too, catapulting into the air in enormous chunks of brick and masonry. The study of science at Harvard would go boom, all these practical buildings for biology and geology and physics that had cropped up since the time of Louis Agassiz. Agassiz had collected specimens for his University Museum of Comparative Zoology with the help of people like Henry Thoreau. And Asa Gray had started the Herbarium. But of course, they weren't the first scientists at Harvard. The study of natural philosophy had been an accepted discipline for years before that. And chemistry. There had been chemists here forever too, like young Charley Flynn, the buccaneer. Charley Flynn would know how to blow up a building. *BOOM BOOM,* so much for Mallinckrodt! *KABOOM KABAM,* farewell to the Science Center! *KABOOMITY BIM BOM BAM,* good-bye to the University Museum with its glass flowers! Oh, no, not the glass flowers! Oh, no, not *tinklety-klinklety-smashity-*

crash! all those fragile botanical specimens of hand-blown glass, all blasted into a billion pieces by the mad bomber Charley Flynn! Hastily Homer glued all the billion pieces of the glass flowers together again in his mind and looked around for 42 Oxford Street.

The Buildings and Grounds Department for the North Yard was at the end of a side lane next to the Engineering Sciences Laboratory. Forty-two Oxford Street looked like a train going around the bend. It had once been a cyclotron, that was the reason. They had fired atomic particles around a curving track, splitting atoms into pieces, until the project ran out of federal money. So now the big magnets had moved out and Donald Maderna had moved in.

Maderna's phone was ringing when Homer walked into his office. He picked it up and waved Homer to a chair. "North Area Maintenance Office," he said. "Oh, yes, the clock. You mean the four clock faces on the tower of Memorial Hall. Yes, I know, we've had a number of complaints that the clock is now too fast. I've sent somebody over there to shut it off. We thought we had it fixed the first time. We must have had a hundred calls the first day. Everybody was ten minutes late to class. We had to get this expert back again, the specialist who got the thing running in the first place. He travels all over the country, you see, adjusting big public clocks. Only he got the thing going a little fast this time, so now we've got to get hold of him again to slow it down. Don't worry. We'll attend to it." Donald Maderna put the phone down and turned to Homer.

"The clocks aren't running right?" said Homer. "The clocks on the tower of Memorial Hall?"

"Oh, it's just a matter of getting the fine tuning straightened out, so to speak. A big clock like that, if the compensation is off a little bit, the whole city of Cambridge is five minutes early or late. Oh, I'm sorry." His phone was ringing again.

Homer got up and crossed the room to look at the charts on the wall, while Mr. Maderna talked to a representative of the

Cambridge Exterminating Company. "It's cockroaches this time. Cockroaches in Richards Hall."

Mr. Maderna's charts were fascinating. The names of the seventy-five buildings in his domain ran up and down the left side of the chart and the fifty-two weeks of the year ran from left to right across the top. Mystic symbols were written in the squares of the chart to show what needed to be done to each of the buildings and on what particular date. Another wall was covered with a job order board. There were rows and rows of wooden pegs hung with green slips of paper under the headings PLUMBER REFRIG STEAM ELECT LIGHT GLASS MASON KEY CARP ROOF MILL.

"My God, Donald," said Homer, when Maderna at last put down the phone, "this is a big operation you run here. I mean, you're a sort of four-star general with armies of colonels and captains and privates defending the health and physical well-being of Harvard University, keeping the whole place running smoothly, right? How many people are there in Buildings and Grounds, all told?"

"You mean altogether? The whole university? Oh, there must be, oh, maybe as many as fifteen hundred people, if you include the Business School and the Med School. Now, what can I do for you, Homer?"

"Well, I just wondered if you've got some plans and layouts of Memorial Hall here that I could see. And I'd like to know if anybody has been using them lately."

"Why, certainly. I've got them right here." Donald Maderna rose from his chair and pulled open a file drawer in a cabinet beside his desk. It was a wide cabinet with shallow drawers. "This drawer is all Memorial Hall. Nobody's been looking at them, not so far as I know. Here, we can spread them out on the table. Which plans are you most interested in?"

Homer lifted the corners of the big sheets. He didn't know what he needed. He was greedy and wanted to see them all. The topmost plans showed elevations of the new tower roof by the firm of Bastille and Neiley, with diagrams of the four clock faces and the clock works and circuit diagrams of the wiring and a cross section showing the system of fire protection in the tower. Below the plans for the tower roof the big sheets of paper went back in time, growing older as Homer groped lower and lower down. *Putnam and Griswold, alterations to the basement of Memorial Hall, 1946.* That was for the Psychology Department. Professor Skinner had put his pigeons in Skinner Boxes in the basement of Memorial Hall. *Densmore and LeClear, proposed addition for serving room and kitchen, 1905-6. Van Brunt and Ware, plans and elevations for Alumni Hall, Harvard University, 1871-8.* That was the beginning. Van Brunt and Ware had designed the original building. He had come to the bottom of the pile.

Homer pulled a chair up to the cabinet and pored over the thick sheaf of plans, riffling through them from bottom to top, and top to bottom, while Donald Maderna answered his telephone and responded to the beeper attached to his belt, keeping his finger on the pulse of life in the North Yard, making sure that keys turned smoothly in the locks of doors, that elevators ran up and down in perfect safety, and that all the physics and chemistry and biology laboratories and experimental research projects scattered by the acre across the length and breadth of his territory were supplied with their multiplicity of individual needs, the proper flow of gas and water and air both hot and cold, and electromagnetic waves traveling along wires and cables at something like the speed of light.

Densmore and LeClear, 1905–6. Homer pulled out the big plan of proposed additions to the serving room and kitchen of Memorial Hall and laid it on the table. The addition had been built on the north side of the building in 1906 to make the task of preparing and serving thousands of pounds of food to the students in the great hall a little easier, in the days when that enormous room had been a student commons. Homer stood over the table and spread his hands on the plan. There had been a meat room down there in those days, and an apple room, a milk room, a bakery with huge walk-in ovens, a laundry and a vegetable cold room. And a room full of tables: *White help dining room.* White help? Homer was stunned. He looked further. Sure enough, there was the *Colored help dining room,* and here were the separate locker and toilet rooms for white and colored help. Of course. Good lord.

"What's so funny?" said Donald Maderna, looking up from his desk.

"Oh, it's not funny. That was what you call an ironical sort of laugh. More like a snort. I'm appalled, that's all. Here you've got a building, a giant building, a huge colossal pile of brick erected in memory of the gallant graduates of Harvard who died in the Union cause in the Civil War. And what did they fight the Civil War for? To free the slaves, wasn't it? Well, at least it was partly to free the slaves. And look at that, will you? They've got the colored help segregated from the white help in the basement.

And the white help was probably mostly all Irish, I'll bet. I'll bet my own great-grandparents were down there with the rest of them, stirring the pots and passing the plates, while upstairs in the dining hall the students were all white Anglo-Saxon Protestants. Well, nowadays the students are pretty well mixed up, but otherwise it's just the same as modern Boston. Oh, the human race. Oh, alas, for humankind. Oh, Donald, how one despairs. All that blood, all the names on those gallant marble tablets. And to think, Donald, just to think of Henry James standing in front of those memorial tablets with his hand on his heart, rejoicing that the place was erected to duty and honor, that it spoke of sacrifice and example, that it was a kind of temple to youth, manhood, and generosity. Generosity! and right there under his feet were the toilets of the colored help. Oh, it makes you think, doesn't it, Donald, of the fall of man, of the lost last hope of— What's it mean, here, *Fan Room*, next to the toilets? What was the fan room?"

"Well, I suppose it was part of the ventilating system. I guess it collected all the smoke and steam from the kitchen and blew it up through the big ventilating shafts in the tower, and then pulled the fresh air down. It was a big interconnected system of pipes running around into all those little spaces down there. The spaces are rearranged now, ever since 1946, when they did the basement over. But we've still got those ventilating shafts. It's just more of the same thing. Of course, part of those shafts in the tower now are for the air-conditioning system in Sanders Theatre."

Homer pulled more plans out of the drawer. "Here, Donald, this is the way it looks now, right? All these little rooms? Look, this whole plan is just plumbing. And this one is wiring. My God, what a complicated mess. What's this thing here at the west end? It looks as if a piece of the basement goes right off the map."

"Oh, that's the tunnel. The service tunnel. For the utilities. It goes all the way to the Cambridge Electric Company down by the river."

"A utility tunnel? But it's so big."

"Oh, sure. You could drive a small car through most of it. Except where it crosses the Charles by way of the Weeks Bridge to the Business School. And under Mass Av."

"It goes all over the place? Right under Mass Av?"

"Sure. Right there behind Widener. It's only about four feet high under Mass Av because of the subway under the street. They've got this little cart there. You lie down in the cart and pull yourself across with a rope."

"Is that a fact?" Homer was dumfounded. "Well, how do you get into the tunnel in the first place?"

"Oh, there are entrances from all the buildings along the way. They're kept locked, of course. We don't want the students to have access to the tunnel. I mean, when you think of the mischief they'd think up to do." And then Maderna told Homer a story about the time all the inhabitants of Lowell House had flushed the toilets at the same time and flooded the sewage system. "Of course, we have to use the tunnel for visiting dignitaries and important speakers sometimes. So they can get in and out of buildings without going through crowds of students. Like when Henry Kissinger was here, during the war in Vietnam. He was supposed to give a talk in Langdell Hall. There were a lot of hostile students collected outside the building, but Sloan Tinker brought him in through the tunnel."

"Well, I'm flabbergasted." Then Homer began trailing his finger over the plan of the basement, searching for the row of little rooms that ran from north to south below the memorial corridor. Here they were. There was a separate little hallway under the corridor. It must drop down to a lower level than the rest of the basement rooms, because it had its own pair of staircases at either end. The bundle of dynamite must have been fastened to the ceiling of one of those little rooms along that hall, room 197 or 198. That part of the basement was boarded up now, but he had actually looked down into those rooms from above on the day of the bombing. He had seen them shattered and demolished, with

168

the marble tiles from the floor above collapsed all over their fallen walls (along with splattered fragments of the great kindly mind of Hamilton Dow). Glumly Homer stared at the huge sheet of paper on the table. "Has anybody else taken a look at these plans, Donald? I mean, lately? Anytime in the last year?"

"No, I don't think so. Of course, we don't have the only set of plans. The Harvard Planning Office has some. And I suppose they've got the originals in the archives in the Pusey Library. Say, that reminds me, Homer. I meant to call Crawley. He was having a lot of trouble with a knocking radiator. Or a pipe. Something was making an awful racket over there in his office. Only we couldn't get anybody over there because of the emergency we had in William James Hall. All our plumbers were tied up for a week, and a lot of other people too. All fifteen floors flooded, because the solder gave way at one of the elbows on the fifteenth floor. But if Crawley's got a knocking pipe, it might be water in the steam line. It could be dangerous." Mr. Maderna picked up his phone again and dialed a number. "Hello, there, Mr. Crawley? I just wanted to tell you we're free to come over now, if that radiator of yours is still knocking. I mean, I've got a couple of men I could send over there right now. No? Not since last week? Hasn't been giving you any trouble for five or six days? Well, fine. I'm glad to hear it. I won't send anybody over, then. Let me know if anything else gives you trouble."

At the other end of the line, Mr. Crawley hung up the phone, leaned away from his desk, and stretched out in his chair. The chair at Mr. Crawley's desk was one of those office armchairs that tip comfortably backward. He tipped it back as far as it would go and lifted his feet up on his desk.

It was a good thing that damn pipe had stopped knocking. He wouldn't have to be bothered with no plumber. They'd probably want to go downcellar and poke around and find out where the pipe came from and want somebody to hold their goddamn tools and help them pry up the goddamn floor or do some other goddamn thing. It was bad enough when the police and the FBI were running around all over the place, asking him questions, making him run errands all over the place during his lunch hour. And what for? There wasn't going to be no more bombs. They were probably bombing Paris, France, by now, for Christ's sake.

Homer was through with the plans in Donald Maderna's file. He rearranged them in the drawer and patted them neatly into place and shut the drawer and then explained to Donald Maderna his new understanding of the entire physical and metaphysical nature of the university, because he now perceived the truth, that the whole whimsical intellectual superstructure of professors and students and scholarship and learning and all the libraries chock-full of books, all that tonnage of verbiage weighing down a thousand miles of bookshelves—he was now aware for the first time that it was all only the flimsiest, most ethereal gauzy bit of thistle-down floating on the great undergirding bedrock of the Buildings and Grounds Department, that firm foundation supporting the airy universe above, that vast intricate interconnecting sub-cosmos of cables and pipes and wires and ducts tunneling through dark corridors underground, in the perpetual care of a stalwart army of craftsmen, wise in the lore of a thousand arcane professions and secret skills. And Mr. Maderna said, well, yes, he supposed you could look at it that way if you wanted to, and Homer beamed at him and said good-bye and went away. And then the telephone in Donald Maderna's office rang again.

"Mr. Maderna? This is Sloan Tinker. I wonder if you could help me out. I've just learned that the Harvard Planning Office hasn't reopened yet after the Thanksgiving break. I understand that you have on file a duplicate set of plans and elevations of some of the buildings in the North Yard. By any chance do you have a set of plans for Memorial Hall?"

"Why, yes, Mr. Tinker, we do. As a matter of fact—"

"Well, good. I'm meeting with the Vice President for Alumni Affairs. We'd like to look over the plan of the basement to see how extensive an office could be set up down there on the site of that explosion when work on reconstruction resumes in the spring. We're looking for more floor space for alumni affairs, and we just wondered if the space in Memorial Hall would be adequate."

"Well, yes, of course, Mr. Tinker. You're welcome to anything you want."

"Very good, Mr. Maderna. I'll come over to examine them later this afternoon."

"You know, it's funny, Mr. Tinker. You're the second person today to want to look at those very same plans. Professor Kelly was in here just now, looking at them too. It never rains but it pours."

"Mmmm, is that so? Oh, Mr. Maderna, it occurs to me that I may be tied up a little later this afternoon. What if I came over to look at them now?"

"Well, certainly, Mr. Tinker. Come on over. I'll be right here."

Chapter Thirty-two

He trusted in God that he would deliver him; let him deliver him, if he delight in him···

He carried his broom down the steps of the basement entry beside the south door and pushed it along the corridor, staring upward at the ceiling. According to the plans in Maderna's office, the pipe in Crawley's room had once been part of the ventilating system for the old kitchen, back in the days when the basement under the great hall had housed a whole underground population of kitchen staff. The ducts to the fan room had come from every direction. The one from the small dining room off the great hall, the room that was now Crawley's office, should have run along a line right about here. But if the duct still existed up there over his head, it was now hidden by the low ceiling. Well, then, where would it change direction? Somewhere it would make a ninety-degree turn into the room upstairs.

The ticket office. He turned around and looked at the window of the office belonging to the Harvard-Radcliffe Orchestra. Then he leaned his broom against the wall and peered into the window, holding his hands beside his face to diminish the reflection from the surface of the glass. The room looked abandoned. Good. The orchestra must have moved its headquarters somewhere else.

Then he smiled in triumph. There was the pipe, as big as life. A fat round pipe emerged from the northwest corner of the room and turned upward, disappearing in the ceiling. That was it. Upstairs it would reappear in the corner of Crawley's office.

So it was just a matter of disconnecting that elbow joint. Then, if there was any more banging on Dow's end of the pipe, the sound would be cut off right here. That is, if the fellow was still alive enough to hit the pipe at all. Chances were, he was gone by now. The knocking had apparently stopped. Maderna had told him, in response to the discreetest of inquiries, that there was no problem with Mr. Crawley's pipes any more. Dow's strength had been phenomenal, but after all, the interval had been so long— what, six weeks? Longer than six weeks. He couldn't have held out much longer. By now he was probably . . . So this maneuver was just for the sake of a little insurance. And then later on one would come back again and provide still another little increment of safety, that extra little push of effort that a good job required. It was only a matter of taking the trouble to be thoroughgoing. After all, that was what had got him where he was today. He wasn't a genius, he knew that. He didn't even have a long string of degrees after his name. It was just thoroughness, that was it. Doing a job well, no matter how big or small it might be. That, and a commonsense understanding of how to choose the simplest means to an end, whether the task at hand was the selection of a president of Harvard or the repair of a blown-out fuse. *Economy of means for maximum effect.* The only question remaining was what means to apply in this particular case. Something odorless, of course—that was beyond question. Odorless, but highly effective. Carbon monoxide would do the trick. It was so simple, after all, so perfectly simple. People committed suicide with it every day in the week by merely shutting the garage door and starting the engine of the family car. As soon as he could lay his hands on a small pressurized tank of carbon monoxide he would come back, reconnect the pipe in the ticket office, and let himself into the room upstairs during Crawley's lunch hour so that he could work unobserved. The broad pane of glass in the ticket window of this basement room was too thin and transparent a barrier. Two doors protected Crawley's room from observation, and the windowless outer door could be locked. Then it would simply be a matter of tapping the pipe in Crawley's office and inserting the nozzle of the tank into the hole.

He unlocked the door of the ticket office, stood on a chair, jerked the elbow of the pipe free at both ends, and stuffed the open ends of the pipe with wadded sheets from a newspaper that was lying on the counter.

Now let Dow hit the pipe with all his might and main. Nobody would ever hear him again. The pipe went nowhere at all. It was connected to nothing.

Chapter Thirty-three

BASS SOLO

...the peo - ple that walk - ed, that walk - ed in darkness have seen a great light...

It was Miss Plankton's last lesson before the concert. Miss Plankton sat in the middle of the stage on one of the old Sanders chairs and struggled through the most disastrous of the rapid passages for the second violins.

"No, Miss Plankton," said Vick, "you start upbow here, you see. Look, I've got an idea. Why don't you just leave out this prestissimo part altogether? I'll put a parenthesis around it, and you just stop playing when you come to the parenthesis, okay? Then you can come in strong on the quarter notes at measure 77."

Jane Plankton's cheeks were pink with disappointment. "Oh, too bad. Oh, don't you think if I were to practice harder? That part, it's so thrilling! I mean, where he's singing about the refiner's fire and the violins are like little flames! Oh, I do love that part! I feel so sure I could do it with just a teeny bit more practice!"

"Well, all right, then. Let's just take it again. Slowly. *TEEdeedeedee deedeedeedee, TEEdeedeedee deedeedeedee . . .*"

SQUEEscrawscrawscraw scrawscrawscrawscraw, SQUEE-scrawscrawscraw scrawscrawscrawscraw. Vick leaned back and watched Miss Plankton's bow flop across the string. Miss Plankton was pretty bad, but it was the altos who really worried Vick. She felt her fingers stiffen with worry as she thought about the

175

altos. There were places where they brayed like donkeys. And they just couldn't seem to manage those long passages of sixteenth notes in *He shall purify* and *Unto us a child is born*. The sopranos were just great. They could lilt out those sixteenth notes like little pieces of icicles. But the altos were sloppy and heavy. They blurred the sharp edges and messed the whole thing up.

There was only the one rehearsal left, that was the trouble. She should have had plenty of time to prepare the Christmas concert, they had begun working on *Messiah* so early in the fall. But the Collegium had been invited to join the Glee Club in the football concert with Princeton, and then she had been so worried about the performance with the Boston Ballet that she had set aside a lot of rehearsal time for that—too much, because the *Carmina Burana* had turned out to be child's play. Well, she had planned the entire schedule badly. The last rehearsal would be the first one with orchestra and chorus together. There simply wouldn't be time to go over those sloppy melismas again. She would just have to hope the altos would somehow turn over a new leaf.

Miss Plankton's lesson was over. She jumped up, loosened her bow, popped bow and fiddle into her violin case, and began pulling layers of sweaters and jackets over her moth-eaten tweed suit. Then she pulled on her brown rabbit-fur hat, and her small face peeked out beneath it like that of some clever little forest animal.

"Oh, Miss Plankton," said Vick, "wherever did you get that wonderful hat?"

"It is wonderful, isn't it?" said Miss Plankton. "It's Brother Wayland's. He shot the rabbit himself, as a boy. When Cambridge was all woods and fields out where all those traffic circles are. And Brother Evvie caught fish in Fresh Pond. Isn't that remarkable? So different now! Thank you so much for the lesson, dear Victoria. Oh, how I shall practice!"

Vick followed her to the door. "Where do you live now, Miss Plankton?" she said. "In the same house? Do you live in the same one you grew up in?"

"Why, yes, of course." Miss Plankton swept her violin case in a generally westerly direction. "It's over there a ways."

"You know, if you wanted to, you could live here." Vick spoke cautiously, looking over Miss Plankton's head at the pointed arch above the north door. "There are all these rooms downstairs, and I think I could probably fit you into one. It's rent-free, you know. It's just a matter of—"

"Oh, goodness me, my dear, thank you. But I have a *perfectly* good home of my own."

I'll just bet you do, thought Vick. A cold-water flat somewhere. Some bare little walk-up. Miss Plankton was probably living on next to nothing. Too proud to admit she needed help. In the great gray rectangle of the open door she was a queer silhouette, all angles and knobs beneath her furry hat. "Oh, doesn't it look like snow?" gushed Miss Plankton. "Oh, I do hope it will snow! Oh, doesn't it feel like Christmas?"

The dear old soul. How brave she was. What a hard life it must always have been for her. Even in the old days. The family must have kept themselves alive by hunting and fishing. They must have lived like pioneers in the old days in Cambridge. Oh, if only the old dear could stay on pitch. If only she wouldn't try to play the tricky parts. If only the altos would shape up . . .

Vick pulled the string of her key out of the neck of her blouse and ran the whole length of the corridor. She turned the key in the lock of the instrument storage closet and took out her cello. She would practice for a while to fill up time. She had to do something to keep her mind off the concert until three o'clock, when Rosie Bell and Mr. Proctor were coming to work on Mr. Proctor's aria. Rosie was perfect on the trumpet part, of course, positively dazzling, but Mr. Proctor went all haywire there at the end, so Rosie had volunteered to help him out.

Vick carried her cello back to the stage, jerked it out of its case, set up her music, tightened her bow, tuned her strings, flipped the pages of her music, and began practicing the most fiendish of the Popper exercises Ham had assigned at his last lesson. Popper would take her mind off the concert. Oh, those God-awful double stops in thumb position. Vick jammed the side of her thumb down hard across the A and D strings, working her way up the scale of D flat in thirds, diminishing the interval a fraction of an inch as the scale rose higher and higher. Oh, look out, that G flat was sharp. Watch out. Try again. *Thuck, thuck, thuck, thuck, thuck, thuck, thuck, thuck.*

"You know, I just don't see how you do that."

Vick jumped, and screamed a small scream.

"Oh, sorry," said Homer Kelly. He came around her chair and stood in front of her. "My God, it looks difficult. I should think those strings would cut right through your little pinkies."

Vick laughed and held up her left hand. "Oh, no, not any more. See there? Look at the calluses. Along the side of my thumb. And all across the tips of the other fingers. You get really hard calluses after a while."

"Oh, is that it." Homer took Vick's hand and felt it. "I see what you mean. That's not exactly the soft sexy flesh one expects in a female. That's a mean leathery little paw. No offense."

"Well, if you think my hands are hard, you should have felt Ham's. He put all the power of his big strong left arm behind those fingers of his, so they had real knots on the ends."

Homer looked at her. "Ham played the cello. That's right. I guess I knew that. He played the cello too."

"Yes, of course he played the cello. He was my teacher."

"Ham played the cello. So he had calluses on his fingers."

"Well, of course he did. That's what I said. On his left hand anyway. You don't get much of anything on your right, where you hold the bow."

"But the man at the funeral parlor said—" Homer picked up Vick's hand again and looked at it. "That certainly is a hard, hard hand."

"The man at the funeral parlor said what?"

"Oh, nothing." Homer dropped Vick's hand. "He said Ham's hands were flabby."

"Flabby?"

"Mr. Ratchit, the funeral director. He showed me his own hands, all tough and callused from hard work, he said. He said the body had white puffy hands. Flabby, he said."

Vick looked at Homer. She stood up and set her cello down on the floor on its side. She put the bow on the chair. "Ham didn't have flabby hands."

"Well, I suppose he had fat pudgy hands, only the funeral guy didn't notice they had calluses on the ends."

"And on the side of the thumb. Here. See, right here."

"I'll call him and ask him again. It's too bad they didn't take fingerprints. Maybe they did. I'll find out." Homer turned and started down the stairs.

"Homer, let me talk to him. I just want to ask him—" Vick tripped over her cello. She left it lying flat on its face. She ran after Homer. "Ham didn't have flabby hands, Homer. He didn't."

Homer called Mr. Ratchit from the pay phone at the north end of the transept. He looked up at the shadowy wooden vault high overhead and asked Mr. Ratchit about calluses.

"Calluses?" said Mr. Ratchit. "Who do you mean? Oh, the guy at Harvard, the bombing victim, the guy without any head? Oh, right. Right you are. Now, what was that about calluses?"

"On his hands. I said, do you remember whether or not he had calluses on his left hand?"

"Oh, no. I remember him well. He was a big corpulent guy, right? He had these real white fat soft hands."

"But, Mr. Ratchit, the point is, he might have had white fat hands, only he played the cello, so his left hand would have had hard calluses on the ends of his fingers, where they come down on the strings, you see, when you play. Maybe you were just looking at the fingers of his right hand?"

"Oh, no. There weren't any calluses on that corpse. Not anywhere on his entire physique. Except corns. He had these big corns on his feet. But nothing else. You could tell he didn't get any kind of exercise. I looked him over good. Because of my hobby, see, being physical fitness. I mean, I'm in a state of perfect physical fitness myself. But you take a person like that, never takes any exercise. He's bound to get flabby all over. His hands were just soft like spaghetti. You know what I mean. Big flabby pieces of cooked macaroni."

"Both hands, Mr. Ratchit?"

"Well, sure, both hands."

"I don't suppose they took any fingerprints, Mr. Ratchit? I mean, because it never occurred to anybody that there was any doubt about the identity of the body."

"Fingerprints? No, nobody took any fingerprints."

"Here, just a minute. I'm going to put Miss Van Horn on the phone. She's a cellist. She knows what the calluses should be like. Here, Vick, it's your turn."

"Mr. Ratchit? I just want to be sure. Do you remember whether or not it was the fingers of both hands that were soft and flabby, or maybe you just noticed one hand, because, you see, the right hand might not have had calluses, because you just hold the bow with the right hand, do you see?"

"No, no, there weren't any calluses. Like I said to Mr. Kelly, I told him, both hands. They were like marshmallows all over. Both hands."

"Well, then, it couldn't have been Ham Dow! Homer, it wasn't Ham! His hands weren't like marshmallows! Nobody could say that about Ham's hands. Never! Oh, Homer!"

"Hey, there," said Mr. Ratchit, "are you still there?"

"Mr. Ratchit? This is Kelly again. Look, I think this is probably a difference in language more than anything else. Just a semantic confusion. But just out of curiosity, tell me, if we went to all the bureaucratic trouble of getting an exhumation order, would they still be able to take fingerprints? And do you think a doctor would still be able to tell whether or not a person had calluses on his hands after this amount of time has gone by? It's been six and a half weeks."

180

"Well, I don't know. It was you people who didn't want him embalmed. I mean, I told you he should of been embalmed. So I don't know how fast he might have decomposed. I mean, he was beginning to sort of deliquesce already. Fall apart into, like, a jelly. But anyway, I'm telling you. I told you before. There were no calluses on that corpse. He was a big flabby slob of a swollen piece of bloated disgusting—"

"Right. I get the picture."

"Whereas, if he'd only gotten some exercise. Just a few minutes of the day. In the privacy of your own home. Or you climb the stairs instead of take the elevator. Now, you take me, for instance . . ."

Vick clutched Homer's arm when he hung up the phone at last. Her eyes were blazing. Her skinny body shook. "It wasn't Ham! Homer, it wasn't Ham!" She pounded his chest with both fists. "I told you that shoe didn't belong to Ham Dow. Remember that shoe? I told you!"

"Now look here, Vick. Don't get excited about it. It's a small thing. A very small thing. I don't have any way of knowing how reliable an observer that Ratchit guy is. He's a crank. A faddist. He may have taken one look at the body and just decided it was too fat and flabby to be anything but a horrible example to the world, and he's making the most of it. And besides, you're forgetting the most important thing. If the body isn't Ham, then who was it? Has anybody else turned up missing? Not a soul. And then too, if it wasn't Ham, where *is* he? Where the hell is he? Before the explosion he was alive and well and present among us. After the explosion he was gone."

Then Homer had an unhappy thought. Maybe there had been two people killed in the explosion instead of one, but the second one had been blown into pieces so small they had been sprayed all over the walls and floor and the high wooden vault of the building in tiny invisible irrecoverable fragments. He opened his mouth to say this, and then thought better of it. "So tell me, what could have become of him? We know he wasn't buried in the debris, because they went all through the rubble with a fine-tooth comb."

"Maybe he ran away." Vick flung out her arms to show the wide world Ham had run away to. "They were after him. He knew they were after him. He's somewhere in hiding." She looked up as the north door burst open and a flurry of snow blew into the dark corridor, followed by a cluster of people streaming in the door, laughing with the excitement of the first snowfall, their breath steaming in front of them. Vick pointed past them at the open door. "He's out there somewhere. He's not dead. The dead man wasn't Ham. He's still alive, I tell you, Homer. He's still alive somewhere, somehow. I don't know where, but somewhere."

A snowball flew the length of the long hall. It smacked against the pale patch of new cement in the middle of the floor and disintegrated.

Homer put his hand to his brow. "Well, oh, God, all right. I'll see. I'll look into it. I'll try to get an exhumation order. I'll probably fail. But I'll try."

Chapter Thirty-four

Homer and Mary Kelly were still in bed when the phone rang on the morning of December second. "Mr. Kelly? This is Oliphant at Cambridge Police. I just thought you might be interested in something that's turned up at the Harvard Motor House on Mount Auburn Street. Somebody who was there overnight back in October went out in the morning after paying his bill and left his attaché case behind. Then he never came back for it. So they kept it for a while the way they always do, but then when nobody called for it, and he never answered their letter, they opened up this attaché case, and when they saw what was in it they called us. Dynamite sticks and coils of wire and God knows what all. Wait a minute, I've got a list here. Wire, heavy-gauge. Electrician's tape. Miscellaneous clock parts. Staple gun. Sweater. Wrist watch."

"A sweater? How big was the sweater?"

"Oh, really big. You know. Huge. Couple of petrified bananas. Bag of candy. Toolbox. Tools. Couple of keys. Map of Harvard. Piece of paper with a number on it—198."

"That could be the room number in the basement of Memorial Hall where the bomb went off."

"That's what we thought. And there was a Philadelphia newspaper, dated—listen to this—October fifteenth."

"October fifteenth! The day before! From Philadelphia?"

"Right. We're getting in touch with the department down there. He was registered as—you won't believe this—John Smith of New York City. Funny thing, Mr. Kelly, the wrist watch was still going."

"Still going? After six weeks?"

"It was one of those really expensive electronic watches. You know. You set it by the stars once a year or something. Really accurate to the second."

"Was it still keeping good time?"

"Right on the button."

"Well, thank you very much, Mr. Oliphant. Did you tell Peter Marley over at Harvard Police?"

"Oh, sure. He's the one said to call you. Thought you might be interested."

"Oh, I am. I certainly am. I'm very much interested indeed."

Homer put the phone down. Then he put his legs over the side of the bed and picked up the receiver again. He stared out the window for a minute. It was snowing again. It was going to be an early winter. He reached for the phone book, but then he remembered the number by himself—1111—because it looked like a row of tombstones.

"Oh, Mr. Ratchit, I'm sorry to bother you again so early in the morning. It's me again, Homer Kelly. Did I wake you up? I did? Oh, I'm terribly sorry. There's just one more thing. Did that guy who got blown up in Memorial Hall have a watch on his wrist?"

Mr. Ratchit was peevish. "A watch? No, he didn't have a watch. Did he have a pink ribbon in his hair? No, he didn't have a pink ribbon in his hair. Did he have a tattoo on his chest? No, he—"

"You're sure? You're absolutely positive he didn't have a wrist watch?"

"Listen, mister, are you accusing me of stealing a wrist watch from the dead? Because if you are, you can just—"

"Oh, no, no, no, oh, certainly not, Mr. Ratchit. I know you're the soul of integrity. Old family firm. Totally reputable establishment. There was no wrist watch, then. That's all I wanted to know. Thank you again, Mr. Ratchit. I'm really deeply grateful."

Mary was sitting up in bed, hugging her knees. "What was that all about?"

Homer looked at her. "You know what I think? I think he blew himself up."

"Who blew himself up? Not Ham Dow?"

"No. The man from Philadelphia. Somebody came up from Philadelphia the day before, a hired killer, I think, and he got the thing all set up. He stapled his dynamite sticks up on the ceiling of Room 198, with the timing device set to go off the next day at eleven-thirty. And then the next day he went back to Memorial Hall for some reason, only he forgot his watch, so he made the mistake of getting too close at the wrong moment, and he got himself blown up for his pains. He was a big fat guy like Ham, so when his head was blown off, everybody assumed this giant dead body was Hamilton Dow."

"But it wasn't?" Mary jumped out of bed and threw her arms around Homer. "Oh, Homer, then Ham Dow is still alive. Vick's right. He's not dead after all."

"Well, if he's not dead, where is he?" Homer rubbed his face in his wife's thick hair. "You know, I feel nothing but foreboding about that. I'm afraid nothing good can have happened to the man. He wasn't the kind of guy to just up and disappear. I must say, I'm not really very hopeful."

Mary picked up her bathrobe and stuck one arm in a sleeve. "Homer, I don't see why he came back to Memorial Hall at all. I mean, the man from Philadelphia. You'd think he'd know enough to stay away. Especially when he didn't have a watch and didn't know what time it was. Wasn't that an awfully foolish thing for him to do?"

Homer put his hands on the window sash and stared at the snow piling up on the railing of the back porch. Then he slammed the window down with a crash. "But he did know what time it was. He knew! Only he was wrong! The clocks, the new tower clocks, they were wrong! They had just been set into motion the day before. There was a little ceremony the day before in Sanders Theatre, and Cheever made a speech and pushed the button, and then the clock works began whirring for the first time, only they were sluggish, and the whirligigs were still in the clutch of inertia, and the two spiral coils that wind back into the past and forward into the future weren't working right yet, and the little gears weren't really loosened up and twirling around fast enough and notching their little notches into the little slots on the other little gears, and the sprockets and spindles and thingamabobs were all delayed just a whisker, so the whole damned mechanism was slow by ten whole minutes the next day, and all four clock faces, looking east, west, north, and south over the city of Cambridge, were wrong, and everybody in the whole city was late to class or to work or they missed their trains and planes and opportunities for advancement and who knows what all. So the man from Philadelphia thought he had another ten minutes before the thing would go off, only he was wrong. Dead wrong. The deadest wrong of all."

"I see," said Mary. "He had just come up from Philadelphia, is that it? So it didn't occur to him that the clocks weren't accurate, since he didn't know how new they were, and he'd be bound to think that any clocks as big and important-looking as they were would certainly be exactly right, so he trusted them, only he shouldn't have."

Homer shook his head and laughed. "Too much respect for Harvard. These outsiders, they really think this ancient institution is dedicated to *veritas*, the way it pretends to be. They think it's dishing out *veritas* by the bushel. Only of course Harvard is just

186

another bunch of fallible fools working on lucky hunches or wild guesses or august mistaken theories inherited from the past. Just a miscellaneous batch of mortal souls scattered all up and down the great chain of being from the bottom to the top."

"Oh, Homer, look at it snow. Doesn't it make you think of Christmas. Homer, darling, what do you want for Christmas?"

Homer looked balefully at the snow blowing in small whirlpools between their own back porch and the porch of the house next door. "I'll tell you what I want for Christmas. Hamilton Dow. I'd like to find a big slob of a man named Ham Dow stuffed into my Christmas stocking. The trouble is, I may meet him altogether sooner than I'd like to. I'm going over to the Cambridge City Hospital first thing this morning and talk to that pathologist. The exhumation order finally got handed down by the judge and they've dug up the poor wretch from Mount Auburn Cemetery and taken him over to the hospital."

"Oh, Homer, let's hope it's the man from Philadelphia."

"I hope to God it's the man from Philadelphia. But if there are any calluses on those decomposing fingers, I'll get my Christmas present a whole lot sooner than I want."

When Homer left the house on Huron Avenue, snow was still falling in flurries, collecting in the branches of the spindly trees, blowing eastward in gusts from the flat roofs of the three-deckers. But when he came back from his mission to the Cambridge City Hospital and stepped shakily off the bus at Harvard Square, the low winter sun was beginning to glare through the thinning clouds. The tinsel bells hanging over Boylston Street and Brattle swung sparkling in the sunlight. The bells and the tawdry Christmas decorations entwined around the light poles were the contribution of the city of Cambridge, and therefore they were Town, whereas the square itself was really a province of the university, and therefore it was Gown, so the tinsel bells didn't fit in at all. But in a vulgar way they added something to the particolored daftness of Harvard Square at this season of the year. The place

throbbed and palpitated with its own skewed version of the Christmas spirit.

Homer's own mood was sepulchral. He walked feebly across the street when the light said WALK, telling himself that of course he should really be rejoicing, because, after all, that pathologist had found no calluses on the hands of the corpse dug up from Mount Auburn Cemetery. He hadn't found any fingerprints either, but he had looked at Homer solemnly over the putrefying mess on the table and said that if there had ever been calluses on those hands he would have found evidence of them still. So that was good news. But, oh, God, the body of the man from Philadelphia had been unspeakable. Those damn kids and their idealism about embalming and their sanctimonious opinions about just letting nature take its course! Homer staggered up on the sidewalk on the other side of Mass Av and groaned aloud. It was his blood sugar, he told himself. He had thrown up his breakfast, and his blood sugar was down. It needed pumping up with something really solid and substantial, like a nice little second breakfast at Elsie's. And after that he would run right over to Memorial Hall and tell Vick the results of the exhumation. Vick would be conducting a final rehearsal of the orchestra and chorus, getting ready for tonight's performance. She would be overjoyed by Homer's news.

But no. There was something else he should do first. Before he went over to Mem Hall to talk to Vick. Just for the hell of it. Just a crazy notion. Just a nutty crazy thing he felt like doing.

Chapter Thirty-five

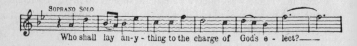

SOPRANO SOLO

Who shall lay an-y-thing to the charge of God's e-lect?——

Homer had never seen Elmwood before. He had lived in Cambridge most of his life without ever finding himself on this short byway off Brattle Street. And yet he should have had a historical curiosity about the place, because James Russell Lowell had lived there. Lowell had been Longfellow's successor at Harvard. And he had been one of those truculent abolitionists who had made everybody so mad. Well, his house was a splendid residence for the President of Harvard. Homer pushed through the front gate and walked boldly up to the front door. It was still early. The President of Harvard would probably still be eating a leisurely Saturday-morning breakfast.

But James Cheever was just coming out. He paused in the open door and looked blankly at Homer.

"Oh, good morning, sir. I was just passing by. I thought I would drop in and make a brief report on a new development in the matter of the bombing at Memorial Hall." Homer looked inquisitively over Cheever's head at the presidential front hall, and caught a glimpse of a table on which was displayed a small piece of alabaster sculpture, something picked up from the rubble of a ruined temple, a broken torso through which the lamplight shone. Homer wanted to exclaim in wonder, but Cheever was closing the door in his face, shutting off the view.

"A new development?" said President Cheever. "What new development?" He moved away from the door and started down the brick walk.

"Well, sir, I'm sure you'll be as amazed as I was to learn that the man who was killed in the explosion was not Hamilton Dow."

James Cheever stopped in his tracks and looked sharply at Homer. "It was not . . . ? Surely you are mistaken."

"No, sir, it's a fact. It was a man from Philadelphia. The bomber himself. He planted the bomb the day before, and then blew himself up by mistake."

Cheever began walking quickly forward again. He pushed through the gate and slammed it shut against Homer's knee. "But if that's true, then where is Hamilton Dow? Whatever happened to Dow?"

Doggedly Homer opened the gate. "Who knows? Beats me. Maybe he's still buried under all that brick."

President Cheever slipped on the snowy sidewalk, then regained his balance and drove his legs forward once again. "But they searched the debris so thoroughly. I have been assured of that. Unless of course"—Cheever looked at Homer and uttered a dry laugh—"unless he was buried and rose again. Perhaps he rolled away the stone. Sloan Tinker is of the opinion that the man had a messiah complex, so of course that sort of thing would have come naturally. Perhaps he simply rolled away the stone."

"Oh, yes, ha ha. He rolled away the stone." Homer tripped on the sidewalk too, and nearly lost his balance. The old slate blocks along Brattle Street had been heaved up unevenly by generations of winter frosts and thaws, and Homer caught his big foot on a lifted corner, pitched forward, stumbled a few paces, and then caught up with Cheever again. "What did you say, sir? I'm sorry. I didn't hear."

President Cheever had been mumbling to himself. Now he flung out one hand in a gesture of irritation. "But what about the

plaque? I'm supposed to dedicate a plaque in Dow's memory during that concert in Memorial Hall this evening. What shall I do about the plaque? Nobody tells me anything. Nobody keeps me informed."

"Well, you see, sir, this new piece of information isn't common knowledge. I don't know when it will be made known to the public at large. Perhaps it would be just as well to keep it under your hat. At least for the time being."

And then Homer began rambling in a genial way about what an awful responsibility it must be to assume the presidency of so vast and various an institution as Harvard University. Surely it must be difficult enough to deal wisely with the ordinary intramural problems of the day, without random violence from the outside world throwing everything at the university into a tizzy. But how fortunate it was that through the wisdom of the forefathers, some of the heavy burden of responsibility could be carried on the shoulders of the Harvard Fellows and the Board of Overseers! So many loyal hands clasping the rod of authority! In union there was strength! How wonderful to think of the good will and self-sacrifice of the men and women who—it truly struck Homer as remarkable—would even gather from across the face of the land to meet at the very moment of the Harvard-Yale game. The fellows and the Overseers. Truly extraordinary devotion to duty.

Again the President of Harvard stopped short. "The Harvard-Yale game? What are you talking about? The Fellows and the Overseers? They had a meeting during the Harvard-Yale game?"

"Why, yes, I believe they did. You mean, they didn't tell you? Strange. I suppose it was just some slip-up in the normal processes of communication. A mistake, no doubt."

James Cheever's steps quickened. He began puffing and jogging in his haste. Homer suspected he was frantic to arrive at the presidential office in Massachusetts Hall and begin throwing his weight around. Counter-conspiracies would be set afoot with Sloan Tinker. Heads would roll.

Homer galloped easily along beside the President of Harvard, adjusting his long-legged gait to the shorter span of Cheever's. They were more than halfway to the square. Cold puffy clouds were boiling across the brilliant blue sky. A chartered bus was pulling up at the Longfellow House. Homer was suddenly possessed by a demon. He raced ahead of Cheever and stopped beside the bus just as the door opened to discharge sixty members of the Historical Society of the North Shore. Throwing out his arms and bowing from the waist, Homer welcomed them all to the gracious house that had once been the headquarters of General Washington during the siege of Boston! the home of Longfellow! author of "Evangeline!" and "Hiawatha!" and "The Village Blacksmith"! and "The Courtship of Miles Standish"! and "The Wreck of the Hesperus"! And then, as James Cheever drew abreast, his face turning pale with horror, Homer took his arm and thrust him gently into the middle of the enraptured throng. "Allow me to present to you the President of Harvard," cried

Homer, "who wishes to welcome you to Cambridge, to sign his name for any of you who would like his autograph, and to answer any questions you may wish to put to him about this historic city and our ancient university!"

Then Homer stepped gracefully aside and waved good-bye and hurled himself away in the direction of Mason Street and the brisk west wind whipping across the Cambridge Common in the direction of Memorial Hall.

Chapter Thirty-six

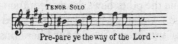

Vick's final rehearsal was nearly over when Homer walked into Sanders Theatre. She was standing on the podium on a platform built out from the front of the stage, leaning across the crowded orchestra, waving her arms at the chorus massed behind it. "Not *wus*," cried Vick. "Not unto *wus* a child is born. Unto *us*. Start again, sopranos."

The sopranos started again, lofting the good news of the birth of Christ, and then unfurling a fluttering banner of sixteenth notes. The tenors came next, and soon the basses too were running joyously upward. Even Homer's tin ears could distinguish the separate voices of the tumbling fugue. He sat down on one of the benches at the side, and then flattened his spine against the back as the chorus burst out in a sudden thunder of major chords. *Wonderful, Counsellor, the Mighty God, the Everlasting Father, the Prince of Peace!* In the balcony over the stage someone lowered a microphone on a pulley, then reeled it in again.

Homer caught Mary's eye and winked at her. Jennifer was standing beside her, looking more swollen than ever, as if she might fulfill the obstetrical prophecy of the chorus at any moment. Betsy Pickett sat in a chair at the front of the stage, wagging her head in time with the beat, and beside Betsy Mrs.

Esterhazy's great red face was suffused with joy. The long stringy kid beside Mrs. Esterhazy was the tenor soloist, Tim Swegle, and the barrel-chested man in the sweater was the bass, Mr. Proctor. Jack Fox was playing a small organ instead of a harpsichord. Rosie Bell was leaning back, reading a book, her tiny trumpet idle in her lap. And there in the very back row of second violins was that funny little old Cambridge lady, her hair ribbon fluttering, her beaming face pressed against her fiddle, her bow rising steadfastly all by itself while the other bows descended, then sturdily plunging as they rose. "Upbow, Miss Plankton!" cried Vick.

The rehearsal was over. Vick dropped her arms. "Now listen, everybody," she said. "It's going to be a long evening, because we need plenty of time to get warmed up before any of the audience comes in, and then, don't forget, the second intermission is going to be a long one because President Cheever is going to dedicate a bronze tablet in Ham's memory. Well, okay, it's all right to put up a tablet, but you know as well as I do that Ham would care a lot more about the concert we're going to do tonight than he would about having his name out there in bronze forever and ever. So you'll be singing for Ham, not me. Is that clear? Anyway, we've got to start early. Be here promptly at seven o'clock."

Homer walked up the five steps at the front of the stage and slapped Vick on the back. "Good old girl. You've really got the thing in shape. It's going to be just great."

Vick laughed and scribbled something on her score. "I don't know. I just don't know. I mean, I think they're all right now, if they just don't get careless. But, oh, God, Homer, it's me I'm worried about. I've never been all the way through the whole thing from beginning to end, and I'm really scared." Then Vick's face changed, and she gripped Homer's arm. "Homer, the pathologist. What did he say?"

"No calluses."

"None? None on the left hand? Oh, Homer, then that means . . . !"

"Listen, my girl, all it means is another person is dead. Why don't you feel sorry for the other guy? Maybe his mother loved him. Maybe he showed great promise in his youth. But as a matter of fact, you know what I think? I think he was the bomber and he blew himself up by mistake." Then Homer told Vick about the attaché case in the motel, and explained his theory about the forgotten wrist watch and the unpunctual tower clock.

Vick was thrilled. Mary Kelly was pushing through the thicket of departing violinists, and Vick squealed at her, "No calluses."

"No calluses?" said Mary. "Oh, terrific."

Vick turned back to Homer, her eyes flashing. "Now listen, Homer, where do you think he is? I mean, Ham's a missing person now, not just a dead body buried in a cemetery."

"After all, Homer," said Mary, "it isn't as though he were exactly inconspicuous. Somebody like Ham Dow couldn't just melt away in the crowd."

They were both looking at him, demanding a plan of action. Homer sighed, suppressing his own suspicion that the man had been entirely blown up and completely disintegrated. "Well, of course, there are ways of tracing missing persons. I'll get to work on it. But who knows, it might be in the man's best interest never to turn up again. Have you thought of that?"

"No," said Vick. "We've *got* to find him."

"Now look here, Vick, dear," said Mary. "When are you going to get some rest? Look at you. You're trembling."

"Rest!" Vick threw back her head and laughed. Then she clutched her shivering arms and shook her head. "I couldn't possibly. Besides, you know what? Of all the really dumb incredible things, I've got a test in Chem 2 on Monday. I've got to study. I'm flunking. I know I'm flunking. So I'm going to hole up in Mr. Crawley's office and go over my notes for Chem 2. He's not there. He must be goofing off again today. Just when I needed him most this morning, he wasn't there. I had to set up the risers all by myself. So I went downstairs and found the Esterhazy boys running around in the basement. Those little kids are all muscle, except, oh, ouch"—Vick hopped on one foot and made a face—

"one of those damn little kids dropped a riser on my toe. Anyway, I'll have Mr. Crawley's nice comfy office all to myself."

"Can you get in there?" said Homer. "Doesn't Mr. Crawley lock his office when he's not there?"

"Yes, but he gave me the key to the instrument storage closet, and guess what, it turns out it's a master key. It opens everything."

"Well, I'm going home right now and have lunch and take a nap," said Mary firmly. "What are you going to do, Homer? Are you coming with me?"

"No, I'm going to stick around here and keep an eye on things. I had something to eat at Elsie's. I never felt more wide awake in my life."

But left to himself, Homer yawned. He felt an overpowering impulse to lie down. He controlled a desire to run after Mary and go home and share her bed. Something held him, an air of excitement in the building, a sense of forces gathering, of preparations coming to fruition. He walked down the steps at the front of the stage and looked at the long cushion on the bench in the front row. The sound-absorptive capacity of one meter of Sanders Theatre seat cushion had once been a standard scientific unit; Homer had read that somewhere. Right now the cushion looked capacious enough to absorb his entire six and a half feet, stretched on it flat from head to toe. Homer lay down and covered himself with his coat and went to sleep immediately.

Chapter Thirty-seven

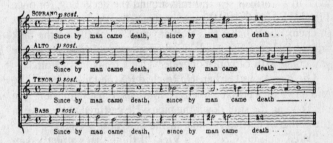

At the south door Vick said good-bye to Mary Kelly, after promising her faithfully to eat a good supper and try to get a little rest if she possibly could. Then she hurried across the hall to Mr. Crawley's office, put her book bag on the floor beside the door, pulled the key on its string over her head, fitted the key into the lock, and opened the door. She threw open the inner door. Then she stopped short.

The room was not empty. A man was kneeling in the corner with his back to the door.

"Oh," cried Vick, "you surprised me." It wasn't Mr. Crawley. It was that old man who must be his assistant. Vick was always seeing him pushing a broom down a hallway or swabbing the floor with a wet mop.

The man was as startled as she was. He stood up suddenly and dropped something. It clattered to the floor. It was a tank, a small tank of gas under pressure, and the gas was still hissing from the valve. The tank skittered violently across the floor and whammed against Vick's sore foot. She shrieked. The man lunged at the tank, but before he could lay his hands on it, Vick snatched it up and turned the stopcock.

The hissing stopped. For an instant the two of them stood staring at the tank. "Oh, wow," said Vick. She laughed shakily. "It was like one of those movies, you know? Where a cannon gets loose in a storm at sea and rolls around the deck. Boy, for once I'm glad I'm taking that course in chemistry. We use these things in chem lab. What is this stuff anyway?" Vick turned the tank around and read the label. "Carbon monoxide? Gosh, what are you doing with carbon monoxide? That's really nasty stuff."

The man looked at her. He reached for the tank. "A rat," he said. "I've got a big rat cornered downstairs. I'm just finishing him off. Sending the stuff down the pipe." He gestured at the pipe in the corner. There was a hole in the pipe near the floor.

"Well, but, my God," said Vick. "I think that's a pretty dangerous way to go after a rat. You might finish off some of the other kind of rats instead. You know"—Vick laughed again—"rats like me."

The man turned away. "Well, I think I've finished the job anyway." He took a rag from his pocket and stuffed it in the hole. Then he picked up his box of tools and his tank of carbon monoxide and left the room.

Vick shook her head and shrugged her shoulders and followed him out into the hall to get her books. But then it occurred to her that carbon monoxide was as odorless as it was poisonous. She ran back into Mr. Crawley's office, unlocked the window, threw it open, hurried out into the hall, slammed the door, locked it, picked up her book bag, marched into the great hall, found a table under the balcony, and sat down. Taking a sandwich out of her book bag, she began flipping through her chemistry textbook.

Mr. Crawley's assistant walked along the basement corridor until he found the boarded entry to the subbasement. Cradling the tank carefully in his hands, he looked at the boards he had hammered back into place so securely. On the other side of the boards the stairs led down to a door against which the litter from the explosion was piled high. And behind the door . . . The question was, had the administered dose been enough to do the job? He wasn't sure how much of the stuff it would take. Did that room at the bottom of the stairs still harbor a very stubborn rat? Probably not. The man was surely dead by now. Dead as a doornail. But what if one had miscalculated again? It was better to be sure. He must be ready to finish the job. To provide that extra increment of security. To be thoroughgoing. Again it was just a matter of thoroughness and economy of means. It would be wise to prepare his equipment. Readiness was all.

One only had to know where. And he did. He knew precisely where to place his material, at the four corners of the tower, high on the basement walls, hidden in the forest of pipes that ran along the ceiling. He was pleased to observe that after all these years he still had an instinct for the job. (Well, it was an instinct based on a hell of a lot of experience). And then he would only need to lay a single wire. The stuff was right there in the closet where he kept his change of clothing. He would take care of that part of the job right now. And then later on if there was any need, he would be ready at a moment's notice with the control switch. The switch was one of those clever little wireless gadgets the size of a man's hand. It had belonged to his nephew George. Poor feckless simple-minded George! The boy was his mother's despair. He would never make it to any institution of higher learning, never mind Harvard. Flying model airplanes was the only thing the poor kid cared about at all. Well, for once it was a good thing. The shaft of the rudder servo from one of George's old kits would turn at a flick of the transmitter switch and connect the battery with the detonator. The wretched boy was about to be of some unwitting service to the world at last.

Chapter Thirty-eight

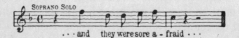

··· and   they were sore a - fraid ···

Homer woke up smiling. A little nap always made him feel like a newborn babe. He sat up and looked around the empty forest of Sanders Theatre. His watch said one o'clock. He still didn't feel like going home. He decided to go downstairs where the Rats lived and find somebody to talk to. His nap had made him feel friendly and talkative, eager for the society of his fellow man.

The first person Homer ran into downstairs in the basement was a chap who was fixing something behind a door. Jolly-looking feet were sticking out of the doorway. Some competent fellow was down on his knees doing something in the corner. *Bzzzzzzzzz bzzzzzzzz*. Whine of electric drill.

"Hello, there," said Homer, all geniality and willingness to serve. "Do you want some help? I'd be glad to lend a hand."

The feet jerked, but they stayed behind the door. "Just rewiring in here," mumbled the person attached to the feet. "Putting in more outlets. Old building. Not enough electrical outlets anyplace down here."

Homer poked his head around the door. It was Mr. Crawley's right-hand man again, drilling a hole in the baseboard. A great coil of black cable lay on the floor beside him. He had his back to Homer. He didn't look up. He just went right on drilling the hole.

"Oh, say," said Homer helpfully, "I don't know if you noticed it, but there's an outlet a couple of feet down the wall. See there? You've got your drill plugged into it."

"Wrong voltage," mumbled Crawley's assistant.

"Oh, I see," said Homer, who didn't know voltage from wattage, or AC from DC. "Well, if you need any help, just holler." He backed out of the room again and tripped over the cable, which ran out the door and down the hall. Homer followed the cable to Mr. Proctor's room. Mr. Proctor's door was open. Mr. Proctor was sitting in an upholstered chair reading the paper and eating a bowl of soup. "Mind if I come in?" said Homer. "Mmmmm, doesn't that smell delicious."

"Oh, come right in, Professor Kelly." Mr. Proctor was delighted. "Won't you join me? Just canned soup, I'm afraid." He stood up and waved Homer into the chair.

"Oh, no," said Homer, "I couldn't take your chair."

"Oh, that's quite all right. I'll just sit on the bed." Mr. Proctor took a pan of steaming soup off his electric hot plate and poured another bowl for Homer.

"My, my, doesn't that look good. Say, isn't this a nice room you've got here."

"Oh, yes, we're very comfortable down here. I've even got a window. See my window? I can watch the world go by. Nice and warm. All the comforts of home."

"You bet," said Homer. "Nice lamps and everything. A hot plate. Is that new wire going to come in here? No, I guess you have enough outlets already. Plenty of voltage of one kind and another, right?"

"Yes, sir. I'm just as comfortable as a bug in a rug."

Homer chatted with Mr. Proctor until he had finished his bowl of soup and eaten several large sticky buns, and then he said good-bye and wandered upstairs and out of the door at the northwest corner of the basement and in again by way of the cloister porch into the great hall.

At first Homer was blinded by the broad column of colored

light falling across the dusty air from the high west window over his head, spreading out in an immense pattern on the floor. But then the dim hollows of the enormous room revealed themselves, and he saw a little figure staring at him far, far away at the other end. It was Vick Van Horn, sitting at a table under the balcony, studying her chemistry. The crazy kid. She'd wear herself out. She was standing up, calling to him.

"What's that?" shouted Homer. "Wait a minute." He galloped the full length of the hall, while Vick put her hands to her mouth like a megaphone and kept right on talking at the top of her lungs and gesturing, but the sound of her voice kept ricocheting all over the room. "I'm sorry," said Homer, pulling up a chair and sitting down on the other side of the table. "What did you say?"

"I said, don't you think carbon monoxide is dangerous stuff? I've been reading about it in my chemistry textbook. It's really terrible. What's Mr. Crawley's assistant doing with carbon monoxide in Memorial Hall?"

"Carbon monoxide? Mr. Crawley's assistant?"

"He was in Mr. Crawley's office a little while ago. He had a tank of carbon monoxide. He drilled a hole in one of the pipes and he was putting it into the pipe. But I think that's just an incredibly dangerous thing to do, don't you? The stuff could go all over the building. He said he was exterminating a rat downstairs. But he shouldn't be running around loose with a tank of carbon monoxide, sticking it into a pipe like that, should he?"

Homer frowned. "I saw him just now. He was downstairs drilling another hole." Homer looked at Vick thoughtfully. "You know, the man gives me the heebie-jeebies. Who is he anyway? Another one of Ham's Rats?"

"No, I don't think so. I mean, I'm not sure. I never laid eyes on him until after Ham was gone. Doesn't he work here? I thought he was Mr. Crawley's assistant. You know, you never see Mr. Crawley doing any work himself. I thought this guy was Mr. Crawley's second in command or something."

"Well, let's see if Crawley's back in his office and ask him."

Mr. Crawley was back. He was angry. "The place is a refrigerator. I had this funeral to go to, see, so what happens behind my back? Somebody gets in here and opens the window. What's the big idea?"

"It was me," said Vick. "The room was full of gas. Your assistant was doing something to the pipe."

"My assistant? I don't have no assistant."

"But, Mr. Crawley," said Homer, "what about that man who goes around here cleaning the halls and fixing things up? Isn't he your assistant?"

"Oh, you mean that old guy? Oh, sure. Well, you know. I let him hang around. I mean, a poor old guy like that. I let him think he's being a big help. He don't do no harm."

Homer drew Vick out of the room and closed the door softly. His cheery mood had vanished. "Listen here, Vick, I'm worried about that guy with the broom. He's up to no good. What in the name of God was he trying to do with the carbon monoxide but poison everybody in the building? Those pipes go all over the place. I saw the chart of all those plumbing and ventilating pipes in Mr. Maderna's office. The man must be mad. What on earth do you suppose he's up to? I'll find him. I'll get a straight answer this time. He says he's putting new electrical outlets in the basement. But that's not what he's doing. There are plenty of outlets in the basement. Maybe he's planning to flood the whole place with poison gas."

But Mr. Crawley's assistant was not in the basement. Homer looked up and down the hall outside the doorway where he had seen the man working half an hour before. "Hey, you," he shouted.

There was no answer. The man was gone. They looked for him up and down the basement corridors, then went upstairs and ransacked Sanders Theatre and looked around once again in the memorial corridor and the great hall.

"He must have gone away," said Vick, after Homer came out

of the men's room and shook his head at her. "And we don't even know his name."

"I don't like this at all," said Homer gloomily. "There's something very strange and unpleasant about it. I think we need help. A whole lot of help. Right now. Look here, I want you to call up everybody you can think of, and get them back here. Immediately. But the first person I need is that chemist. What's his name? Flynn. Charley Flynn. I've got to be sure the place isn't roiling and boiling with poisonous fumes. Do you know how I can get hold of Charley Flynn?"

"That's easy. He's my chem lab instructor. He practically lives in Mallinckrodt. Try the office there. I'll get busy on the others right away."

"Get hold of my wife first, would you? I'll use the pay phone. You can use the one in Crawley's office. And if he objects, just yell, and I'll come in and knock him down. It would be a pleasure. A service to mankind."

Charlie Flynn came over with a pump and a plastic bag and took a sample of the gas in the pipe back to the infrared spectrophotometer in his laboratory. A few minutes later he came running back into Mr. Crawley's office. "It was there alright," he said. "Carbon monoxide dissipates quickly, but there must have been more than enough to kill a whole mess of rats." Charley looked at Homer soberly. "Are you sure the man isn't still in the building?"

"The tower," said Homer. "What if he got up in the tower? The place is one huge jungle of ventilating pipes. All those air-conditioning ducts from Sanders Theatre."

"All those people," said Charley Flynn, "coming to the concert this evening. Just five or six hours from now. If this nut decided to pipe carbon monoxide into the air-conditioning system in Sanders Theatre, he could kill a thousand people. Look, we've got to get up there and take a look."

"Right," said Homer. "We'll start right now. Say, Mr. Crawley, have you got a key? You know, another one of those master keys?"

"Well, I don't know." Mr. Crawley shook his head. "I've only got a few left. I'm not giving out no more keys."

"The hell you're not." Homer shoved Mr. Crawley against the wall. Mr. Crawley whimpered, and turned over his entire collection of keys. Homer put them in his pocket and strode out of the office.

He found Vick marshaling her forces in the hall. She had collected Mary Kelly and half the chorus and most of the orchestra. Mrs. Esterhazy had brought her two little boys. Jane Plankton was dithering with excitement, eager to help out.

Homer quickly began sorting them into search parties. "Vick, you and Mary take a bunch of people downstairs and search the basement. Every single cubbyhole and room down there. Here, I've got a bunch of extra keys. Now, who wants to go upstairs with Charley and me to search the tower?"

"Me, me." Putzi and Siegfried Esterhazy were jumping up and down.

"No, no," thundered Mrs. Esterhazy. "You vould fall down and be keeled."

"Me," squealed Betsy, beaming at Charley Flynn.

"Me," growled Tim, glowering at Betsy.

"Well, all right, then," said Homer. "Come on, you people. Good Lord, Charley, I've just thought of something. What if he comes in from outside?"

"Oh, my God," said Charley, "that's right. We've got to guard the doors."

"Every bloody door. How many doors are there? Jesus, there are doors all over the place. There must be fifty doors."

"No, no," said Vick. "Not that many. And I've got more people coming. We've got the Organ Society. The whole Organ Society is coming, and Betsy has this friend in the band. Her friend is calling up the whole band."

They went over the list of doors. "There's these two here," said

207

Miss Plankton, flapping her mittens at both ends of the memorial corridor.

"Zuh two vuns at zuh end of zuh great hall," said Mrs. Esterhazy.

"The copy center door," said Tim.

"The one that goes downstairs past the ticket window," said Jennifer.

"The fire escape," said Charley Flynn. "Don't forget the fire escape up at the top of Sanders."

"And the door that goes right into WHRB from Quincy Street," said Vick.

"And the service entrance on the other side," said Mary.

"How many is that?" said Homer. "Two, four, five, six, seven, eight, nine. We need one person at every door. Now look, if he comes in, don't try to stop him. Just keep track of him until you can get help from the rest of us. Now, how are we going to search the building and cover all the entrances at the same time? We haven't got enough people." There was a trumpet blast and a thump at the door. "Aha! Here comes the band."

Homer's second expedition to the tower was noisier than the first, because Betsy wanted to hear the echoes in the great open spaces of the tower. She sang all the way to the top of the ladder stair, showing off as hard as she could for Charley Flynn. "Rejoice, rejoice," warbled Betsy. Her voice rattled against the trap door to the bell chamber and battered back at them.

"Oh, can it, Betsy," said Tim.

"Oh, damn," said Homer. He poked at the lock of the trap door with his finger. "Look what I've done now. I broke the key off in the lock. It's stuck in there. It won't come out. I always was a clumsy fool with keys."

"Here, let me try it." Charley Flynn squeezed past Homer on the narrow ladder stair. Charley couldn't fix it either.

"Well, never mind," said Homer. "I suppose they'll have to get some locksmith up here on the top of the ladder to fix it. Come on. Let's go down."

And then on the way down Betsy discovered the upside-down vaults, and she screamed with delight. "Oh, isn't that fabulous! Oh, don't they look really incredible! Oh, isn't that disgusting, the way people throw things into them! Just look at those disgusting old lunch bags and popcorn boxes. Oh, I wish I had a penny. It's like a wishing well, where you throw a penny in and make a wish. Oh, Charley, give me a penny!"

Charley Flynn gave Betsy a penny. Tim Swegle gave Betsy a quarter. Betsy threw the penny and the quarter down. They clattered on the sloping sides of one of the wooden vaults and disappeared among the trash in the narrow tapering cavity at the bottom. Betsy leaned out from the ladder and shrieked, summoning the spirit of the upside-down vaults. "I wish to sing like an angel so everybody will love me!"

"Watch it there, girl," said Charley Flynn.

"Oh, for Christ's sake, Betsy," said Tim Swegle. "Come on down before you break your fool neck."

Chapter Thirty-nine

SOPRANO SOLO

There were shepherds a-bid-ing in the field, keeping watch over their flocks by night.

Jennifer's post was the south entry. She sat on a folding chair just within the doorway, squinting at her sewing. In the dim light of the chandeliers she felt drowsy. She didn't know what she would do if the man she had seen poking a feather duster at the benches in Sanders Theatre should come in the door. She didn't much care. All she could think of was the baby thumping around inside her.

"You look like Madame Defarge," said Homer.

"Oh, no," said Jennifer. "Madame Defarge was a knitter. Besides, I don't know how she knitted all those names into a sweater anyway. I don't think it's possible at all. I think Dickens was really just bananas."

"Well, keep an eye on everybody going and coming. Good for you, Jennifer."

Homer went down the broad south stairs and crossed the bridge over Cambridge Street. Then he turned around and looked back at Memorial Hall. To the northwest above the snarl of traffic the sun was setting like some barbarous jewel, shining on the west end of the building. The bricks glowed a violent harsh red. A cold sea breeze from the east was blowing sea gulls in a flock away up over the roof. That way too lay the moon, nearly full, looming over

East Cambridge, dented like a hammered salver. Salome's plate, thought Homer, red with blood.

Had he really covered all the entrances? On the cloister porch at this end Homer could see Mrs. Esterhazy marching up and down like a general, shouting at her children, who were running back and forth, little blobs of green and blue. Mary was on the other side, sitting on the steps inside the service entry to the basement, reading over a typed sheaf of index pages. Mr. Proctor was holding the fort at the north door. Jennifer was there at the south. A couple of bassoonists were supposed to be taking care of the entrance to the copy center and the lecture hall. Miss Plankton was camped on a folding stool at the basement entrance to WHRB, keeping her ears warm in her big fur hat. Rosie Bell had parked herself in the balcony of Sanders Theatre beside the door to the fire escape. Betsy and Tim were plainly visible at the ticket office entrance, and above the traffic Homer could hear Betsy's canary voice. She was showing off again to the whole world.

It was a three-hour shift. At seven o'clock Vick's warm-up exercises would begin on the stage of Sanders, and a new batch of sentries recruited from the Organ Society and the band would take over the watch. Homer lifted his head. Who was that, moving around the building, carrying something? Oh, of course, it was just Jack Fox. He had passed the hat. He had made a trip to Elsie's for emergency rations. He was going from door to door, passing out sandwiches. And someone else was scuttling out of the south door, running down the steps, hurrying away up Cambridge Street, a small crouching figure. "Rats desert a sinking ship," murmured Homer. But it wasn't one of Ham's Rats, of course. It was Jerry Crawley. Homer looked at his watch. Four-thirty. Hardly quitting time yet, but it was typical of Crawley.

The wind was really whistling down Cambridge Street. Homer wedged himself into a niche where a fountain was attached to the wall, and looked at Memorial Hall, half closing his eyes against flying pieces of grit. As usual the building impressed him with its bulk. It was immense. Today it looked less like a church than a fortress. A mighty fortress, a bulwark never failing. The trouble was, it was a besieged fortress. But besieged by whom? And from what direction? And for what reason? Something nagged at Homer. How good a bulwark was it really? Had he covered all the entrances? The enemy was invisible so far, but nonetheless Homer suspected his craft and power were great.

Bulky it was, Memorial Hall. Enormous. Henry James had called it majestic. *It sprang majestic into the winter air.* Well, it was majestic, all right, but it certainly didn't spring into the air. It was too heavy for that. It squatted like a beast on its great comfortable haunches. It was a vast cow of a building. No, not a cow. In the ruddy light Memorial Hall seemed once again like some dreaming mythical monster, some elderly sleeping dragon with a secret fire in its belly. Sleeping? Yes, it was sleeping, but any day now it would wake up, open its dreadful eyes, and breathe flame from its cavernous jaw.

Chapter Forty

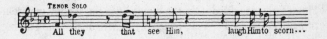

TENOR SOLO

All they   that see Him,   laugh Him to scorn...

"Let it all go," said Vick. She stood at the front of the stage and bent over, letting her hair pour down on the floor and her arms flop loose. The chorus bent over too, and flapped dangling hands. Vick stood and threw back her hair. "Ready now, chorus? Okay, let's go. *Mee-meh-ma-mo-mooooo* . . .

Where was Mary? She wasn't standing in her usual place at the back of the chorus. Homer wandered out into the hall and found his wife standing beside the ticket table talking to Charley Flynn and another tall woman, wearing a red cloak.

The woman in the red cloak was Julia Chamberlain. "Oh, Homer, hello, there. I'm so glad to meet your wife. I was feeling so restless I came early. I don't know what got into me. What can I do? What the hell's going on? Who is this guy you're looking for?"

"We're not sure. That's the trouble. We've got all the doors posted. We'll get our hands on him and find out."

"Only we're running short again, Homer," said Charley. "Mary's taking over for some piccolo player who had to leave. I'd do it myself, only I don't know what the man looks like."

"It's not the mad bomber?" Julia Chamberlain was thrilled. "Let me help. I'll stand watch with Mary, and the two of us will wrestle him to the floor." She sailed down the hall with Mary and Charley Flynn, her red cloak billowing behind her, while Vick's choristers finished their exercises and began running through transitional passages, and the instrumentalists drifted out of the great hall carrying cellos, violins, oboes, flutes.

"Oh, good evening, Mr. Kelly." Jane Plankton was waggling her bow at Homer. Her black velvet evening gown trailed behind her on the floor. Her hair ribbon was spangled with gold. A beaded purse dangled from her belt. She looked vaguely medieval. Homer was delighted. Oh, the dignity, oh, the shabby grandeur of genteel poverty! "Well, hello, there, Miss Plankton. The big evening arrives at last."

Miss Plankton's cheeks were bright knobs of joy. She pointed with her bow at a curtain high on the wall. "Oh, the whole thing is so exciting," she said. "Did you see the memorial tablet? We're going to have a little ceremony!"

"So we are," said Homer, noticing the curtain for the first time.

"President Cheever is going to pull the string during the second intermission. After the 'Hallelujah Chorus.' You know, Mr. Kelly, it reminds me of my girlhood. When I christened Brother Wayland's sailboat. He named it after me. The good ship *Jane!*"

"A gallant name for a gallant craft," said Homer, smiling at Miss Plankton. "Does the *Jane* still sail the seven seas?"

"Oh, I do hope so, Mr. Kelly. Brother sold her to the Duke of Windsor." Miss Plankton bowed and nodded and trailed away, her train dragging behind her on the floor.

She was mad as a hatter, the old dear. But then Homer had to admit to himself that the place was full of lunatics. Someone was tugging at him from the rear.

"Hey, Homer, there's this crazy guy!" It was Putzi Esterhazy. "There's this really crazy guy trying to get in. Come on!"

"What do you mean, crazy?" Homer followed Putzi into the great hall, and then he saw the scuffle at the west end, and began to run. Putzi's brother Siegfried was clutching someone around

214

the middle, dragging him this way and that with his short sturdy arms.

"Oh, no," said Homer. "Freddy Fulsom, what are you doing here? I thought you went home to stay with your mother." It was the Messiah of Memorial Hall. He was wearing his white sheet.

"I'm simply attending the concert," gasped Freddy. "What's wrong with that?"

"It's all right now, Siegfried," said Homer. "You can let him go."

Reluctantly Siegfried loosened his hold. "He was trying to sneak in. Only I saw him. I snuck up in back of him and jumped him from behind."

"Well, good work, Siegfried. Good for you too, Putzi. Only you can see perfectly well this isn't the man we want."

"Well, maybe he's the bomber," said Putzi eagerly. "Look under the sheet. Maybe he's got a bomb hidden under the sheet."

Freddy smiled gently and parted the sheet, revealing a padded jacket and a pair of corduroy trousers. Putzi and Siegfried made a thorough job of going through his pockets.

"His suitcase. That's where it is, I bet," said Putzi.

Freddy picked up his satchel from the floor, opened the top wide and displayed the contents. The satchel was full of pamphlets. Freddy extracted one and handed it to Homer. "For you," he said. "A free gift."

Homer glanced at the pamphlet.

Christ Reborn
into
Every Generation!
Where Is He Now?
Behold, He Walketh Among You!

"Oh, good Lord, Freddy."

"You see," said Freddy, "the moment has come. The time to announce my incarnation."

"Now look here, Freddy, you don't have any intention of interrupting the concert, do you? Because if you do—"

"Interrupt! Oh, no." Freddy wiped his glasses with a corner of his sheet and smiled. "After all, the concert is on my behalf. I mean, the whole thing."

"For you? Oh, you mean because it's Handel's *Messiah*. Because you're the Messiah reborn in human flesh. Oh, yes, I see. Oh, of course. Oh, well."

"Hallelujah, you see," explained Freddy modestly. "The Lord God omnipotent reigneth."

"Is he kidding?" said Putzi.

"No, no, he's not kidding," said Homer. "You see, Putzi, Mr. Fulsom is proclaiming a revolutionary new theological doctrine. It is his opinion that Jesus is reborn into every generation. I mean, you should really study this fine pamphlet here, Putzi. Now look here, Freddy. You can stand out in the lobby there if you want to. That's fine. You can hand out your nice pamphlets. That's just great. But there will be no proclamations from the balcony. No speeches. No standing up during the concert in Sanders Theatre to warn of doom and destruction or the end of the world or anything like that. In fact, just stay the hell out of Sanders Theatre altogether. Have you got a concert ticket? I thought not. All right, then—look here, Freddy. If you so much as poke your nose into Sanders Theatre, I'll have you arrested. Because, you see, Freddy, I should explain something to you. Something that fits right into your theory. Maybe Pontius Pilate gets reborn into every generation too. Did you ever think of that? So just watch it."

216

Chapter Forty-one

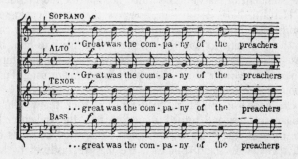

It was going well. Vick grinned at the sopranos and tenors as they swung into the next-to-last chorus of Part Two. She was unconscious of any effort. She hardly needed the score. Her arms were moving of their own accord, and the chorus was singing as if it had no other life on this earth but in Handel's *Messiah*, and Mrs. Esterhazy's arias were round fruit on a plate, and Mr. Proctor had raged and roared, his great chest cavity engorged with wrath, and Betsy had filled the theatre with her fine-spun threads of glass, and Tim had handled his awkward passages of sixteenth notes better than ever before, and the orchestra had been nearly perfect so far. Even Miss Plankton was all right, because she was completely drowned out by everybody else.

Let us break their bonds, sang the chorus. They were casting away their yokes in a tumult, they were a controlled riot, thousands of voices were crisscrossing and intermingling, it was a great crowd all milling and pushing. Behind her Vick sensed the audience filling the twelve hundred seats on the floor and in the balcony and in the rising tiers of seats under the balcony. They were silent, listening, drinking from this bountiful source, all other life functions stilled. Homer Kelly was standing in the shadows beside the door, his arms folded, his head down. Off to one side Vick had caught a glimpse of the President of Harvard. She cared nothing for the President of Harvard. Now it was Tim Swegle's turn. Vick could see him bracing himself. Poor Tim, his voice was too thin for the wrath he needed to sing the next aria. But listen to him, he was getting off on the right foot. He was shaking with fury, almost like Mr. Proctor. *Thou shalt break them,* sang Tim, *Thou shalt break them with a rod of iron.*

Oh, good for you, Tim, good for you. Vick threw Tim a brilliant glance, and turned around to face the audience. It was time for the "Hallelujah Chorus." She lifted her arms to tell them all to stand. But then the massive rustle of twelve hundred bodies rising, the great soft whisper of clothing leaving benches, the dropping of coats and the fluttering of programs to the floor, made her catch her breath. To her horror she almost sobbed. She smiled hugely instead, and gave a great encouraging upbeat. Instantly the twelve hundred white faces became twelve hundred open mouths. They roared back at her, *HALLELUJAH, HALLELUJAH.* Standing at the focal point of the circular chamber, she was bombarded. Twelve hundred pairs of lungs had puffed themselves up with the amber air, and now they were letting it out in shouts of *Hallelujah.* Vick swung her arms in a tremendous beat of four. They were too lusty, too loud. But it didn't matter. They had been waiting all evening for this chance to stand up and bellow at the tops of their lungs. Behind her the chorus too was letting itself go, shouting in competition with the people in the hall, and Rosie Bell was lifting up her little trumpet, and the timpani were volleying like cannon. The great harmonious noise shook in every tiny crevice in every stick of wood in the forest of lumber that was Sanders Theatre, it trembled in the walls and wooden dome, and in the supporting timbers of the floor, reverberating again and yet again, *HALLELUJAH, HALLELUJAH, HALLELUJAH.*

Chapter Forty-two

The buzzing of insects irritated him awake. He had been asleep for a long time. A dreamless solemn suspended sleep like death. Slowly, very slowly, Ham fought his way out of nothingness and opened his eyes. Tiny rhythmic mosquito-like noises were whining in his ears, and some sort of bumblebee was thudding and rumbling inside his head.

His lips were cracked. He put out his thick tongue and tried to lick them. He was terribly thirsty. For some time he had been too weak to do much more than lie in the corner, growing feebler every day. Every day he had tried to get up and walk a little, to clear his head, but it had been more difficult with each attempt. The last time he had swayed to his feet he had suddenly been overcome with a strange light-headedness. He could remember laughing as his legs gave way beneath him. He had fallen across the wooden beam in the corner. Now he could feel the sore swollen place throbbing on the side of his jaw where his face had struck the beam.

He must have water. He was too weak to stand. He hunched himself up on all fours and crawled in the direction of the pipe. His shaking hands could no longer lift the basin. He lowered his head and lapped from the dish. He drank and drank, paused and drank again. Then he sat back on his knees to rest, letting his head fall forward and his hands trail limply on the floor. The bee was still thudding in his head:

babaBUMbum! babaBUMbum! babaBUM, babaBUM, babaBUMbum!

The mosquito crooned:

ooa-ooa, ooa-ooa!

Ham opened his eyes and stared into the dark. It was the "Hallelujah Chorus." Somewhere over his head they were playing and singing Handel's "Hallelujah Chorus."

Feebly Ham picked up the brick that lay beside the pipe.

221

It would be the last time. Lifting the heavy brick took the last ounce of his strength. It had been a kind of miracle that the thread of his life had spun out so far, that he had lasted so long in the dark underground. But now he could feel the thread trailing off into nothingness. It had spun itself out. Clumsily, fumbling at the brick, dropping it and picking it up again, Ham began pounding the timpani accompaniment to the "Hallelujah Chorus":

bingbingBANGbing! bingbingBANGbing!
bingbingBANG, bingbingBANG, bingbingBANGbing!

Chapter Forty-three

Vick dropped her arms, and the last *Hallelujah* rang in the air. There was a minute of quiet before the applause began, but then it was another great assaulting noise. Vick stood aside as the soloists brushed past her, hurrying off the stage through a narrow passage between crowded rows of violins, and then she ran after them. Mrs. Esterhazy had taught them how to do it proudly ("Up zuh head, up zuh boozum"). Then Vick strode back and swept her arms at the chorus, at the orchestra, at Rosie Bell. She flung out her hands at the audience, to tell them to applaud themselves. She ran off and came in again with the soloists. Safely out in the hall for the third time, she shook her head at Betsy, who was ready to plunge forward again. Enough was enough. "Vonderfool," said Mrs. Esterhazy, throwing her arms around Vick. "You were great," said Vick. "You were all just great." Betsy threw herself at Tim, at Mrs. Esterhazy, at Vick, at Mr. Proctor. They were all flushed with triumph. But Vick was keyed to so high a pitch she didn't trust herself. She would cry, or laugh. She would laugh too hard. She had to get away.

The second intermission was going to be a long one, long enough for President Cheever to unveil the bronze tablet behind the curtain on the wall. In a moment the place would be crowded. People would be packed together on the staircases at either end, looking on. Where could she go?

Mr. Crawley's office. Of course. It was just right. There was even a sofa in Mr. Crawley's office where she could rest, where she could force her rushing brain to slow down. Somehow she had to be ready for *Messiah*, Part Three. Part Three was serene and contemplative, with choruses of thanksgiving and arias rejoicing in redemption. Vick was feeling anything but serene and contemplative. She would just lie down on Mr. Crawley's sofa and try to pull herself together. She pulled the key out of the neck of her dress and opened Mr. Crawley's door. Quickly she closed it on the rising hubbub in the hall, clawed open the inner door, and felt her way in the dark to the sofa against the wall.

The radiator was knocking.

She lay down on the sofa. Her body was still shaking with the rhythms of the "Hallelujah Chorus." She forced herself to close her eyes, to unharness the stringy tensions in her arms and legs. Outside the door she could hear the voice of President Cheever, beginning his presentation. ". . . to the memory of the man who made the walls of this building echo with the music of the masters . . ." Vick stuffed her fingers in her ears. What did he know about Ham Dow? What did he know about Ham's music? Nothing. Nothing at all. For President Cheever, Ham was dead. But here in the dark, right here in her head, he was alive.

It was no use. She couldn't shut out the sound of Cheever's voice. She couldn't rid herself of the tremendous pulsing beat of the "Hallelujah Chorus." She couldn't shut out the sound of the knocking radiator. Vick sat up impatiently and lay down on her left side. Even the radiator seemed to be knocking with the rhythms that were shaking her from head to foot.

bingbingBANGbing! bingbingBANGbing!

It was ridiculous. Vick cursed the radiator and turned over on her right side.

bingbingBANG, bingbingBANG, bingbingBANGbing!

She sat up.

BANG bingbangbing! BANG bingbangbing!
bingbingBANGbing! bingbingBANGbing!
bingBANG bing BANG, BANG!

"Oh, dear God," breathed Vick.

She stood up, blundered across the floor, turned on the light, and stared across the room at the pipe rising in the corner of the wall.

The pipe was knocking with the rhythm of the "Hallelujah Chorus."

It stopped.

Had she dreamt it? With trembling hands, Vick pulled off her shoe and approached the pipe slowly, reverently, as if it were alive. For a moment she held her shoe poised beside the pipe, hesitating, and then she began pounding.

bingbingBANGbing! bingbingBANGbing! bingbingBANG,
bingbingBANG, bingbingBANGbing!

She dropped her arm and stared at the pipe. Did it hear? Was it listening?

The pipe was silent.

Vick's shoulders sagged. She turned away and dropped her shoe. Oh, what an idiot she was. Oh, why couldn't she lie down and get some rest? The blood was still rushing through her head. The noise outside was worse than ever. The President had finished his speech, and now everyone was clapping. He must have pulled the string of the curtain and displayed the bronze tablet. The dumb stupid idiotic tablet.

The *Hallelujahs* began again in the pipe.

> *BANG bingbangbing! BANG bingbangbing!*
> *bingbingBANGbing! bingbingBANGbing!*
> *bing BANG bing BANG, BANG!*

Vick whirled around and dropped to her knees on the floor. She snatched up her shoe and struck the pipe. *For the Lord God Omnipotent reigneth:*

> *BANG BANG BANG BANGbingBANGbingBANG BANG*
> *BANG!*

Then she sat back on her heels and waited for the pipe to take its turn.

But it was pausing again. It seemed to be considering, thinking. When it began again she was puzzled. It should have continued with the *Hallelujahs* once again. But it didn't. It was rattling in an unfamiliar rhythm, hasty and unclear. The pattern was repeated over and over. It was dying away. It was only a fluttering in the pipe. And then she understood.

> *bingbingbing BANGBANGBANG bingbingbing!*
> *bingbingbing BANGBANGBANG bingbingbing!*

There was no doubt about it any more. It was Ham, calling for help. It was Ham at last. Tears welled up in Vick's eyes. She sobbed aloud, "It's all right, Ham. It's all right. We're coming, we're coming." She gave the pipe three comforting final mighty blows, and rose to her feet and stumbled across the room to the door, pulling on her shoe. She must find Homer Kelly. She must find Homer right away.

But outside the door in the high corridor the crowd was thick. Someone touched her arm, put something in her hand. Shiny round glasses goggled at her. A man in a white sheet was leaning over her, speaking in her ear. "Did you know that Jesus Christ has been reborn?" Behind the man in the white sheet the President of Harvard was pressing forward, attended by important-looking people, all milling along in a thick crush, pushing in the direction of the doors of Sanders Theatre.

And then Vick saw Homer. He was moving along with the rest, shoulder to shoulder with Charley Flynn, and Charley was talking to him, but Homer was paying no attention to Charley, he was looking back at Vick over the heads of the man in the white sheet and the President of Harvard. His face wore an expression of concern. It occurred to Vick that she must look wild, mad, bedraggled. She laughed. She threw her hands over her head and beckoned at him. Come, come. Come quickly.

He came. Charley Flynn came too. Rudely they pushed past President Cheever and knots and clusters of Overseers and Vice Presidents, and Homer grasped her by the arm. "Are you all right?" he said.

"Oh, Homer, listen." Vick could hardly speak. "It's Ham. He's still alive. He's down in the basement somewhere. He's been down there all along. He's knocking on the pipe. I can hear it in Mr. Crawley's office." She tugged at Homer. She was all elbows and shoulders. She dragged Homer and Charley Flynn past a protesting President Cheever into Mr. Crawley's office. She slammed the door and took off her shoe and gave the pipe a mighty whack. "Sssshhh, now, listen," said Vick. "Just listen."

The pipe began knocking again. Rattling faintly.

Charley Flynn jerked his head up. "SOS," he said quickly.

Homer took a deep breath and closed his eyes. "So it is, by God."

"I told you. I told you." Vick clawed at her hair. She smoothed her dress. She pulled her shoe back on. She ran out the door.

The memorial corridor was empty again, except for a tall woman in a red cloak guarding the south door. Through the windows in the doors of Sanders Theatre Vick could see the audience on the benches. They were settled down. They were waiting for her. She smiled at the woman in the red cloak, threw back her shoulders, tossed her hair, and marched back into the theatre, while everyone clapped and then stopped clapping and

227

sat back to listen, and the orchestra picked up its instruments, and the chorus stood quietly waiting at the rear of the stage.

Homer would know what to do. She would leave it up to Homer and Charley Flynn. Vick picked up her stick and cast all her attention upon the score in front of her. She nodded at Betsy. Betsy stood up and lifted her music and began to sing, *I know that my redeemer liveth.*

Chapter Forty-four

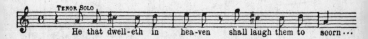

TENOR SOLO

He that dwell-eth in hea-ven shall laugh them to scorn ···

In the vestibule outside the men's room, a white shape flapped up at him from the doorway to the great hall. It was carrying a satchel. "Sir, would you like a pamphlet?"

No, no. He brushed the pamphlet aside.

"But I do think you should know. It is terribly important. Jesus Christ has returned to earth. He stands before you in the flesh."

"Go away. Get out of here. Take that thing off, and get out."

"Take it off? But it is Christ's seamless garment." The madman dropped his satchel and jerked at the sheet. He pulled it off and displayed it back and front. The sheet had no seams, that was true. Only hems, and a label in one corner: *Wamsutta Percale.*

"Get away from me. Go on. Get out of my way."

The madman dropped the sheet and picked up the satchel. "But I must hand out my pamphlets. I must proclaim my coming to the world."

"You heard what I said. Get out of the building."

"Not until I distribute my pamphlets. They are of such tre-

mendous significance, you see, to the whole world." The crazy
fool began tossing pamphlets in the air as if he were feeding
pigeons. He walked away in a flutter of flying pamphlets, leaving his white seamless garment behind him on the floor.

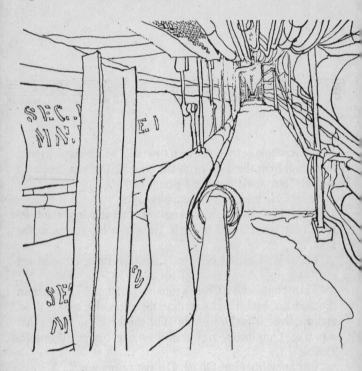

Chapter Forty-five

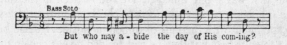

But who may a - bide the day of His com-ing?

Tinker entered the tunnel through the door in the basement of Langdell Hall. He had kept the key to the door ever since the Kissinger episode, ever since that time during the war in Vietnam when Kissinger had come to Harvard to speak in the Law School. Some of the more hostile undergraduates and Law School students had been waiting outside Langdell Hall, howling for Kissinger's hide. So he had conducted the great man into the building by way of the tunnel.

They had simply finessed the encounter. It had been a perfect example of his favorite maxim, *Economy of means for maximum effect.* And during the walk underground, as they had strolled along side by side, he had entertained Kissinger with the story of the occasion in his own life when that maxim had proved its enormous effectiveness, way back during World War II, during the Battle of the Bulge.

"There were only three of us left, you see, sir, out of the entire 325th Engineer Combat Team, and all we had left in the way of ordnance was a couple of satchel charges, and yet the 325th had been given the task of blowing up a bridge over the Meuse in the face of the advancing German army. Well, sir, the other two men said it couldn't be done, but I was determined to carry out our mission. I took one look at the bridge, and I knew what to do. It was a lift bridge, you see, sir, and it had this tiny little control tower. So we simply forced our way into the control tower, lifted the bridge, left our entire cache of explosives in the tower, and blew up the tower. The entire bridge remained in perfect order, you see, sir, but the German army was faced with a little problem. The bridge was up and not down. Do you see?"

And Kissinger had been impressed, you could see that.

But that was a long time ago. He hadn't been in the tunnel since. This time he was just going to check up on the success of his experiment with the tank of carbon monoxide. He had been about to go to bed, but then he had decided he just couldn't rest until he knew whether or not the situation was under control. Jim was taking it so badly. He was beside himself. It was a thousand pities he had ever found out that Dow had not after all been killed in the explosion. Damn that interfering fool Homer Kelly. There had been no need at all for Jim to know that the permanent removal of Ham Dow had been somewhat delayed. What mattered, after all, was that the thing should be accomplished. And accomplished it would be. He would see to that.

This was the time to make sure. Everybody in the building would be in Sanders Theatre. He would be able to pull those boards out of the way again and listen for signs of life behind the door without fear of interruption. If there was no sign of life, then all well and good. He would go home to bed and forget the whole miserable episode. Dow's body would come to light sometime in the spring, when some workman discovered it during the reconstruction of those basement rooms. Then, of course, there would be general shock and dismay, but it would be no concern of his. However, if, in spite of everything, it was apparent that the man was still alive, it would be necessary to take action at once. And this time there would be no mistake. That thug from Philadelphia had made a mess of the job, and blown himself up for his pains. Well, after all, one should have remembered that if one wanted a thing well done one must do it oneself. In a case of this kind it was by far the safest plan. The little control mechanism was in his pocket. It was a very simple affair. He would go back home immediately, say good night to his housekeeper, climb into bed, and then press the button in the small hours of the morning.

Economy of means. It had been so simple. It hadn't been necessary to bring in tremendous quantities of explosive material. He had simply applied his forces where they would do the most good, at the foundations of the tower. The whole building would fall in upon itself. Gravity would do the work.

Tinker quickened his pace. The light bulbs in the ceiling stretched on and on, disappearing around the curve. The distant perspective was strange and dreamlike.

Gravity! Gravity would do the work! He had figured it out, starting with the weight of a single brick, calculating the number of bricks in walls that were, say, two feet thick and forty feet wide and one hundred and sixty feet high. A wild approximation, but close enough. It came to ten thousand tons. Ten thousand tons of brick would fall toward the center of the earth in obedience to the law of gravitation. Ten thousand tons of brick would take care of Ham Dow. And it would take care of the threat to the Harvard community that was implicit in Dow's continued existence. He would be perishing in a good cause. Tinker smiled to himself as he approached the exit from the tunnel into the basement of Memorial Hall. He said it aloud. *"Moritur pro suo collegio!"*

Chapter Forty-six

TENOR SOLO

But Thou didst not leave His soul in hell · · ·

What they needed, of course, was a wrecking bar. They had found a small tool kit in Mr. Crawley's closet, but it contained no wrecking bar. Charley pried at the edges of the boards with a claw hammer, lifting the nails, hammering the boards down again to free the nailheads, jerking the nails out with the claw of the hammer. Homer stood to the side, getting in the way, trying to tear at the other ends of the boards with his bare hands.

"That's enough, I think," said Charley. "See if you can get through. Here, wait a minute, I'll do one more. Look, get that wire out of the way. What's that wire doing there? Good for you. If you can get through that little hole, so can I."

They crawled through the opening. "I can't see a thing," said Homer.

"Maybe there's a light switch," said Charley. "Yes, here it is."

Light flooded the sub-basement. And in that instant they beheld the door to Ham's prison. It faced them at the foot of the short flight of stairs. The other rooms were a rubble of fallen walls and broken timbers littered with chunks of marble from the floor of the transept up above. A mountain of debris had been shoveled to this end of the short corridor. It was piled in front of the one remaining door. Only the top of the door was visible. The wooden panels were shaking in the doorframe.

Homer stumbled after Charley down the stairs. He was laughing, waving his arms. "The fine-tooth comb," he said. "So much for the fine-tooth comb."

They tore at the debris. They picked up chunks of concrete and brick and hurled them aside. They were shouting at Ham, saying they knew not what, that they would have him out in no time, that he would be out of that goddamned hole in half a sec. They scooped up handfuls of plaster dust and flung it behind them. They kicked at piles of brick. They dug and scrabbled and shoved their way down to the doorknob. Homer tried to turn it. It wouldn't turn. Maybe it was caked with plaster dust. Maybe the door was locked. Charley snatched up more handfuls of clotted plaster. Homer slapped his pockets for another one of Mr. Crawley's keys. He found one and stuck it into the lock and turned it. He tried the knob. It turned easily in his hand. The door was unlocked. He pressed against it with his shoulder. But something was holding the door shut. The door panels had stopped shaking. He raked his fingers through the rubble once again.

"What do you think you're doing?"

Homer looked up. Charley looked up. Sloan Tinker was standing at the top of the stairs. Homer could see at once that he was the man with the broom. He was not holding a broom now. There was something else in his hand, something small. He was holding it carefully, like a precious dish. "How did you get in?" said Homer.

"I must ask you to leave this area at once," said Tinker. "It has been officially closed off. It is out of bounds. It is highly dangerous."

And then Homer remembered an entrance where they had failed to post a guard. "The tunnel," he said, looking at Charley Flynn. "What a fool. I forgot the entrance to the tunnel." He looked back up at Tinker. "It was the tunnel, wasn't it? You came in by way of the tunnel."

Tinker gestured with the thing in his hand. "I tell you, you are to leave at once. This part of the building is scheduled for reconstruction. It is in a dangerous condition. Come out of there immediately."

The thing in Tinker's hand was a little wireless contraption. Homer recognized it, and he cursed himself for being twice a fool. It was a little control panel of the kind that makes a model airplane dip and soar or land gently in a field. They had been wrong about the man, altogether wrong. He had not been poisoning the ventilating system. He had been running a loop of electric cable around the entire foundation of the tower.

"Did you say reconstruction?" said Homer. "Scheduled for reconstruction? Or do you mean demolition?" He picked up a brick and threw it at the man at the top of the stairs. His aim was wild. Charley's was better. Charley heaved up from the floor a lump of bricks embedded in concrete the size of his head. He hurled it at Tinker. Tinker fell backward with a cry, sprawling on his back halfway down the stairs.

And then the room went dark. A pale shape was bending over Tinker, flapping down above him like a shroud. "Take it, you fool," cried Tinker, "take it, take it. Do you know what it is? Go on, take it."

The dim white shape was gone again, flipflopping through the gap in the boarded entry at the top of the stairs.

"After him," shouted Homer. "He'll blow us all to kingdom come. It's that crazy Freddy Fulsom."

Chapter Forty-seven

TENOR SOLO

...Thou shalt dash them in pieces like a pot- - - - - - - - ter's ves - sel...

They had been careless fools. They had left all the doors open when they had finished exploring the tower that afternoon. Freddy Fulsom was in the tower. He had run up the stairs to the balcony, as if he were heading for his old room, and then he must have seen the dark orifices of the open doors at the summit of the ceiling. One of the doors was swaying. The crazy half-wit was climbing all the way up into the tower.

"Freddy, come down," shouted Homer. His voice was hoarse. He was exhausted. He stumbled slowly up the last flight of stairs, taking his time. "Oh, come on, Freddy. It's not time yet for the end of the world. Not now. You're not supposed to come in glory now. Why don't you just come on down?"

Where were the guards at the west doors of the building? They were nowhere in sight. They must be waiting out of doors on the stone porch in the cold. And where was Charley Flynn? Charley had started after Homer. He had followed him through the opening in the boarded doorway, but he had fallen behind. He was gone. Homer was dogging the footsteps of an irresponsible fool or a homicidal maniac all by himself. Timidly he stepped into the dark emptiness of the turret room at the top of the stairs, leaving behind him the huge lighted volume of the great hall, and began climbing from one turret room to the next, feeling his way, aware of a prickling sensation on the surface of his skin and a feathery feeling in his chest. It was all very well to chase a lunatic through brightly lighted corridors, but it was another thing entirely to blunder after him in dark attics in total blindness. At any moment Homer expected to be fallen upon by a madman with destruction in his hand. He felt his way along the narrow boardwalk in the direction of the wooden bridge across the great open space over the vaults, then stood for a moment with his hand on the railing. The full moon was shining somewhere in the sky beyond the high south window. Homer was reluctant to come out of the darkness into the bright cluttered space of the tower, where he could be seen, but where he himself could not see into the shadows behind the shiny surfaces of the ventilating shafts. Through a hole in the east wall he could hear the chorus in Sanders Theatre. Soft voices were drifting solemnly out of the hole, drawing out long grieving notes in a rising scale—*Since by man came death.*

Homer began walking heavily along the shaking catwalk, looking over the railing at the shadowy crevasses of the wooden vaults below. He told himself he was an imbecile to accompany this madman, to climb up and out so far on the topmost fractured limb of the shattered tree of his lunacy. But he kept going in spite of himself. He set his hand on the railing of the steep ladder stair on the east wall and began to climb, feeling the whole framework of the stairway spring and shiver beneath his feet. The hushed voices of the chorus floated through the hole in the wall: *As in Adam all die.*

Yes, there was Freddy, climbing above him in his white sheet, moving more and more slowly. Poor crazy Freddy. He must be tired too.

It was no good. It was no good at all. It was altogether grotesque. It was like some evil sort of nightmare, that he should find himself climbing higher and higher in the dark, that he should be trapped in a corner like a common criminal. The man in the white sheet paused, looked down, and then started climbing again, nearly catching his foot in his encumbering garment. He had seen the white sheet lying on the floor. He had picked it up and thrown it over himself in the first moment of his panic, like a child hiding his face in order to become invisible. Because invisibility was his due. It was unthinkable that he should be seen. But he had been overwhelmed by a furious impatience, by the need to find out for himself if what the girl had said was true. "Oh, yes," Tinker had said, "there's been a hitch. It's being attended to. Just trust me." Trust him! Trust Tinker! But he had had nothing to do with Tinker! It was Tinker's doing, not his!

He had fled. *Run, run, and cover your head.* He would have run to the ends of the earth. But instead he had been pursued by this ruffian, and it had been *dodge, twist and dodge, dodge and turn,* until now at last he found himself climbing this perilous ladder in the dark toward no escape, no hiding place at all.

The matter was not of his doing! He had made a decision, that was all. At a particular moment a long time ago he had made a certain decision, and it had been the only right course, the only possible resolution of the issue for the good of the institution. It had been the kind of difficult judgment that one had to make from time to time, a man in his position. A strong measure was absolutely necessary. It was required by circumstance. It was the only proper solution. After all, he was not himself a man of action. He had never pretended to be a man of action. He had always looked upon his task as one of perceiving the issues, of leaning slightly in this direction or that, because the whole future of the university depended on the direction in which he tentatively set his foot. It was entirely a matter of vision, of having the foresight to guess the probable shapes looming beyond this alternative or that. And this possible outcome had seemed to him so dangerous, so menacing. He had agonized over it with Tinker. They had tried in every traditional way to put a stop to it. But, one by one, the customary means had failed. The moment had come at last when no other course had been left to them. And therefore it had been necessary for him—sole guardian as he seemed to have become of the precious thing he had inherited, whose stewardship had been so universally abandoned by almost everyone else—to do something drastic. He had recognized the moment, he had made the decision, and then he had turned the matter over to Tinker, as was only correct. It was the kind of delegation of duty that was perfectly routine, that came up a dozen times a day. And Tinker had merely said, "Good. I'll see to it," and slapped the table and walked out of the office. Nothing more had been said. They had never discussed it further. Tinker had gone out and done what had to be done.

But unfortunately he had failed.

So it was Tinker's fault. Tinker had been entrusted with a matter of the gravest importance, but Tinker had proven untrustworthy. The job had been bungled from beginning to end.

Once again he pulled his awkward garment out of the way. He took a last cautious step upward. There was a trap door over his head. He pushed at it feebly with his free hand. The trap door was locked. He could go no farther. Below him he could hear that barbarian blundering up the ladder after him. Homer Kelly was another one of them, just one more of the rabble that had begun to close in from every side.

There was no way out. He had been driven into a corner. Slowly he turned around on the steep open stairway, grasping the railing with his right hand, shifting his feet one at a time, until his back was braced and he could look down at the man ascending below him. Carefully he shifted the object in his left hand to his right, and held it out into the void over Homer Kelly's head.

It was not Freddy Fulsom at the top of the ladder. Looking upward as he climbed, Homer could see the man crouched above him. The jag ends of the sheet drooped down like the wings of an albino bat. It was not Freddy. And then the moon slipped across the flat brick face of the tower and reached the window in the south wall and sent a long finger pointing past the giant ventilating shaft to touch the face of the man who was hunched on the top of the ladder with his back pushed up against the trap door. At the summit of the tower his robe was dazzling in the moonlight. He squatted there like a caricature of an angel at the pinnacle of a cathedral. He had removed himself as far as it was humanly possible from Ham Dow at the bottom, from the brute beast who had refused to perish in his subterranean cave.

But when the man at the top of the ladder spoke, it was not of angels or beasts. He reached his hand down to Homer as if to hand him something, and addressed him.

At the top of so many ladders, Homer felt dizzy and light-headed. In a careless trance he reached up obediently and took the thing. "What did you say?" he said.

"I said, he rolled away the stone." And then the man in the white sheet leaned forward and dropped into the air, falling away from Homer. The tumbling white shape plummeted, grazing the iron side of the ventilating shaft in the center of the tower, sliding down its vertical flank, and then falling perfectly, headfirst, into the very center of the tapering vault below.

It was the northernmost vault of the five that crowned the high memorial corridor. Homer had often thought of the compartments of the arching wooden ceiling as treetops, their towering ribs meeting like the branches of trees in a forest. But now, looking down at the dark cavity of the inverted vault below him, he could see again that it was like an immense empty wastebasket for sandwich wrappers and paper coffee cups, for a president of Harvard who had thrown himself from the top of the chain of being.

Chapter Forty-eight

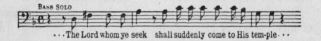

···The Lord whom ye seek   shall suddenly come to His tem-ple···

Ham had lost consciousness again. He woke to find himself slumped against the door. Had he dreamt it, the hammering and the shouting on the other side? He dropped his head back and stared at the top of the door. The line of light was gone. He sank his face in his hands and rubbed his eyes. His fainting brain had played on him one final savage trick. Then he fumbled at the handle of the door. In his dream, the knob had turned. It turned again. It turned all the way around. Slowly he dragged his haunches an inch away from the door and pulled.

The door opened.

Mary Kelly had given up her place in the chorus to sit halfway down the stairs inside the basement entrance beside the south door. She was falling asleep. She had been sitting in one position with her head against the railing for two hours. What if she were to stretch out on the floor at the top of the stairs and take a nap? If anyone came in, if anyone tried to step over her, going up or down, she would wake up. She shook her drowsy head and stood up and stretched, and then she stopped with her arms over her head.

"Oh, Ham," she said, "it's you."

She said nothing more. She ran down to the man who had fallen into a huddle of rags along the wall at the bottom of the stairs. He was trying to get up. She helped him to his feet, and then slowly they worked their way up the stairs and out of doors. Ham lifted his head and gulped in drafts of cold night air.

"Who's that?" said Julia Chamberlain sharply, staring down at them from the south door. "Is that you, Mary?"

"It's Ham," said Mary softly. "Help me. You hold him on the other side."

"Good God," said Julia. She ran down the steps and took his arm and together they half guided and half carried him inside. "An ambulance," said Julia firmly. "We'll just put him down in that chair and I'll call an ambulance."

Ham tried to speak up and say no, but he was shaken by a palsy of trembling and nothing would come out. He shook his head and tried to shuffle forward by himself. From Sanders Theatre he could hear Rosie Bell's trumpet trilling and flourishing. Mary shrugged her shoulders at Julia, and together, two tall strong women, they bore him between them into Sanders Theatre. With Julia at one elbow and Mary at the other, Ham stood in the amber air looking up at the pale intent face of Vick, who was beating a majestic pattern of three, *pomposo, ma non allegro,* smiling at Rosie Bell, nodding to Mr. Proctor, and now Mr. Proctor was standing, closing his eyes, opening his mouth to sing the first words of his last triumphant aria.

The audience saw Ham first, and a few of them shouted and rose in their seats. The basses and altos were standing on the right side of the stage, and they all began surging forward, blundering between the chairs and music stands of the second violins. Mrs. Esterhazy was screaming. And at last Vick glanced around to see what was going on, and saw Ham's face turned up to her, and she dropped her arms and burst into sobs. With one swift motion Jack Fox and Tim Swegle reached for her and lowered her gently to the floor. Only Mr. Proctor kept his eyes firmly shut. *The trumpet shall sound,* sang Mr. Proctor, *and the dead shall be rais'd incorruptible.*

Chapter Forty-nine

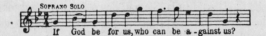

SOPRANO SOLO

If God be for us, who can be a-gainst us?

The reading room of the Faculty Club was the kind of place where Homer felt ill at ease. The slightly stuffy air of quiet splendor made him want to upset little trays of sherry and say unspeakable things at the top of his voice. He huddled beside his wife at one end of a sofa. But before long he found himself warming and expanding in the comfortable presence of Julia Chamberlain, so that when he dropped his little glass it was only a typical blunder rather than an act of defiance and rebellion. "Whoops, there I go again." Homer sprang to his feet and swabbed at the rug with a paper napkin.

"Oh, Homer, you poor clod," said Mary.

Julia laughed and summoned another glass.

"Now look here, Julia," said Homer, sitting down again. "The only thing that still puzzles me about this whole thing is the connection between Dow and Cheever. I mean, I figured it out about Cheever. You people were pulling your forces together two years ago to get rid of Cheever, isn't that right? But then you were going to dump Ham Dow too. Whatever for?"

"We were going to what?" Julia looked at Homer in surprise. "What makes you think we were going to dump Ham Dow?"

"Oh, you know, Julia," said Homer. "It was at that emergency meeting of the Corporation and the Board of Overseers, the day of the Yale game. I was hanging around there in the hall, eavesdropping, remember? I heard you in there, all of you. I heard you say, if only Harvard had got rid of Ham in time, then he never would have been blown up, or words to that effect."

Julia laughed again, and slapped her glass down on the table. "That's what happens, Homer, dear, to people who listen at keyholes. They don't get the whole story, you see. They don't see it right out plain on the table. We weren't going to get Ham Dow out of Memorial Hall by firing him. The faculty does all the hiring and firing. We were going to get him out of there by promoting him."

"Promoting him?"

"Promoting him as far as we could promote anybody. Well, of course, we couldn't do it by ourselves. There would have had to

be a big search committee, and a long process, with everybody getting a whack at nominating somebody, and then, of course, it would have been up to the Corporation to make the final decision. But two years ago there was a consensus of opinion among the Fellows, and most of us Overseers felt the same way, that we should get rid of James Cheever and put somebody an awful lot like Ham Dow in his place. Sssssshhh, sssshh—it wasn't ever supposed to be common knowledge."

"You wanted to make Ham Dow the President of Harvard? Jee-*eee*sus." Homer giggled at Julia and tried to take it in. "So that's it. Ham was a personal threat to Cheever's job. And Cheever knew it. And Tinker too. Right? I knew there was some reason they hated his guts."

"Oh, yes, Tinker too. Tinker was Jim's man, of course. Two years ago he was the big voice of opposition when we were all so determined to ask for Jim's resignation. I mean, the first time. Oh, we tried to be discreet about the whole thing, but Ham's name kept right on coming up as somebody who could put the place back together again if we asked for Jim's resignation. We didn't discuss the matter in front of Jim. We weren't far enough along for that. But of course Tinker was always there, and he passed everything along to Jim, naturally. So I suppose it was natural that Jim and Tinker would feel that way about Ham. That they feared and hated him, I mean. You can't blame Jim. It wasn't personal, really. I know that. He really did think Ham would destroy the place. Harvard, I mean. You know. He thought Ham would change the whole character of the university and destroy all it had stood for in the past. Oh, he meant well, he really did. I know he did."

"So it was only Tinker who supported him?" said Mary. "The others were all for forcing Cheever's resignation?"

"All of them. All of them except Tinker."

"But then why didn't it go through? Two years ago, I mean, when it came up for the first time."

"Oh, it was Tinker again. Tinker can be pretty eloquent. He

persuaded two or three of the Fellows and some of the older members of the Board of Overseers to wait awhile, to think it over, before doing anything so unheard of as asking for the resignation of a president of Harvard."

"After all," said Homer, "it wasn't as if he were an Antipedobaptist, or anything like that."

"What?" said Julia. "Oh, you mean like President Dunster. That's right. And Increase Mather. There haven't been many enforced resignations of Harvard presidents in three hundred and fifty years. That's a long time. So the Fellows finally agreed they would wait awhile, and in the meantime we would all speak to Jim and make it very clear to him about the necessity for a broader, more generous kind of spirit, for accepting a majority vote with good grace, and he wasn't to go behind people's backs any more in a foolish effort to get what he wanted. Well, anyway, the upshot was, we waited around for the transformation to take place. Only it didn't. That Decorative Arts Building of his was the last straw. A Curator for Porcelain and another one for Objects of Silver and Gold. We all got sick to our stomachs. I mean, it just made you want to smash something. You know, like a Ming vahz or something." Julia laughed her great laugh. Then she straightened her big face and leaned forward grimly and stared at the table. "So we were gathering our forces again. I snatched the opportunity and then *we* met behind *his* back, for a change. Not something we would normally ever dream of doing. But we'd been driven too far. And he could see the handwriting on the wall. They knew what was coming, Cheever and Tinker."

"So Tinker hired the man from Philadelphia," said Mary softly.

"Yes, I suppose they decided it was the only thing left. Of course, they were fools to think the removal of one man would make any difference."

"But what went wrong? Why didn't it work? Oh, I know your theory, Homer, about the clocks being ten minutes slow, and how the man from Philadelphia forgot his wrist watch. But I really don't see what he was doing on the scene at all. Why didn't he just set the thing to go off at a certain time and go back to Philadelphia?"

"Because he had to be sure the job got done. Tinker told me. If Dow didn't get blown up, the hired killer didn't get his hundred thousand in small bills. The money came from some discretionary fund of Cheever's. I don't know who the alumnus was who supplied Cheever's office with money like that. Maybe they'll squeeze that information out of Tinker, although I don't suppose there was anything illegal about that kind of gift."

"But how did the hired accomplice manage to blow himself up?" said Julia. "Pretty clumsy of him, if you ask me."

"It was Ham's fault," said Homer. "Ham didn't cooperate. I saw Ham this morning in the hospital. He told me it all began coming back to him, little by little, there in the dark in that little room in the basement. There had been some stranger. Just before the explosion he had been talking to a stranger. A big man. A big fat man. A perfect stranger. Ham was supposed to meet Cheever in the memorial transept at the entrance to the great hall at eleven-thirty. They were going to have lunch in some hotel. Tinker had called Ham and made the appointment on Cheever's behalf. So Ham decided to wait for Cheever outside in the sunshine, because it was a nice day. And then this stranger came gasping up the steps and dragged him back indoors, saying Cheever would be there any minute, and then the guy rushed off again, and then, of course, Ham drifted cheerfully out onto the steps again, and this poor guy rushed back again, sweating and fuming, and tried to jockey him into position again, only his clock mechanism went off ten minutes sooner than he expected it would, because he was judging the time by the new tower clocks, and the clocks were wrong. The damn thing went off and killed him and dropped Ham into the cellar."

"But I still don't understand why Tinker— I mean, everybody thought the dead man was Ham," said Mary. "So I should think

Cheever and Tinker would have been satisfied. What was Tinker doing later on, hanging around Memorial Hall the way he was, pretending to be a janitor?"

"Oh, Cheever was satisfied, all right," said Homer. "But not Sloan Tinker. I talked to Tinker yesterday. He was perfectly frank and open about the whole thing. Seemed resigned to his fate. Fortunes of war, you know the kind of thing. Anyway, he told me he had had an appointment with the man from Philadelphia for one o'clock. The man was supposed to show up and collect his fee. But he never came. So Tinker began to worry. He went over there to Memorial Hall with Cheever on an official expedition of administrative concern, and then while Cheever was pulling his chin and staring at the hole in the floor and falling on his face in the blood and turning green, Tinker was looking under the sheet. And then he saw that the blackened headless remains could belong to the man from Philadelphia just as well as they could to Ham Dow. And he began to fret. Only he didn't tell Cheever. Cheever thought Harvard was rid of its incubus at last. But poor Tinker was left with the whole thing to do over again. And of course the burning question was, where in the name of God was Dow? It haunted him, day and night. He began to pick at his coverlet and gnaw at his blanket. He began to hang around the building. At first he thought Ham might be hiding out in the basement along with all of those Rats of his. But then one day he wandered into Crawley's office and heard him calling for help by knocking on the pipe. And then he knew what had happened."

"You know, it seems awfully strange to me," said Julia, "that nobody in Memorial Hall recognized Sloan Tinker. I mean, you say he was walking around in plain sight all the time. He wasn't even wearing false whiskers or anything like that. Why didn't somebody say, 'Why, Mr. Tinker, whatever are you doing with that mop and that bucket of dirty water?'"

"It's just a matter of expectation," said Homer. "If you're used to seeing a man in a business suit behind a desk, you just don't expect to find him pushing a broom. Vice presidents of Harvard don't push brooms in the basements of university buildings. And it works the other way around. Old broom-pushers don't guide the planets in their courses. Not in this university. And of course he fooled me too. I kick myself for not even trying to see him face to face. Well, I'm black and blue from kicking myself about one thing or another."

Mary Kelly put her hands to her head. "Oh, Homer, it really sickens me to remember how they went through all that debris down there, and didn't find Ham. How could they have missed him? They kept saying they had examined everything so carefully. I mean, they came up with tiny pieces of dynamite caps, but they missed Ham entirely. I just don't see how they could have made such an awful mistake."

"There were a few teeth missing from that fine-tooth comb," said Homer. "That was the trouble. And it just never occurred to any of us that they could have made a mistake. I asked McCurdy how it could have happened, and he said it wasn't his fault, *he* didn't look behind the door, it was supposed to be Tom that was going to look behind the door, and he asked Tom, and Tom said *he* didn't look behind the door, because Bert was supposed to look behind the door, and he asked Bert, and Bert said *he* didn't look behind the door, because somebody else said he'd already looked behind the door. And you know who it was? Only he didn't look behind the door either. He just said he did. Who do you think it was?" Homer looked drearily at Mary.

"I don't know, Homer. Who was it?"

"Crawley."

"Crawley!"

"Crawley. That vile, peevish, careless, dead letter Crawley."

"But—" Mary flapped her hands in horror. "Oh, Homer, there was Ham, right there on the other side of the door. You mean, because of Crawley, he was sealed up for almost two months, all that time without food or light or any hope of discovery, there in the dark? Oh, Crawley, Crawley."

"That's right. It was old creepy Crawley." Homer clenched his fist and pounded it on the table and quoted "The Man with the Hoe," dropping his voice an octave, ominous and dire:

> "Who loosened and let down this brutal jaw?
> Whose was the hand that slanted back this brow?
> What gulfs between him and the seraphim!

I mean, talk about bestial creatures snuffling about at the bottom of the great chain of being! Crawley is the bottom, the very bottom. And if Ham Dow hadn't been carrying around a lot of extra fat, he never would have made it. I asked the doctor this morning. He told me he'd seen people go for a year without eating, if they were terribly overweight. Only, of course, people like that are under supervision, and they're given vitamins and protein supplements. It was the protein that mattered most, he said. The body breaks down protein to get glucose. The brain can't get along without glucose."

"The brain," said Julia. "But does that mean . . . Homer, is he all right?"

"Oh, you bet. I talked to him. He was obviously his old self. Well, of course, I don't know what his old self was like. But I don't see how it could have been any better than the man I met this morning. And he told me he hadn't been entirely without protein because he had some candy in his pocket. Peanut brittle. The peanuts had a little protein and a little salt. The candy gave him a little sugar. It may have saved his life."

"Well, thank God, his ordeal is over." Julia reached into her bag and pulled out a copy of the Crimson. "Of course, things are never going to be the same again. Did you see this?" She held up the front page.

Mary leaned forward. "What is it? Some kind of map?"

"It's the tunnel. It's a map of the entire tunnel system under Harvard University. What are we going to do now? I ask you. We'll have people pouring into the tunnel from all over. Donald Maderna told me he's going to have to change every one of the locks on all those doors, just to be sure nobody but authorized people have the keys."

Homer reached for the paper and laughed at the picture of Assistant Professor Charles Flynn. "Look at Charley. That chase through the tunnel after Tinker, it's made him a hero. Poor old Charley; he told me he thought Tinker wasn't going to give him any more trouble, because he had just finished knocking him down with a brick. But then Tinker got up and threw Charley down the stairs and disappeared down the hall. Charley picked himself up and ran after him and then they had another tussle at the entrance to the tunnel, and Tinker got away again and tried to lose himself in the labyrinth of branching corridors down there. But he made a big mistake. He headed for the part of the tunnel that goes under Massachusetts Avenue with a little cart."

"A little cart?" said Mary. "You mean, under the street?"

"That's right. A little flatbed cart. Because of the subway. The tunnel is shallow under the street because the subway runs right underneath. So Tinker jumped on the cart and started hauling himself across with the rope. But good old Charley just pulled out his trusty pocket knife and cut the rope, and then he hauled the cart back hand over hand and nabbed him. Look at those head-lines, will you. They must be six inches high. CHEEVER DIES IN TOWER PLUNGE. ASSISTANT PROF TRACES ROUTE OF HEROIC CHASE."

"You know, Julia"—Mary laughed—"we thought coming to teach here might be a little bit tedious. I mean, to tell the truth, we thought the place might be too genteel and academic and refined for red-blooded people like us. We'd be bored, we thought, and want to go back home and do exciting things in Concord, like canoeing on the river and looking for pitcher plants in Gowing's swamp—staggering things like that. We never guessed we'd be in the middle of anything like this."

"Well, I don't know when things will ever quiet down," said Julia. "Our Search Committee is getting to work, looking for new candidates for president. Nominations are already pouring in.

252

Half of them are for Ham Dow. Of course, the fame of his sensational survival hasn't hurt his chances any. Oh, good heavens, that reminds me. Did you hear about our other tragedy? The news of what happened to President Cheever was too much for one of the Fellows, and the poor thing is gone."

"Oh, dear, not Mr. Bowditch?" said Homer.

"Oh, no! Mr. Bowditch is fine, just fine. It was the youngest Fellow, Pendleton Waterhouse. Pendleton apparently heard the news over his car radio, and he promptly stopped at a local bar and downed the first glass of liquor he had ever drunk in his life, and then on the way home he ran into a telephone pole."

"Good Lord."

"So they've got to appoint a new Fellow. It's not common knowledge yet, but I'll let you in on a secret, because I know who it's going to be."

"Who is it? We won't tell."

"Me. I don't know if I'm going to like it or not. Well, of course, it will strike a blow for womankind."

"Oh, Julia, congratulations," said Mary.

"Hail, Fellow—!" began Homer.

"Oh, shut up. It gives me a pain, it really does." Julia put both hands on her head and looked at them mournfully. "There's so much to do. The place is in an uproar. I don't know when we're going to get back to nice normal simple little problems like whether or not to replace the stained glass in Memorial Hall."

"Why, Julia Chamberlain, of *course* you're going to replace the stained glass in Memorial Hall!" Someone was planting a kiss on Julia's cheek, brushing Julia's forehead with a great furry hat.

Mary jumped up. "Oh, Miss Plankton, how nice to see you again."

Homer rose too and shook Miss Plankton's eager little outstretched hand.

"Oh, wasn't it *thrilling?*" said Miss Plankton. "Didn't we all just go *wild?*" She clasped her hands, then sat down firmly beside Julia Chamberlain. "Now, Julia, dear, do tell me, what's all this about the stained glass? I heard some horrid rumor about corrugated plastic. Dreadful! You wouldn't do that? Surely not! Oh, that would be perfectly frightful!"

"But, my dear Jane, the trouble is the same as always. You know. That damned stained glass costs two hundred dollars a square foot. That comes to three hundred thousand dollars altogether. That's what it would cost to reproduce every little fragment and lead it together and put it back up in the right place. And the powers that be have got their backs up about it. Nobody wants to raise three hundred thousand dollars for a useless expenditure like a couple of enormous old stained-glass windows. It's too bad, but that's the way it is."

Miss Plankton lifted her hands in dismay. "But, Julia, they were so beautiful! So red! So blue! Oh, the mystery, the splendor! Oh, how they always made me think of Chartres! Our grand tour back in 1932!" Miss Plankton's eyes shone with rapture. She snatched up her bag and tugged at the string. "I'll write an I.O.U. This very minute. You'll have a check for three hundred thousand dollars this afternoon. Why not?"

"But, Jane, dear, I can't ask you to do a thing like that. Not on the spur of the moment. I didn't mean that you should—"

But Miss Plankton, her face flushed with pleasure, was scribbling in a rumpled little notebook, tearing out a page, thrusting it at Julia. "There, now. That settles it. If it isn't enough, just let me know. Brother Wayland and I just made a killing. It was something about the way the apple tree in the back yard cast its shadow on the snow this morning. I just had a hunch. And then, you know what? The New England Cider Syndicate went up fifteen points."

Julia protested again, and tried to give the piece of paper back, but Jane Plankton put her hands behind her and giggled, and then Julia hugged her, and Miss Plankton trotted away, hallooing to a portly man who was coming in the door, taking off his coat.

Homer laughed and sat down again. "What an old darling. It must give her a lot of satisfaction to pretend to be a public benefactor like that, going around writing colossal I.O.U.'s. I only hope nobody ever tries to cash in on them. Then she'd be in terrible trouble, the poor old thing."

"Cash in on them?" said Julia Chamberlain. "You bet your life they cash in on them. When Jane Plankton says she made a killing, she means it. That's the Jane of Janeway and Everett, the most successful firm of investment people in Boston. Her two brothers have the know-how, Wayland and Everett Plankton. Jane has the intuition. You see that man she's with right now?"

Homer was dumbfounded. "Haven't I seen him before somewhere?"

"That's Eliot North. Treasurer of Harvard College. Eliot has lunch with Jane Plankton here every Friday. Of course, he depends on her two brothers for sturdy dependable blue-chip advice, but it's Jane's pixie audacity and derring-do that really count." Julia Chamberlain snapped her pocketbook shut on Jane Plankton's three-hundred-thousand-dollar I.O.U., while Homer with dropped jaw sat stiffly upright on the edge of the sofa.

"Upbow, Miss Plankton," cried Mary, collapsing backward.

"You bet your boots I'm going to cash in on it," said Julia Chamberlain.

Chapter Fifty

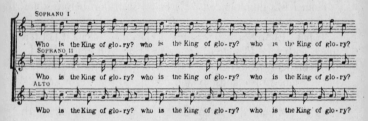

Ham was back. The word went up and down the basement corridors, and in and out of the nine doors. It flooded all over Mem Hall 201, where Homer was lecturing on the last day before the Christmas break. He threw up his hands and dismissed the class, because everybody was leaving anyway. They were all surging out of their seats and running out of the building and around to the north entry and in again, shouting a welcome. Homer went too, trailing Mrs. Esterhazy, who was pounding up the stairs carrying a tray of Viennese pastry she had manufactured by some kind of witchcraft in her room in the basement.

They found Ham leaning against the wall in the corridor with his arm around Vick. Jack Fox stood in the balcony over his head, playing a saxophone in triumphant screeches and blats. Betsy was singing at the top of her lungs.

"Shut up, everybody, shut *up. Quiet!*" shouted Tim.

There was a sudden silence, and then Ham made a deprecating

face, and they all laughed. Mr. Proctor poked him in the stomach. "Why, the poor man is nothing but skin and bone."

"Well, I was working on getting my stomach back," said Ham, "eating everything I could lay my hands on. But then Vick said she wouldn't have me unless I stayed thin. Keeps talking about my health. Good heavens, Emma, what's that? Sort of a choco-late-lemon-meringue-whipped-cream delight, is that it?"

Mrs. Esterhazy was holding a tray under his nose, beaming at him. "For you," she said. "I vork my fingers to zuh bone."

"Oh, Mrs. Esterhazy, that looks really incredibly delicious," said Vick. "Oh, Ham, go ahead, eat all you want. Any time Mrs. Esterhazy wants to give you something to eat, take it, take it! Oh, mmmmm, Mrs. Esterhazy, this is really just fabulous."

"Come on, everybody," said Ham, "pitch in. Put some in your pocket. You never know when one of Mrs. Esterhazy's little tidbits is going to save your life. What about Putzi and Siegfried, Emma? What mischief are they up to today?"

Mrs. Esterhazy frowned. "Zey are in school. Zuh city of Cambridge, zey made me put zem in school."

"Well, I'll tell you what I'll do. If I ever get to be President of Harvard, I'll pull a lot of strings and throw my weight around and get them admitted to the freshman class as child prodigies. How would you like that? Of course, I'm not at all sure I really want to be President of this place or not."

"Oh, I hope to *God* they pick somebody else," said Vick. "I don't know if I could stand it, being married to the President of Harvard. I mean, I'm still young. I've got my whole life ahead of me. Tea for the faculty wives! Oh, it would be so incredibly ghastly."

"Say, listen," said Ham, "where's Jennifer? I don't see Jennifer Sullivan. Did she have her . . . ?"

"Nine pounds," squealed Betsy. "She had this really darling nine-pound baby boy. And guess what, Ham? She named it after you."

"Oh, no, she didn't. Oh, my God, she didn't name it after me?

257

Oh, well, what the hell, who wants to be President of Harvard? Not me. No, sir. I'll tell you what I do want. Lunch. A bottle of beer. Who wants a beer on me? Come on, you Rats." Ham put his head back and shouted up at the balcony. "Say, Jack, do you know 'He That Drinks Is Immortal'?"

"No," said Jack, leaning over the railing. "How does it go?"

"Like this." Ham began to sing.

> He that drinks is immortal,
> He that drinks is immortal
>   and can ne'er decay,
> For wine still supplies,
> for wine still supplies
>   what age wears away.
> How can he be dust,
> how can he be dust
>   that moistens his clay?

"Hey, what the hell's going on?" Mr. Crawley popped out of his office. Ham took Vick's hand and began running down the hall. He grabbed up Mr. Crawley and carried him along, and Vick snatched Mrs. Esterhazy's hand, and Mrs. Esterhazy caught Tim's, and everybody else ran after them hand in hand. They all burst out the south door, singing Purcell's praise of wine.

Homer watched them go. He couldn't help thinking, one last time, about the great chain of being, and James Cheever's way of looking at the world. Those people running across Cambridge Street, all linked together, they were a chain too, a chain chockfull of being, only it was horizontal. Nobody was climbing up over anybody else to sit at the right hand of God. They weren't on any kind of ladder at all. It was all on the flat.

At the north door Homer turned to go outside, but then he stopped and looked back again at the full length of the memorial corridor in which so much had happened since last October, since

258

that day when he had first set foot in the place and found Vick Van Horn and demanded to know where his classroom was.

"Excuse me." A girl with her arms full of books was brushing past him, lugging a suitcase, running the whole length of the hall, her hair blowing in front of her. She was taking a shortcut to Quincy Street and the Yard. When she went outside, a gust caught the south door too, and blew it open, and then the wind went blustering through the building, sucked from one end to the other, barreling particles of old snow before it, and scraps of wastepaper and clumps of wet dead leaves.

Homer went out of doors too, by the door on the north side. Carefully he clapped that door shut behind him, because the building was too huge and hospitable for its own good. It was altogether too big and prodigal and open to the weather. Then he went in again by way of the service entrance, and down the stairs to the basement.

Who was living downstairs now? Homer guessed some of the Rats would be moving back into the house on Martin Street—Mrs. Esterhazy and her children, Jennifer and son. Before long Ham would be squeezing new vagrants into crannies and cupboards and lofts in Memorial Hall to fill the empty rooms when the old trespassers left. There was many a corner in the spacious hold of this enormous creaking ship that was hove to in the squalls and crosscurrents rolling down the broad cold wastes of Cambridge Street and Kirkland. . . .

Homer strolled along the corridor, looking once again for somebody to talk to. There was an open door at the end of the hall. A wisp of smoke was trailing out of the door. The smoke smelled strongly of incense. The incense was fragrant with the mysterious East and the temples of the Ganges. A familiar voice was chanting a mystic succession of syllables.

Maaaandaaaalaaaa. Maaaaaaaandaaaaaaaalaaaaaaaaaaaaaaaa.

To whom did that reedy voice belong?
"Good God," said Homer, looking around the door. "Is that

you, Freddy?"

Freddy Fulsom was taken by surprise. He jerked to his feet. A small brass incense burner clattered off a stand, emitting coils of greenish smoke. In a blur of saffron robe and shaved head and skinny arms clanging with bangles, Freddy made a rush for the door, and shut it with a shivering slam.

Homer stood in the hall and stared awe-struck at the door. Beside it the white card on the doorframe was dog-eared and grubby, but it still said ADMINISTRATIVE ASSISTINT. Homer put his face close to the door. "It's all right, Freddy," he said loudly. "I do not require administrative assistance. But listen here, are you a Buddhist or something now?"

Silence.

"But what about your theory, Freddy? You know, your idea about Jesus Christ being reborn into every generation? The Messiah returned to earth? Who's going to take care of that sort of thing from now on?"

Freddy wasn't telling. Homer shook his head and turned away. The chanting began again. At the other end of the corridor a baby cried.

Acknowledgments

Many people have helped this book along. I could not have written it without the help of Michael Lane, the energetic custodian of Memorial Hall, who is the opposite in every way of his fictitious successor, Jerry Crawley. I am also indebted to Frank Marobella, Mechanical Foreman for the North Yard; David Gorski, formerly Director of University Police and Security; Elizabeth Rigby, Librarian in the Planning Office; Kenneth John Conant, Professor of Architecture Emeritus; Louise Ambler, Curator of the Portrait Collection; Elizabeth Keul, Administrative Assistant to the President; James Sharaf, Attorney in the Office of the General Counsel; and F. John Adams, Director of Choral Music at Harvard and Radcliffe. The kind instruction of John Ferris, University Organist and Choirmaster, was most important of all. I have tried to correct most of the mistakes some of these patient people uncovered in the manuscript, but of course they are not to blame for the ones I clung to.

Others whose advice and assistance were invaluable were Allen Lannom, Conductor of the Masterworks Chorale; cellist Philip Moss; William Cremins, Chief of the Cambridge Fire Department; Sergeant Robert Rigollio of the Boston Police Department; art historian Robert Shaffer; Dr. George Hewitt; Dr. Gordon Winchell; and Robert Lunning of Bastille-Neiley, the architectural firm which recently restored part of Memorial Hall.

Included in the plans for this restoration was a new roof for the tower, to replace the one that burned in 1956. The first stage of the work has been completed, but unhappily the forlorn stump of the tower continues to loom over the city of Cambridge. Since my story is set in some near but vaguely defined future, I have written it as though the reconstruction of the roof had been accomplished. I hope the money will someday be found to crown the old tower with a new steeple in actual fact, so that Memorial Hall will at last be restored to its old dignity and grandeur.

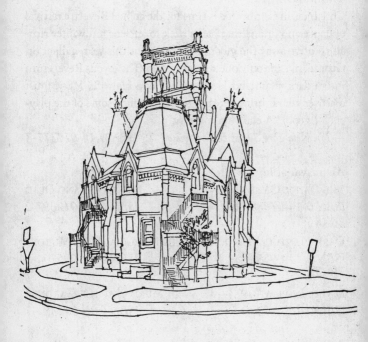

Read more Homer Kelly mysteries by Jane Langton, "today's best American mystery writer."
—*St. Louis Post-Dispatch*

THE SHORTEST DAY
Christmas in Cambridge is time for the annual Revels, a festival of dance and drama that harks back to ancient midwinter rituals to drive away the gloom of winter. But this year, gallant St. George isn't the only one who gets slain. The joyous Revels turn into a dark affair, and Homer Kelly and his wife, Mary, must discover who is bringing the curtain down on some of the players for good. "A cheering mystery."
—*The New York Times Book Review*   ISBN 0-14-017377-3

Also Available:

THE DANTE GAME	GOOD AND DEAD
ISBN 0-14-013887-0	*ISBN 0-14-012687-2*
DARK NANTUCKET NOON	THE MEMORIAL HALL MURDER
ISBN 0-14-005836-2	*ISBN 0-14-005704-8*
DIVINE INSPIRATION	MURDER AT THE GARDNER
ISBN 0-14-017376-5	*ISBN 0-14-011382-7*
EMILY DICKINSON IS DEAD	NATURAL ENEMY
ISBN 0-14-007771-5	*ISBN 0-14-013393-3*
GOD IN CONCORD	THE TRANSCENDENTAL MURDER
ISBN 0-14-016594-0	*ISBN 0-14-014852-3*